Allan Pinkerton

The Model Town and the Detectives

Allan Pinkerton

The Model Town and the Detectives

ISBN/EAN: 9783337333133

Printed in Europe, USA, Canada, Australia, Japan

Cover: Foto ©Andreas Hilbeck / pixelio.de

More available books at **www.hansebooks.com**

THE MODEL TOWN

AND

THE DETECTIVES.

BYRON AS A DETECTIVE.

By ALLAN PINKERTON,

AUTHOR OF

"THE EXPRESSMAN AND THE DETECTIVE," "CLAUDE MELNOTTE
AS A DETECTIVE," "THE DETECTIVE AND THE
SOMNAMBULIST," ETC., ETC.

NEW YORK:

G. W. Carleton & Co., Publishers.
LONDON: S. LOW & CO.
MDCCCLXXVI.

THE MODEL TOWN

AND

THE DETECTIVES.

PREFACE.

THE history of all places which have had a rapid growth is full of startling incidents of crime. Particularly has this been the case in the western country, where the incoming population has been of such a mixed character, and opportunities for criminal deeds so numerous, as to sometimes create an epidemic of wrong-doing.

Almost every community has known one or more periods when the dissolute elements of the place have seemed to be unusually active, and the majesty of the law so little regarded and feared as to cause a perfect carnival of crime. Under such circumstances, the honest portion of the population become bewildered and disheartened, and the rogues apparently take charge of affairs, until some sudden discovery brings to punishment a number of the guilty men, and then order returns.

Such was the experience of "The· Model Town." It was a very pleasant and thriving inland place, the law-abiding people far outnumbering the law-breakers; yet previous to the time when my services were engaged there was a period of almost total disregard of law and authority in the place. In a few weeks my detectives were successful in identifying the ringleaders of all the evil-doers of the town, and I was able to gather them in for punishment in small groups, without exposing my plans or alarming the others, whose guilt was yet to be discovered. At length, having effectually broken up all the parties of thieves, counterfeiters, burglars, and incendiaries, I left the place to enjoy a career of peace and prosperity.

There are many persons yet living who will remember the circumstances herein related, and they will recall how complete the reformation was worked by the arrest and conviction of the criminals. From the moment it was revealed that Pinkerton's detectives were at work in the town, the orderly character of the place was assured for an indefinite length of time, and the good effect lasted many years after my men had been withdrawn.

As the story of "Byron as a Detective" may call forth some discussion, I merely desire to say that, concerning his being the son of Lord Byron, I have no means of determining the truth or falsity of the claim; and only give the facts, which were then common among his associates, to the public for what they are worth. There were doubtless hundreds of other men of legitimate, as well as illegitimate, birth, each one of whom chance might have thrown into habits of reckless adventure resulting in crime, the temperament and mental conditions of each of whom might have given rise to the theory of being Byron's son, especially when the claim was so persistently put forward and so commonly accepted as in this case.

But I will personally vouch for the truth of this much: that Augustus Stuart Byron *claimed* that Lord Byron was his father; was a man of good learning and manners; was possessed of a thorough education and more than ordinary culture and refinement; was addicted to those strange bursts of brilliancy and joyousness, alternating with utter despondency and savage moroseness, which were such a distinguishing affliction to the great poet, and, I might also add, to his friends; that he naturally drifted into the half-literary, wholly-vagabondish life of the journeyman printer; and that while such, he was himself known among the fraternity as a poet of no mean order. It is also true, as stated, that Byron had been drawn into the society of young Napier by that natural affinity, or sympathy, which brings the poor or scalawag, relatives of great men together; that they had been into the far North-west, to the then wild, weird, and almost unknown Manitoba, with its famous gipsy-like Red River trains, its gaudy but lazy half-breeds, and hardy Scotch and English population of two hundred years' descent, and had expended nearly all their means in a series of wild adventures; that they had left Chicago on the eastern-bound train, which had been shattered with the one that had shot through it, sending from the wrecks of both trains a score of passengers into eternity; that the two escaped unhurt, and finding an opportunity to suddenly acquire vast wealth, with barely a chance of detection, had, in the very presence of death itself, committed their first great crime, the proceeds of which were almost as quickly wasted as gained; whereupon the couple returned to the locality of their first

1*

successful exploit, and immediately began the perpetration of the fiendish outrages which followed.

On account of the destruction of many of my records in the Great Chicago Fire of 1871, I am without the proof of the identity of young Napier, but will state that I was positively assured of his relationship to the Admiral by another Napier, a well-known and highly respectable citizen of Chicago, who, at that time, resided at No. 130 East Washington Street, in a building erected by Alexander White, and who was cognizant of the relationship, being himself a distant relative of the Admiral, and knowing that the nephew's reputation was that of a profligate among the family.

The subsequent career of the two men, and Byron's arrest and conviction before Judge Wing of Adrian, Michigan, with the latter's remarks when delivering the unusual sentence of ninety-nine years' imprisonment in the Michigan Penitentiary; Byron's incarceration in that institution as Augustus McDonald, on September 25th, 1854, and his final death on the 17th of July, 1857, are matters of record with the Circuit Court papers of Lewanee County, Michigan, and with the penitentiary records at Jackson, in that State, as any curious person or persons may learn by addressing a note of inquiry to the clerk of the former or to the warden of the latter.

ALLAN PINKERTON.

CHICAGO, *March,* 1876.

CONTENTS.

THE MODEL TOWN

AND

THE DETECTIVES.

CHAPTER I.

IN the year 185— I was very busily engaged in the investigation of several cases of great importance, which not only occupied nearly every minute of my time, but also caused me great anxiety. I was thus in no mood to waste precious moments in listening to trivial details of the robberies of country stores and dwelling-houses, and I gave up everything to my superintendent except the operations of great magnitude which I had then in hand. One afternoon, however, having sent my superintendent out for a short time, I seated myself in his office to receive visitors and reports. It was a raw and stormy day in January, and I did not anticipate that I should be called upon for any new business in such weather; but my plans were progressing quite satisfactorily in the most important matter in which I was interested, and I was momentarily expecting to receive some valuable information; hence, when a clerk from the outer office announced that a stranger wished

to see me, I admitted him at once to my own private
office. To my great disappointment, the visitor was not
the person whom I had expected, and at the first glance I
almost regretted having consented to see him. He was evidently a farmer in good circumstances, and I feared that he
would wish me to listen to a long story about some case of
petty larceny or village scandal. He introduced himself as
George R. Nichols, of Mariola, Illinois, and he asked me to
spare him half an hour of my time; he wished to engage
my services, and he would need about that length of time
to state the circumstances which needed investigation.

His direct, business-like style pleased me exceedingly, and
I requested him to proceed with his story. He then stated
that Mariola was a thriving town not many miles distant
from Chicago. It was situated on the line of a new railroad,
and its growth had been so rapid that it had been incorpo-
rated as a city. The surrounding country was thickly settled
by a population of native Americans, and the greatest prosperity prevailed. I knew the city and the vicinity very well
indeed, so that Mr. Nichols merely gave a hasty sketch of
it. He went on to say that there seemed to be a gang of
sneak-thieves, burglars, and incendiaries infesting the city,
and recently they had committed so many crimes that none
of the citizens felt safe. Stores were frequently robbed,
and goods of every description were carried off: hardware,
dry-goods, groceries, liquors, and even such bulky articles
as grain and lumber, were spirited away constantly. But
the worst crime had been arson, and there could be no
doubt, Mr. Nichols said, that at least three instances of

incendiarism had occurred : the Presbyterian church, the public school-house, and the Baptist church had been de-stroyed by fire under circumstances which convinced every one that they had been intentionally fired. In addition to these outrages, various other things had occurred : valuable horses and stock had been stolen, to such an extent that the farmers could hardly retain a fine animal except by the great-est precautions ; finally, the railroad tracks had been tam-pered with for the purpose of wrecking and plundering the cars ; one attempt had proved successful, while several others had been discovered just in time to prevent serious accidents.

Mr. Nichols begged me to go back to Mariola with him in order to detect the criminals who were destroying the peace and prosperity of the city and the adjacent coun-try. He said that he had been appointed to convey this request to me from a committee of the best citizens of Mari-ola. The damages to private property had been so exten-sive as to alarm them very seriously ; but the attacks upon the railroad had developed a still worse state of affairs. The officers of the railroad company whose tracks passed through Mariola were not wholly satisfied with the direction of the road at that point, since a considerable detour from the straight course of the road had been necessary to carry the tracks through the city. Still, the city was growing rap-idly, and the company obtained enough business therefrom to make it profitable to allow the line to remain as it was ; but since these repeated attacks upon the railroad trains, the company's officers had seriously contemplated a removal of the tracks through Mariola. They could thus save abou* five miles, by straightening the line, while they hoped, also, to escape the annoyances and outrages to which their trains were liable in that vicinity.

Of course, any such change would be most disastrous to the future prosperity of the city, and the citizens were determined to prevent the removal if possible. To this end it would be necessary to protect the railroad company from further loss and annoyance, which could be accomplished only by capturing the men engaged in the attacks. Mr. Nichols said further that the citizens had exhausted all their ingenuity in trying to discover the offenders, but no clue whatever had been obtained.

It was the prevalent opinion in Mariola that a "gang" or society of desperate criminals existed in and about the city, who were sworn to act in concert and to create a reign of terror in the county. The respectable portion of the community were in such a state of alarm that no one felt safe, and the value of all property was becoming seriously affected. Mr. Nichols, therefore, begged me to undertake the dispersion of this gang of villains, since the matter was too important to admit any further delay.

I asked Mr. Nichols to give me until six o'clock, as I was very busy. He then went away, and I sat down to think about the facts of his story. Ny first impulse was to decline to undertake the investigation, owing to the pressure of other more important work. On second thoughts, however, I saw several reasons why it would be well for me to give my services to aid the citizens of Mariola in restoring peace and safety to their homes. Moreover, one of the great cases on which I was engaged terminated suddenly that afternoon in the arrest of the criminals and the recovery of a large amount of property. This left me somewhat more free than I had been previously, and I decided to proceed to Mariola myself.

I was influenced to make this decision by two things : in the first place, I saw that the loss of confidence on the part of the law-abiding citizens would greatly encourage crime, and that the actual deterioration in the value of property would be very great; secondly, I wished to explode the theory that there was any organized body of men at work committing the depredations.

It often happens, especially in a newly-settled community, that there are a number of crimes committed in quick succession, in such a manner as to lead honest people to think an organized band has settled down to plunder the neighborhood. The same thing is often stated of large cities, and many people believe that all criminals are united in a league against the rest of the world ; that they have passwords, officers, regular lodges, and degrees of crime, in the same manner as any other secret society. This idea has been carefully cultivated by some writers of fiction for the purpose of adding color, life, and romantic interest to their tales ; but the real facts, in an experience of over a quarter of a century, warrant me in saying that no such organization has ever existed. In the nature of things, it is an impossibility. Criminals, as a rule, are selfish, cowardly, and revengeful: no great number of them could ever remain members of such a society for any length of time.

The first one caught in a serious difficulty would gladly save himself at the expense of all the rest by turning State's evidence; the sentiment of "honor among thieves" has no existence in fact. Besides, crime is essentially solitary in its tendencies, and it is never desirous of having any more participants in its secrets than are absolutely necessary to carry out its plans. Hence, though a few burglars, bank-robbers, or counterfeiters may temporarily unite in the execution of some scheme, their union is never permanent, nor do they regard each other as partners except for the time required to perform their work.

There is an expression common in England to denote the more intelligent criminals, such as forgers, counterfeiters, burglars, etc.: they are called the "swell-mob," and the name is somewhat in use in the United States; but the idea conveyed is wholly an incorrect one. Perhaps it is partly due to this appellation that many people have imbibed the opinion that all criminals act in unison; that they contribute money to defend those who may be arrested; that they manufacture evidence to assist each other; and, in short, that they invariably cling together at all times.

As I saw that Mr. Nichols and the other members of the committee of citizens at Mariola were laboring under this delusion, I thought best to detect the perpetrators of the outrages there, and to show them how little reason they had to fear the presence of any organization of villains.

WHEN Mr. Nichols returned I told him that I would undertake to clear the town of its active scoundrels, on condition that I should be allowed to work in my own way without interference by any one, and that my instructions be obeyed implicitly. Mr. Nichols agreed to my conditions on behalf of the committee, and we then settled the pecuniary portion of our agreement.

The first direction I gave to Mr. Nichols was that my connection with the work should be kept secret.

"But, Mr. Pinkerton, what am I to tell the committee?" asked Mr. Nichols.

"Tell them that I was too busy to come," I replied. " I do not wish to have anything to do with a large committee. There must be only two men to manage the affair on the part of the townspeople, and they must be men above the possibility of suspicion.   I will go to Mariola the first day that I have leisure, and I will meet the two persons who are to have charge of the case, in my room at the hotel.   I shall travel under a false name, and no one must know of my visit except those two.   You must write to me immediately on your return, stating the names of the gentlemen who are to meet me."

" Had you not better give me a letter to the committee?" he asked.

"No ; the less communication I have with them the better. The number is too large : some of them would be sure to let out that they had been in correspondence with a detective agency. Then my difficulties would be greatly increased."

"Well, it shall be as you wish, Mr. Pinkerton ; I have no doubt you understand the matter better than I do. When shall you come out ? "

" I cannot say exactly. You must write to me the names of the managers, and when I am ready to come, I will drop a note to them, giving my assumed name and the time I shall arrive in Mariola. Then the two gentlemen must come straight to the hotel to see me."

" Very well, Mr. Pinkerton ; I hope you will come soon, for we do not know how soon another fire or railroad accident may happen."

" You will hear from me very soon," I replied ; "good day, Mr. Nichols."

Mr. Nichols immediately returned home, and in a day or two I received a note stating that Mr. Lincoln and Mr. Brown would be the persons whom I should meet. As I would be at liberty to go the third day following, I replied in a note fixing the time, and on that day I went to Mariola dressed as a farmer.

The city was a very neat-looking place, having a population of about three thousand people. It contained two banks, one church edifice—the other two having been burned—a substantial railroad depot, and a large grain elevator. The citizens were generally of the more respectable class of society, and the appearance of the town was evidence of a high state of thrift and prosperity. The grain elevator was an important advantage to the place, since it drew trade from great distances. The farmers of the surrounding country knew that they could get the highest prices at the elevator for their grain, and they therefore preferred to trade at Mariola, even when they lived nearer to other towns.

I went to the Mariola House on my arrival, and I soon received a visit from Messrs. Lincoln and Brown. They first gave me a brief account of the various outrages which had caused them to send for me. About two years previous the people had begun to be troubled by the loss of small articles, such as tools, clothing, poultry, and vegetables; then the store-keepers became the victims, and the thefts increased in value and frequency; these were followed by burglaries to the extent of several thousand dollars in the aggregate; a railroad train was thrown from the track and robbed about six months before, and almost immediately thereafter the Baptist church was set on fire. These great crimes drew attention from the smaller ones, though the petty thefts had grown so frequent that they alone would have created great excitement if more serious matters had not occupied people's minds. The Presbyterians soon sustained the same loss as that which had befallen their Baptist brethren, and, as before, there could be no doubt that the fire had been lighted by an incendiary. These two fires had roused the people to a keen sense of danger, since there was no apparent object to be gained by the incendiaries; the churches contained nothing worth stealing, so that no plunder could be obtained by firing them ; hence, the only reasonable theory was, that a spirit of pure malevolence—or possibly revenge—had actuated the criminals. About six weeks previous to my visit, the public-school building had also been destroyed by fire, and this crowning outrage was too much for the endurance of the community. A public meeting was called and a vigilance committee appointed. The members were the most active, intelligent, and respectable men in the city; they were watchful and attentive at all times, some of them being on the alert every night ; but, in spite of their care, they could not prevent the thieves from carrying off a great deal of property from dwelling-houses and stores.   They finally sent Mr. Nichols to Chicago with instructions to obtain my assistance in discovering the ringleaders and officers of the "gang" who, as they believed, were banded together to destroy Mariola.

The story, as above given, convinced me that there must be some reason for the wanton destruction of property : the object of the railroad robbers and burglars was, of course, to enrich themselves without labor ; but I felt sure that the incendiaries, also, had some object which had escaped the notice of the committee. In the course of our conversation I learned that there had been considerable discussion during the last year upon the question whether liquor-selling should be permitted in the city. A revival in religion had taken place, and the advocates of total abstinence had made a great effort to obtain the passage of an ordinance forbidding the sale of spirituous liquors within the city limits. Of course, there had been a bitter fight, and the result had dissatisfied both parties : the council had tried to conciliate the liquor interest by permitting the sale of liquor under license ; on the other hand, they had hoped to please the teetotallers by putting the price of licenses at a very high rate. The result was that neither party was satisfied, and the ill-feeling was deepened. It was possible that either of these parties was guilty : the supporters of the saloons might have become so enraged at the church people who opposed the liquor traffic as to cause them to resort to fire as a means of revenge ; on the other hand, some fanatical temperance advocate might have burned the churches and school-house on purpose to cast suspicion on the other party.

There were a number of saloons in proportion to the population, and each of the hotels kept a bar-room. Mr. Lincoln said that there were no suspicious-looking characters in town, so far as the committee could discover, though there were a good many loafers idling about, without any regular trade or occupation. Several persons had been suspected of complicity in the smaller crimes, but no proof could be obtained of their guilt. As a rule, the loafers were so lazy that the criminals could hardly be among their ranks, since the losses had been too great to have been caused by any but an active, hard-working set of thieves.

Having learned all that my visitors could tell me, I made arrangements which would enable them to correspond with me unknown to any other person, by giving them a fictitious name and address in Chicago. I then cautioned them that they must not allow any person to know that I had under-taken the investigation, and that they must be careful to follow my instructions implicitly. They promised to obey me in everything, and, as it was then very late, they went home.

The next morning I made a tour of the city, and lounged about like a well-to-do farmer examining the place. The Mariola House was the only public hotel of any size, but there were two other taverns which did a fair business. One was called the Tremont House, and the other the Globe Hotel.

The latter was kept by a man named Wolff, who had no family. He was about fifty years of age, rather corpulent, and red in the face. His eyes, deeply set beneath shaggy eyebrows, were restless and wicked; his nose was large and discolored by the excessive use of liquor; he wore full beard, whiskers, and mustache, which gave his face a better appearance than would have been the case had his large mouth and heavy lower jaw been visible. Still, he had a very repulsive expression, and I judged that he would not be very scrupulous if he should be strongly tempted to be otherwise. He had a housekeeper to attend to the domestic affairs of the hotel, and I soon learned that people suspected him of taking a warmer interest in this fine-looking housekeeper than was consistent with strict propriety. She was about forty years of age, but she did not seem to be above thirty. Wolff had no bar-keeper, hostler, nor porter, preferring to attend to all the work himself. There was but one servant, a stupid German girl who could speak very little English. The house was well kept, however, and it was also well patronized; in fact, Wolff was making money fast, as his expenses were very light. He paid cash for everything, and never interfered in the affairs of any one else : hence, he was favorably regarded by many of the best people in Mariola. There were some things about the Wolff House which seemed to me scarcely consistent with a legitimate hotel business, and I made a note of the information I had gained, for future reference.

The Tremont House was not a hotel, but rather a large boarding-house with a bar-room attached. It was very dirty, and seemed to be doing only a moderate business. The proprietor and his wife were equally lazy and careless, so that I readily understood the cause of their lack of prosperity. The boarders were generally laboring men, and there was nothing worthy of notice about any of them.

I made a general survey of all the business houses, and took notes of the state of affairs. They all seemed to be doing well, but I saw that the door-fastenings were very slight, and that many of the stores could be entered by a thief without any trouble. As I strolled into a watch-maker's shop, I saw a man there whom I had previously seen in confidential conversation with Wolff. There was another jewelry shop in the place, which seemed to be well patronized, but the one which I entered contained no jewelry and only a work-bench with a watch-maker's tools. The proprietor's name was Davis, and he sat lazily in his shop doing nothing and looking half-asleep. I sauntered in and asked him what he would charge to clean my watch.

He opened it carelessly, looked at the works, and fixed an exorbitant charge upon it. The watch was in first-rate condition, and the work would not have taken an hour; hence it was evident that he did not wish to do the job. Davis was a villainous-looking fellow, and my object in entering his store was to obtain a good look at him and his surroundings; I felt a natural distrust of him, due to his appearance, and this feeling was augmented by the fact that he seemed intimate with Wolff.

Amongst the restaurants was one kept by a man named Reuben Walker, and I visited it because I saw that it was a resort for some of the worst characters in Mariola. The proprietor himself was a tall, grizzled old man, over sixty years of age. His head showed a great deal of strength of character, and he impressed me at the first glance as a man of more than the average natural ability. His nose was long and straight; his eyes were a piercing gray; his mouth was large and his lips thin; he wore a straggling beard, but no whiskers nor mustache; and his long gray hairs straggled about his neck, falling from a close-fitting cap of dirty velvet, which he wore constantly. He kept his own bar, but the restaurant was under the superintendence of Mrs. Maxwell; the latter did not live in the restaurant, but spent the day there and went home in the evening. I took a drink at Walker's bar and invited him to join me, hoping to draw him out; but, though he was willing to drink with me, he would not talk very much, and I soon went out.

Having made a complete examination of the town, I had another long talk with Messrs. Lincoln and Brown. I asked a great number of questions, and learned all that they could tell me about the various people and places noticed by me during the day. I then told them that I would commence operations in three or four days, and that I would give them, from time to time, such information as would satisfy them that I was represented in Mariola by skilful subordinates ; but they need not expect to know who my detectives were, since I should never allow any one to be aware of their presence.

Mr. Brown thought that secrecy was very desirable, but that there could be no harm in letting the detectives apply to him and Mr. Lincoln for directions and assistance.

I replied that my men could take instructions from no one but myself, and that they would need no assistance except such as they could obtain from each other. If it should become necessary to make any arrests, my men would inform me, and I would instantly send word to Mr. Lincoln.

"Then we shall be wholly in the dark as to your movements ? " said Mr. Brown.

"Yes, gentlemen ; that is the only condition upon which I can consent to proceed."

"Very well, Mr. Pinkerton," said Mr. Lincoln, after a few minutes' private consultation with Mr. Brown ; " we shall be satisfied to leave the matter in your hands, and you can use your own judgment as to the means of discovering the ' gang ' of criminals in and about our city."

Having made all the arrangements necessary, I returned to Chicago and sent for two of my men. Paul Clark, the elder of the two, was about forty years of age ; he was a very agreeable man in conversation, though he had also great tact, and few men could talk more, and say less, on a given subject when it was to his interest to be uncommunicative. Robert Hays was about thirty years old, but he appeared to be hardly twenty-five. He seemed to be constitutionally lazy, and his manner of speaking confirmed the impression; as he drawled out his words, with his eyes half open, he always gave strangers an idea that he was on the point of falling asleep. He had formerly been a bar-keeper, and, in spite of his apparent laziness, he was a thorough master of the work. He was an adroit card-player, also, and he knew every gambling game in existence, so that I felt sure that he would be popular among the drinking men and gamblers of Mariola.

I first gave them a brief account of the condition of affairs in Mariola, and recited the events which had led to my connection with the case; I further gave them copies of the notes which I had made in my tour through the town. I then instructed Hays to get employment in his old trade, if possible, and to make the intimate acquaintance of all the bad characters in the town. I suggested that the Tremont House would be a good place for him to board, since it was surrounded by a number of saloons, and it would, therefore, be a convenient point to start from. I told Clark that I suspected Wolff's tavern of being the rendezvous of a dangerous lot of men, and that he must devote himself to Mr. Wolff, his hotel, and his visitors. For this purpose it would be well to take permanent board there, and endeavor to win the confidence of the proprietor.

Having made all necessary preparations, my men departed by different routes for Mariola. Neither of them went straight there, but one entered on foot from the north, while the other worked his passage on a cattle train from the south-west. They were both dressed meanly 'and had scarcely any money, so that their first necessity was to find a cheap place to board. Following my instructions, Hays found accommodations at the Tremont House, where he was able to pay his way in part by assisting the bar-keeper, while Clark took up his quarters at the Globe Hotel.

The occurrences at Mariola were now reported to me daily with great minuteness ; nothing escaped the notice of my men, and every incident was mentioned with the strictest accuracy. The story as told in the succeeding pages was brought out little by little each day ; but, for obvious reasons, in giving the history of the investigation, it has been necessary to depart somewhat from the exact order in which each discovery was made. Hence, it will be understood that many of these events occurred simultaneously, and were instantly reported to me ; but, for convenience, I have related the operations of each detective continuously in every distinct case.

HAYS soon became well acquainted in many of the saloons, and he was regarded by the "knowing ones" among the drinking and gambling fraternity as a great addition to their society. He sang a good song, smoked and drank sociably, and was so expert at cards as to be a dangerous opponent in gambling games. In fact, he was able to hold his own with the hardest characters in town. He became a regular visitor at Walker's restaurant, where most of the small gambling was done, and the old man soon showed a marked liking for him. Hays always preferred to play for "drinks for the crowd," instead of for money, and this fact made him especially popular with Walker, since he was sure to profit by the game no matter who won or lost.

On the Saturday following Hays' arrival, Walker called him up to the bar and introduced him to a friend named Ben Leitz, whom he characterized as the best man in Columbia County; as Walker rarely praised any one, Hays felt sure that these two old men must be on the most intimate terms, and he felt highly pleased that Walker should have done him the honor to give him an introduction to his crony. In talking together, Walker said :

"Leitz is a man you can depend upon; his word is as good as his bond, and I do not want a better friend. 1

have taken a fancy to you, Hays, and I want you and Leitz to know each other."

Hays returned his acknowledgments modestly, and asked them both to drink. After some further conversation Walker asked him to tend bar awhile, as he and Leitz had some private matters which they wished to discuss. Hays willingly consented, and the two elder men went up-stairs. After they had gone, he commenced clearing up the bar and the lunch counter, and he made such an improvement in the appearance of the place that Walker was quite astonished on his return. He expressed his gratification at the change which Hays had made, and his good opinion of that gentleman was evidently much increased. The weather was bitterly cold, and many customers required attention both at the bar and the dinner-table, so that Hays remained as barkeeper for some time, while Walker and Mrs. Maxwell attended the table. When the customers had finished dinner, Hays sat down with Walker, Leitz, and Mrs. Maxwell; during their meal Walker was in very high spirits, and Lietz also. The latter seemed quite as much pleased with Hays as Walker was, and the whole party, it seemed, were disposed to treat the new-comer like an old friend. It was evident from Walker's manner that the business which he and Leitz had transacted was mutually satisfactory to them.

After dinner Hays said that he must return to the Tremont House, as he had promised to help the bar-keeper there that afternoon. As he turned to go, he said :

" Do you keep open Sundays, Mr. Walker ? "

" Yes ; I allow my customers to come in any time, if they

are the right sort. The farmers have a habit of dropping ir before and after church. They like to slip off quietly to take a sly nip, as it inspires them with great zeal in their attacks upon the whiskey dealers. I know those to whom I can sell with safety; you can come any time, day or night, but I won't sell you anything—you can have all you want free. I am a good judge of men, and I know you are a man I can trust."

Hays thanked him and said that he should try to show that he could be trusted.

"I am a young man," he added, "but I know a thing or two worth knowing; and if you ever want a fellow who ain't afraid of the devil himself, just call on me; I'm your man every time."

"That's the sort I like," said Walker with a satisfied nod. "Hello, Bill Morgan," he went on, as a man entered the saloon, "come here and join us."

Morgan was a middle-aged man of low habits and lazy disposition; it was easily seen that he would never have the ability to plan a scheme of any importance, though he would serve well enough as a tool in the hands of a leader of strong will and nerve. From the way in which Walker first addressed Morgan, Hays knew that they were on familiar terms; but he also noticed a slight tinge of contempt in the old man's tone, which implied a lack of equality between them. Hays and Morgan were introduced to each other, and after drinking together they stood and talked to Walker and Leitz for some time. Although nothing of any consequence was said, Hays learned enough of the characters of his three companions to know that they all had strong prejudices against working, and that they would allow no petty scruples to prevent them from obtaining money dishonestly if the opportunity were given them. Hays knew better than to outstay his welcome, and he preferred that Walker and his friends should show a partiality for his society, rather than that he should appear anxious to have theirs, hence he withdrew to keep his engagement at the Tremont House, although Walker was very desirous that he should remain.

Clark, on his arrival in Mariola, idled about for half a day, hoping to meet Wolff somewhere about town. He knew that he would have no difficulty in recognizing his man, and his intention was to get into conversation with him casually, during which he would give Wolff the impression that he had reasons for wishing to remain in Mariola for a time; then he would ask for some quiet place to board, where people minded their own business; if Wolff asked him to come to the Globe Hotel, he would have no difficulty in settling there as a permanent boarder. Late in the afternoon he was successful; he saw Wolff trying to roll a barrel of whiskey, which he had just bought, into a wagon. He lounged up to the wagon and said:

"Don't you want a lift, friend?"

"I wouldn't mind having a little help," replied Wolff, looking at Clark keenly; "just take hold one side, and I'll take the other; now, together!"

Having thus aided in loading the barrel, Clark turned to go, well knowing that etiquette would require Wolff to ask him to take a drink; and he was not disappointed.

2*

" Hold on a minute," said Wolff; "if you'll come round to my tavern I'll give you a good drink of whiskey. Jump in and ride with me ; it's only a little ways."

" I don't care if I do," was Clark's response ; and the two men drove off together.

Clark improved his opportunity so well that Wolff was very much pleased with him, and it was finally arranged that Clark should take permanent board at four dollars per week. He soon learned that this was a very unusual thing for Wolff to permit : the latter, in fact, said that it never paid to take regular boarders at less rates than transients, and that he was not in the habit of doing so ; therefore he asked Clark not to say anything about it outside. Clark readily promised to be silent, and said that Wolff could trust him to keep his mouth shut at all times.

" I can talk as much as the next man," he said, "when I have no reason to hold my tongue ; but no man can learn anything from me that I don't wish to tell. It isn't always the man who talks most that tells most; I believe, with Talleyrand, that language was made to disguise our thoughts."

"That's true," replied Wolff, approvingly; "there are some who think it is best to say as little as possible. My experience is that those men are sure to say the wrong thing when they have to talk."

" You have my idea exactly," said Clark ; "but please speak a little louder. The fact is, I was near an explosion not long ago, and it has affected my hearing somewhat. My physician recommended country air as very desirable," he added with a significant look, " and so I shall be here for several weeks."

" The longer the better," answered Wolff ; " we'll make you comfortable as long as you choose to stay."

As Clark went out to wash his hands, he heard Wolff say to the housekeeper in a low tone :

" He's a deep one, he is. I'll bet he's a high-toned 'crib-cracker,' for he's too well educated to be after small game. I shouldn't wonder if the explosion he spoke about took place in a safe door."

Clark's method of making Wolff's acquaintance was very bold and risky. A criminal of first-class ability, education, and experience would not have trusted a stranger, as Clark appeared to trust Wolff; hence if Wolff had been more experienced in crime, and more cautious himself, he would have distrusted Clark ; but the latter was a shrewd observer, and he felt sure that he could deceive Wolff. His success was highly gratifying, but on receiving his report I instantly sent him instructions to be doubly cautious in the future, and to let Wolff make all the advances toward intimacy. It was evident that Wolff had a high opinion of Clark, and that, if he should engage in any serious crimes, he would be apt to ask the latter's advice and co-operation.

Clark remained in the hotel a great part of the time and always muffled up his face when he went out. He discovered nothing, however, and no incidents of note occurred until the Saturday night after his arrival. The night was very dark and stormy ; no railroad trains passed over the road after seven o'clock on Saturday nights, and on this particular night few persons cared to spend the evening away from home. Hence the guests at the Globe Hotel that evening were two stock-drovers. Clark and Wolff and these men played cards together until eleven o'clock, at which hour they all went to bed.

Clark stood at his window a moment and listened to the wind as it shrieked about the chimneys and roofs; he had seen nothing as yet to lead him to suspect Wolff of anything in particular, but he had an undefined feeling that Wolff would be ready for any scheme to enrich himself, honestly or otherwise. Avarice was his ruling passion, and he would undoubtedly do anything for money; but it was improbable that he had been engaged in incendiarism, since there could be no profit to him in such work. This train of thought led Clark to wonder whether there would be any more cases of arson; and, as he rolled into bed, the thought passed through his mind: "This would be a terrible night for a fire."

ABOUT one o'clock, Sunday morning, a hoarse voice alarmed the town by crying: ."Fire! fire!" Clark hastily dressed himself and rushed down-stairs, followed shortly by Wolff. The Globe Hotel was situated only a short distance from the railroad track, and the grain elevator was close by. On reaching the street, Clark immediately saw that the elevator was in flames. He was one of the first on the spot, and he tried to discover where the fire had started; this was a hopeless task, however, since the whole structure was burning fiercely. It was evident that the fire had been in progress for some time, and it was impossible to determine its origin, except that it had been on the windward side.

The citizens hurried out rapidly and brought with them the only hand-engine belonging to the city. The extreme cold had frozen nearly all the sources of water supply, however, and the only object which they hoped to attain was to save the railroad depot from destruction. But the total failure of the water soon left them helpless, and they were able to save only the contents of the depot by hard work. The fire could be seen for miles around, and people came from long distances in the hope of lending assistance in extinguishing the flames.

Clark began his investigations as soon as he reached the fire, but he could learn very little. He found that a night watchman was employed to guard the depot and elevator, and it was this man who had given the alarm. It was certain, however, that he must have been asleep when the building was set on fire, since the flames were shooting up to a great height before he saw them at all; he confessed that he sat down in a sheltered spot and dozed a few moments, but he was sure that his nap had not lasted over five minutes when the fire awoke him. Under the circumstances, his estimate of time was not considered very accurate, and there was no doubt in the mind of any one that the incendiaries had had ample time to do their work thoroughly, without fear of interruption.

Wolff talked freely about the fire, and expressed his regret at the loss in a very open, honest manner. He said that the railroad company would now have an additional reason for withdrawing their tracks from Mariola, and, should they do so, his business would be destroyed.

While Wolff was lamenting, Hays, Morgan, and Davis; the watchmaker, came up together. They all lived some distance from the depot, and they were none of them very active men; hence they were among the last of the townspeople to arrive at the fire. Davis was fully dressed and his hair was combed, so that both of my men noticed his appearance. Either he had not gone to bed at all, or else he had been very deliberate in making his toilet. None of this party offered to do any work, and when one of the citizens asked Hays to assist in moving the goods from the depot, he said insolently that he didn't owe the company anything, and he didn't see why he should work on a cold night without any prospect of being paid for his work. Morgan and Davis coincided in this view, as also several other idlers, and Hays rose considerably in their estimation. Morgan talked a great deal about the loss the elevator and depot would be, and said that he supposed the railroad tracks would now be removed from Mariola. Old Walker came up just then and overheard Morgan's remarks. He faced around toward the group of loafers and stood with his back toward the fire. Taking off his scull-cap with one hand, he put the other hand beneath the skirts of his coat as if enjoying the blaze. As he listened to Morgan, he grew very much excited, and began to harangue the crowd in a shrill, vindictive voice.

"Let 'em move their tracks if they want to ! What do I care ? I pay for all the liquor they carry for me, and never ask any favors; but they tap my barrels and steal from three to five gallons from every barrel ; then they fill up with water, and I can't get any satisfaction from them. I don't see what use a railroad is any how. I think we got along well enough before it came, and we shall do better without it. Burn ! burn !" he added, turning to shake his fist at the flames; "I dont care how much you burn."

Morgan stepped up to the old man and said something in a very low tone. Walker looked at him an instant with an almost demoniac look, and then pushed him back contemptuously, saying :

" Morgan, if you ain't able to talk square, you might at least have sense enough to hold your tongue."

Morgan slunk away as if anxious to avoid observation, and Walker, seeing that he had attracted considerable attention, took Hays by the arm and walked away. The latter had noted Walker's excitement and Morgan's attempt to quiet him, but he had only overheard the old man's angry reply. As they went back to the restaurant, Walker was moody and irritable ; he muttered curses occasionally, gesticulated violently at times, and often passed his hand over his forehead, as if trying to clear his thoughts. When they reached the bar-room, Walker poured out a heavy drink of whiskey for each, and seated himself near the stove in sullen silence. At length, poking the fire viciously, he said :

"What a d——d fool Morgan is!" Then he added quickly, as if he had expressed more than he intended : "At cards, I mean, at cards. We got beaten every time this evening, he played so foolishly."

"I should like to be your partner," drawled Hays ; "you have never tried me, but I think we should suit each other."

The old man turned a piercing look upon him, as if to determine whether he had any hidden meaning in his speech. After a prolonged gaze, which Hays bore without showing the least embarrassment, Walker said :

" Well, we'll take a hand together some time. I think I'd get along with you, for I've taken a fancy to you, and I'm a good judge of human nature."

" You will learn more of me by-and-by," replied Hays, " I

have my faults, of course, but I never g♭ back on a friend and I keep my own counsel."

"That's right, that's right, Hays; never talk to any one about your own affairs unless you know that you can trust him. Some day I may talk to you about some matters that are worth knowing, but not just now. I think you are a true man, and I will trust you when the time comes. Now there is that d——d idiot Morgan, I don't know whether he is a fool or a knave. Don't you think when three men have a secret, and they agree to say certain things about it, that it shows a mean spirit for one of them to weaken and attempt to talk against his partners?"

"Yes, indeed, Mr. Walker; a man must be a worthless coward if he cannot live up to his word. Now, I think if you should trust me in anything, I could help you a good deal."

Walker seemed a little disturbed by this remark, and replied quite reservedly, as if he wished to return to the subject of card-playing:

"The only partner I want is a man who can play his hand for all it's worth. Perhaps you would suit me as well as any one else, but that fellow Morgan hardly knows a king from a deuce."

Hays saw that he had gone too fast, and he replied:

"Well, of course, every man plays a different kind of a game; some day, if you will take me for a partner in a good game, I will show you how well we can work together. It is after four o'clock," he continued, with a yawn; "I guess I will go back to my room and finish my sleep."

"Well, come in again this afternoon," said Walker, "and I will tell you about Morgan. It won't do to trust him too much. I am chilled through, and shall go to bed until ten o'clock. I slept through most of the excitement, and didn't wake up until the fire had nearly burned out."

The two men then took a parting drink together, and Hays left the restaurant as the first signs of dawn began to appear in the east. The clouds had cleared off, though the wind still blew with great violence. The smouldering embers of the fire just touched the surrounding houses with a lurid glare, while overhead the clear, peaceful depths of the star-lit skies contrasted strongly with the scene of confusion below. Hays made another visit to the ruins, and, finding nothing new to investigate, he then went to his room at the Tremont House.

Clark remained around the depot grounds until daylight; he assisted in removing the goods, and was thus able to keep a sharp watch upon the whole place. If the fire had been set in the hope of thereby obtaining an opportunity to plunder, the villains had changed their plans, since there were no attempts made to steal anything whatever.

When Clark returned to the Globe Hotel, at breakfast time, he found three strangers in confidential conversation with Wolff. They were all of middle-age and seemed to be partners. Wolff introduced Clark to them and said that they were cattle drovers. Clark did not believe this story, as the men were much more intelligent than most drovers; and in the course of their talk he soon discovered that they did not pretend to keep up their assumed characters.   They went up-stairs immediately after breakfast and did not appear while any visitors were around.

The town was filled with farmers during the forenoon, and many of them left their teams at Wolff's.   They were all greatly excited at the loss of the elevator, and threats of lynching the incendiary, when discovered, were freely made. In the afternoon most of the farmers went home, and at three o'clock Wolff and his boarders had dinner.   The conversation at dinner-time was upon the subject of the fire, and Wolff talked very freely.   He had evidently told his three guests that Clark was trustworthy, for they all treated him like one of themselves.

"I don't know any more about the fire than any one else," said Wolff, "but I have my suspicions.   Old man Walker was there acting like a lunatic, and saying that he was glad to see the depot burn.   Then there was that fellow Morgan, who is as big a scoundrel as there is out of jail.   I have heard a good deal about him, and he and old Walker are always together.   I can't see why Walker trusts him ; for if he should ever be caught at anything, he would 'squeal' on the whole crowd."

"I agree with you," said one of the strangers ; "if Walker puts any confidence in him, he will find out his mistake too late.   Morgan played me a mean trick once, and I would be glad to pay him off if I got a chance."

"But there is Ben Leitz," said another of the strangers ; "he is a safe man, yet he trusts Morgan too."

'Well, that is true," said Wolff; "but probably he has

quit the business ; still, if he has given up the old game, I dont see how he gets along so well."

"Probably he may be working 'on the quiet,' and making it pay better than some others who don't know the ropes so well," Clark suggested.

"Then he has some sharp assistant that I don't know of," said Wolff.

They continued in conversation for some time, but nothing further of any consequence was said.

In the afternoon Hays went back to Walker's restaurant, where he found Leitz and Morgan, who had just dined with Walker. They were all in high spirits, and Morgan seemed to have appeased the old man's anger. He had evidently promised to retract the expressions which had displeased Walker in the morning , for he went out soon after Hays entered, saying :

"I'm going to take a walk 'round town to hear what people think about the fire. I shall talk in a different tone from that I used this morning."

"Mind you do," answered Walker ; "if you hear anybody whimpering at the loss of the depot, just shut 'em up, and tell 'em it's a good thing that it was burned without destroying any other houses. Say that the railroad officers wanted a good excuse for straightening their line, and that they probably set fire to the elevator themselves."

"I'll talk in the right way this time," said Morgan, confidently.

After his departure, the other three men played cards for an hour ; Hays showed such skill in playing, and such extraordinary luck in dealing, as to excite the admiration of both his companions, for, as there were no bets made, they did not mind losing the games. At length Walker and Leitz said that they wanted to take a stroll about town, and the former asked Hays to stay in the bar-room during their absence.

" Don't let anybody in," said Walker, " unless you know they are ' square ' men. Some of these canting church people would like to prosecute me for selling liquor on Sunday if they could get any witnesses to appear against me."

" Never fear," replied Hays; " I can tell the right sort at a glance, and the Puritan Fathers may send as many spies here as they please, but none of them will get a drop from me."

Mrs. Maxwell, the housekeeper, joined Hays after Walker and Leitz had gone out, and they conversed together for quite a long time. Mrs. Maxwell was a fine-looking widow, about forty years of age, and she was quite ready to gossip about anything she knew. Hays learned from her that Walker had been on intimate terms with Leitz for over two years, and that he was even more intimate with Leitz's wife, Lucy. Mrs. Maxwell had two children, and Walker had promised to send them to school during the next year ; but he was strongly opposed to the manner in which the public school had been conducted, and he had really rejoiced when it was destroyed. There had been a strong effort made to prevent the reading of the Bible in the public school, and Walker had been one of the principal opponents of the Sacred Book.

"One could almost imagine that the old man was a prophet," said Mrs. Maxwell, "for he foretold that the churches and school-house would be worsted in the struggle ; and sure enough they have all been destroyed except one church."

Walker and Leitz returned at dusk, and Hays spent the evening playing cards with them ; but they did not again refer to the fire, and it seemed as if they had not been pleased with the loud threats **of** lynching the incendiaries, which they had heard.

M ONDAY morning following the fire I was visited by Mr. Bascom, superintendent of the railroad. I had just received the reports of Hays and Clark, and I was, therefore fully posted upon the recent events in Mariola. Mr. Bascom said that he wished me to investigate the various outrages which had been perpetrated against the railroad, as affairs had now become so serious in the vicinity of Mariola that public attention had been attracted, and the road was suffering considerably. He asked me to go at once to survey the ground, and then to put a keen, intelligent man at work for the purpose of bringing the criminals to punishment.

I told him that it would be unnecessary for me to go there, as I was already well informed of the condition of affairs in Mariola. I would send another man to assist those already there, and they would all work in harmony. I had no doubt whatever that the same men who had fired the churches had also destroyed the railroad buildings. I arranged matters satisfactorily with Mr. Bascom and then sent for Timothy Webster, one of the best men in my employ. I explained to him all the circumstances of the case that were then known to me, and told him my suspicions and opinions. As a number of workmen would be

required to clear away the *débris* of the elevator and depot,
I directed him to obtain a place in the gang.   After he had
worked a short time, he could get discharged ; then it would
be easy to become acquainted with all the loafers in town.
Webster left Chicago the same evening for Mariola ; the
next morning he might have been seen vigorously shoveling
damaged grain into a wheelbarrow in the ruins of the
elevator.   Here he worked about a week ; but, as he grew
more and more lazy every day, he was discharged as a
worthless vagabond.

Meantime Clark was progressing rapidly toward obtaining the confidence of Wolff and his housekeeper, Mrs. Black.
The three strangers disappeared the day after the fire, and
in a few days Wolff told Clark that he thought of going
away for a short time to travel.   He said that he should
need some one to manage the house during his absence, and
that he would like Clark to take charge.

"I shall be gone about a week," he said, "and you will
have plenty to do.   I have a great many customers, as you
know, and I want a man here who knows how to treat my
friends."

"I guess I can tell the right sort," replied Clark.   "I
should expect to give some visitors much quieter accommodations than others."

"That's it exactly," said Wolff ; "if any men come at
night and want to see me, tell them I am away ; if they
choose to wait for me, give them rooms and let them have
what they want.   They can have their meals alone if they
wish ; Mrs. Black understands what to do.   Some of them

won't go out much, and you needn't talk about them outside ; you understand ?"

"Yes ; I think I do," said Clark ; "my idea is that if your boarders attend to their own business and pay their bills, you don't trouble yourself to ask them any questions ; eh ?"

"I see that you know what I want," rejoined Wolff, with a satisfied look. "I shall get ready immediately, so that I can leave at nightfall."

Mrs. Black was present during the conversation, and when he went up-stairs, she said :

"I never saw a man who could manage Wolff as well as you can ; he never has allowed any one to take charge of the house before. I hope you will continue to suit him, for then he will want you to stay. You can make it pay well if you choose, for Wolff makes a pile of money."

"I guess I can keep things pretty straight while he is gone," said Clark, "and I am glad he is going, for we can have a jolly time during his absence."

Mrs. Black blushed and looked very much pleased ; but she said nothing more, as Wolff came in all ready for his journey. He had a small satchel in his hand, which he set down a moment while he put on his overcoat. Clark helped Wolff with his coat, and in doing so he touched a very heavy package in the outside pocket. While professing to be engaged in pulling down the coat underneath the overcoat he succeeded in feeling of this package ; it was cylindrical in shape and was sealed with wax at each end. He also lifted the satchel and found that it was very heavy,

3

much more so than would have been the case had he simply carried his ordinary changes of clothing.

When Wolff was all ready, he went to the stable and
brought out a fine span of mares and a light driving wagon.
Clark helped him to harness them into the wagon, and then
he offered to take the team around to the front door of the
hotel.

"Not much," said Wolff, in reply to Clark's offer; "I
don't propose to advertise that I'm going away any more
than is necessary. Just hold the horses until I bring out
my other span, will you?"

So saying he went back into the stable and brought out
a second pair of matched horses. These were fastened to
the back of the wagon by strong halters, and Wolff then got
in, carefully placing his satchel between his feet. It was
quite dark by this time, but Wolff asked Clark to go to the
street and see whether there were many people in sight. He
was quite elated at something, but still he showed considerable nervousness. As he passed Clark at the front gate,
he said:

"When I have sold these two teams I shall be about
ready to come home. It isn't every day that you can find
such horses as these, and I expect to get a good price.
Good-bye; keep a good watch on your customers, and if you
find any spies hanging 'round, give 'em a good licking to
teach them to mind their own business."

"Good-bye, old man," said Clark; "I shall take good care
of the hotel, and will try to fill your place in every respect."

Wolff drove off at a rapid rate, and Clark returned to the

house to ponder over the suspicious movements and business of the hotel-keeper and his friends. He finally came to the conclusion that the supposed cattle-drovers were horse-thieves, and that Wolff was engaged in selling the horses stolen by the rest of the gang ; he must also be in league with a set of counterfeiters, since the package which Wolff had in his pocket was shaped exactly like a roll of money. Clark therefore determined to direct all his energies toward discovering the place where the counterfeiting was done.

Webster was discharged from his place as laborer about the time Wolff went away. He had made himself well known in all the saloons, and nearly every loafer in Mariola was acquainted with him. He seemed like a lazy ne'er-do-well who would prefer to work as little as possible if he could live at the expense of other people.

One Saturday night he was returning from a visit to a saloon in a neighboring town ; in fact, it was about three o'clock in the morning before he reached the outskirts of Mariola. As he walked along, with the noiseless tread which was habitual with him, he saw two men hurrying down a cross-street, carrying a large bundle between them. They had not noticed him, and he had no difficulty in following them without their knowledge. They walked as rapidly as their burden would permit, and soon left the thickly-settled part of the city. At length they reached a small frame cottage in the suburbs, where they paused ; after glancing around to see whether any one was stirring, they entered the house and lighted lamps in two rooms. Webster crept up and tried to see what was going on, but the windows were all fitted with close shades, which prevented him from discovering anything.   He decided to send a report to me by the express train which passed through Mariola at five o'clock. I received his account therefore the same day, and was able to inform Mr. Lincoln by the Sunday night train that a robbery had probably been committed in Mariola.   I told him that if it should be discovered that any one had been robbed he would find the stolen goods secreted in a small cottage just outside of the city.   I described the premises exactly, and suggested that a warrant be obtained to search them. I urged him to see in person that the search was faithfully made, since the City Marshal might not be wholly reliable ; or, at any rate, he might be careless and inefficient.

Mr. Lincoln received my letter early Monday morning, just after having posted a letter informing me that a dry-goods store had been robbed the night before of a large amount of laces, silks, fine cloths, etc.   The robbers had selected only the best goods and had left no trace by which to follow them.   Mr. Lincoln said that he and Mr. Brown suspected a man named Hays, who was boarding at the Tremont House, of having committed the robbery.   They had learned that Hays was a gambler and a loafer ; he had no regular occupation, yet he paid his board regularly and was well received in all the saloons as a cash customer. They had learned also that he had not returned to the hotel until a very late hour the night before ; Mr. Lincoln therefore asked whether it would not be well to arrest Hays and search his room,

On receipt of this letter I immediately replied that it could do no harm to arrest Hays, since if he was the robber they would be apt to discover something to fasten the crime upon him ; but if he was innocent he would probably be able to prove his innocence, and he would then be discharged.

"It is probable," I wrote, "that he is a hard character, and, like all habitual criminals, he will be satisfied to escape close inquiry into his habits, and will not cause any inconvenience to you for arresting him."

My object in having Hays arrested was to give him an additional claim to the respect and confidence of the criminal element in Mariola society, for they would be sure to regard him as one of themselves as soon as the respectable members of the community turned against him. I knew that his confinement could last only a day or two, and that after his release he would be quite a hero among Walker's followers.

I wrote to Webster also, by the same mail, to see Hays at once, get all his papers, and tell him that he might be arrested at any moment. I preferred to write to Webster instead of Hays, because I was afraid that Mr. Lincoln, who was postmaster, might detain and open Hays' letter. Immediately on receiving my letter Webster called upon Hays and told him what to expect ; the latter instantly turned over his papers to Webster, destroyed all evidences of his profession, and then strolled down to Walker's restaurant to await arrest.

Meanwhile Mr. Lincoln had received my second letter on

Monday morning, and he was perfectly amazed to learn that I had known of the robbery on Sunday evening, when he supposed that it had been committed late Sunday night. He then instituted a careful inquiry, and certain indications which had been observed convinced him that the robbery had taken place Saturday night; but that as no one went to the store on Sunday the loss was not discovered until early Monday morning. Still he could not understand how I had learned about it a day before it was known in Mariola, and he was quite mortified that their own watchmen had been outwitted, while a detective many miles away was aware of the crime.

MR. LINCOLN decided not to search the cottage until after he had received my reply to his letter about Hays. Tuesday morning, on reading my advice to have Hays arrested, he went to see Mr. Brown, and they agreed upon a plan of action. They then sent for the City Marshal and told him that they wished him to arrest Hays on suspicion of having robbed the dry-goods store of Sanders & Co. The Marshal was a large, fat man, good-humored and careless; he was well-meaning, but lazy and easily influenced. He liked to be on good terms with every one, and was too fond of liquor to be an efficient officer.

Mr. Lincoln swore out a warrant for the arrest of Hays, and Marshal Binford went out to search for him. Knowing that Walker's saloon was a favorite place of resort, he went there first, arriving a few minutes after Hays, who had just left Webster. On entering the saloon the Marshal went straight up to Hays and said:

"You are my prisoner; I have a warrant for your arrest."

"I reckon you are joking," replied Hays, without showing any alarm. "What do you charge me with?"

Old Walker was well acquainted with the Marshal, and he instantly came out from behind his bar to see what was the matter.

"What have you got against Hays, Binford?" he asked. "You must have mistaken the man."

"No, sir; I am not mistaken. Here is the warrant, issued by Justice Green; Hays is charged with breaking into the store of Sanders & Co., and the complaint was made by Mr. Lincoln and Mr. Brown."

"When was the robbery committed?" asked Hays.

"The warrant says between the hours of ten o'clock Saturday night and seven o'clock Monday morning.

"Well, I can easily prove an *alibi*," said Hays, "for I was with Mr. Walker most of the time, except when I was abed and asleep at the Tremont House."

"I must take you in charge nevertheless," said Binford; "I must execute my warrant, and you can give bail before Justice Green."

"I'll go bail for you, Hays," said Walker; "you've got plenty of friends here to stand by you."

"Thank you, Mr. Walker, you are very kind, and I shall never forget your offer," said Hays. "When I have proven my innocence I shall make some of these fellows repent having accused me unjustly."

"That's right, Hays," growled Walker; "sue 'em for damages and teach 'em to be more careful in future."

By this time about a dozen persons had gathered around, and Hays seemed to enjoy his notoriety. He told the Marshal that he wished the warrant read in due form, and after the reading he asked the Marshal and the crowd up to the bar to drink. The Marshal had no objection, and the crowd joined them with great satisfaction. Hays and Mar shal Binford then headed a procession which moved from Walker's saloon to Justice Green's office. The arrest was made at the busiest hour of the forenoon, and as soon as it became known that the Marshal had made an arrest for alleged complicity in the latest burglary, nearly every one who could spare the time hastened to the court-room to witness the proceedings. Consequently an immense crowd was present, and the attention of all the spectators was concentrated on Hays and his friends. No one in the whole assemblage was more cool and unconcerned than the prisoner, and he exchanged greetings with his friends as pleasantly as if he were receiving an ovation.

On reaching the court-room Walker told Morgan ro run over to see Ben Leitz and ask him to come to the Justice's office to defend Hays. He hurried away rapidly, and very soon Leitz joined the party.

"What is the matter?" he asked breathlessly.

Walker informed him of the charge, and said that Hays could easily prove an *alibi.*

"Of course he can," replied Leitz? "besides, Hays is too sharp a man to get himself into trouble for a little job like that."

"Certainly not," added Walker; "Hays will have big game or none at all; eh, Hays?"

"That's my style, gentlemen," replied Hays, jauntily putting his thumbs into his vest pockets and tipping his hat forward. "If I should decide to take the hint which Messrs. Lincoln and Brown have given me, I will make a strike for high stakes."

3*

This conversation was carried on in a low tone, being heard by only three or four of Hays' friends. Meanwhile the complainants were at a loss what to do; they had searched Hays' room, but had found nothing to incriminate him, and they had no testimony ready. The Justice at length called the case and asked what was the charge against the prisoner. Mr. Lincoln gave several very trifling reasons for suspecting Hays, and stated that he was not prepared to go on with the examination that day; at his request, therefore, Justice Green continued the case for one day and fixed the amount of bail at five hundred dollars.

Hays, Leitz, and Walker held a consultation upon the question of giving bail. It was finally decided that Hays should refuse to obtain bail, although he could have easily given bonds for treble the amount, with Walker and Leitz as sureties. Hays said that he did not mind passing one night in jail, as he could obtain greater damages from his persecutors by so doing. Leitz therefore addressed the Court in a very extravagant speech, in which he lauded Hays as a model of injured innocence. He concluded as follows :

"My client can give any amount of bail, your honor, but I shall advise him not to do so. He would prefer to pass the night in a noisome cell—yes, even a year if necessary—rather than countenance the illegalities by which he is to be deprived of his liberty. My client, your honor, is ready to go on with the examination this moment, and he can prove an *alibi* without difficulty. In the name of the boasted freedom of our institutions I protest against the commitment of my client on the hearsay testimony which has been offered."

In spite of the protest, however, Hays was remanded to jail. He was accompanied through the streets by all his loafer friends, and Walker, Leitz, and Morgan agreed to stay with him most of the night. The Marshal kindly volunteered to take his distinguished prisoner to get his meals at any restaurant he might prefer, and Hays, of course, chose Walker's. As Hays expected, the result was that the restaurant and saloon did an immense business that day, since every one was anxious to see the man accused of burglary. Walker sent some clean bedding to the jail and fixed up Hays' cell quite decently, so that he was subjected to no discomfort whatever. His three boon companions stayed with him until nearly midnight, and they enjoyed the evening exceedingly. The next morning the courtroom was again crowded, but no one appeared to prosecute the prisoner, and he was therefore discharged. He received many congratulations from the loafers present, and he added to his popularity by treating a crowd of about twenty-five. It was agreed among the Walker-Leitz set that Hays should commence a suit for false imprisonment against Mr. Lincoln, Mr. Brown, Marshal Binford, and Justice Green.

Immediately after Hays' discharge, Mr. Lincoln and Mr. Brown went to Justice Green and called in the City Marshal with them. They then stated that they had strong reasons for believing that Sanders & Co.'s goods had been secreted in a little frame cottage in the suburbs of the town

They thought that a search-warrant should be issued at once
to enable them to hunt for the goods.

Marshal Binford said that the cottage was occupied by
two men named Cook and Wallace. There was a small
piece of ground attached to the cottage, but it did not produce much, and the men were in the habit of working on
farms in the neighborhood during the summer and fall. In
winter they seemed to do very little work, yet they never
complained that they did not have steady employment.
Still the Marshal said that he had no reason to suspect them
of anything criminal, and that he should be very much averse
to searching their house. He tried to persuade Mr. Lincoln
that the affair would turn out as disastrously as the arrest of
Hays ; but the two citizens were determined to follow my
instructions, and therefore they swore out a search-warrant.
Binford was anxious to avoid the responsibility, and so he
said that he would deputize a sharp fellow named Jim Warden to assist him in the search.

Warden was a tall spare man, with a hook-nose, ferret-
eyes, and an insincere expression. He was a man of some
little property, but he had no visible means of support
except gambling, which he carried on in a quiet way. He
affected a dare-devil style, and was quite a braggart. Still
Mr. Lincoln did not know anything against him which
would prevent him from serving as a deputy, and so no
objections were made.

Mr. Brown and the Marshal immediately went out to look
for Warden, and they soon found him playing cards in a
saloon. They called him out quietly and told him the busi-

ness in which they wished his assistance. He ridiculed the idea of searching Cook's house, and said that both Cook and Wallace were decent, honest men.

" What reason have you for suspecting them ? " he finally asked.

" That I cannot tell you," replied Mr. Brown ; "but I and Lincoln have sworn out a warrant and we want you to execute it."

" Oh ! come up and take a drink," said Warden. " I tell you I know that those men are all right."

The Marshal never refused an invitation to drink, and after having accepted he turned to Mr. Brown and said :

"You hear what Jim says, Mr. Brown. He knows all the hard cases in town, and he thinks these men are honest."

" You can depend upon that," said Warden, " and you will get into serious trouble, Mr. Brown, if you act so rashly upon wrong suspicions."

Mr. Brown's courage began to fail him, and he stood for several minutes undecided. At length he said that he would go back to see Mr. Lincoln, and he then left the saloon, where Warden and the Marshal remained to await his decision. Fortunately Webster had been in the saloon and had overheard the whole conversation. He knew that unless Brown acted promptly the alarm would be given to Cook and Wallace, and the goods would be carried away beyond the hope of recovery. He therefore followed Brown out and kept him in sight until an opportunity occurred to speak to him without attracting attention ; then muffling up his face in a large scarf, he came up close behind Mr. Brown and said in a clear voice :

"Don't look 'round, Mr. Brown, nor appear to notice me in any way. You do not know me, and it is better that you should not ; but you must act quickly on my advice. The stolen goods are in Cook's house, and you must insist upon having it searched immediately. Go back to the Marshal and make him commence at once. Don't tell any one where you got your information, but act without delay."

The moment Mr. Brown heard Webster's voice he turned his head suddenly, but he instantly looked to the front again and continued walking, although he listened attentively. Webster darted into an alley as soon as he had finished speaking, so that Mr. Brown was perfectly ignorant of the personal appearance of his unknown adviser. He hurried to Mr. Lincoln's store and told him what had occurred. Mr. Lincoln grabbed his hat and started out, saying :

" Come along as quick as you can. We don't know nor care who the stranger was, but he certainly gave good advice."

The two gentlemen walked rapidly to the saloon, where they found Binford and Warden seated before the stove, drinking and telling stories.

"Mr. Binford," said Mr. Lincoln, "we have sworn out a search-warrant, and have placed it in your hands to be executed ; we insist that you proceed with your duty."

" But, Mr. Lincoln, Jim Warden, my deputy, says that it will get us all into trouble ; if Cook is innocent he will bring suit against us for damages, as Hays is going to do."

" You have no discretion in the matter, Marshal Binfoi d, nor does any responsibility fall upon you," replied **Mr.** Lincoln. "If any wrong be done, Mr. Brown and I are the only ones who will suffer. If your deputy is afraid to help you, you can deputize me, and I will make the search my-self."

"Who says I'm afraid?" said Warden, with an oath. "I ain't afraid of anything; but I can tell you that you'll get sick of searching the houses of honest, hard-working men like Cook. That's your own affair, however, and if you think you can risk another suit for five thousand dollars damages come along. You needn't think I'm afraid, by ——; I'll rip up every mattress in the house if you want the place searched."

CHAPTER VII.

WARDEN'S attempt to intimidate Mr. Lincoln did not succeed, and at length they started out, accompanied by a number of idlers, among whom was Webster. On approaching the house Warden said he would go ahead to see that nothing was disturbed; but Mr. Lincoln had a slight suspicion of Warden, and he followed him very closely. Just as they entered the front door Cook and Wallace dashed out the back way. Mr. Lincoln and Mr. Brown pursued them instantly and succeeded in capturing them both after a long chase. Meantime the Marshal, Warden, and one or two of Mr. Brown's friends were engaged in searching the cottage for the stolen goods, but without any success; hence when Mr. Lincoln and Mr. Brown returned with their prisoners they felt very cheap to learn that nothing had been found to warrant them in arresting Cook and Wallace.

Warden exulted openly and reminded them that he had cautioned them against making the search. The leaders were quite crest-fallen, as they had not only made themselves ridiculous in chasing and arresting two apparently innocent men, but they had laid themselves open to suits for heavy damages. They walked a little way apart from the rest of the party, who were now assembled in the back yard waiting further developments.

Mr. Lincoln and Mr. Brown stood at the front gate in a very dissatisfied frame of mind. Webster saw that the search would fail for want of some one of experience to conduct it. He determined to give them a hint, however, and turning to Warden, whom he knew slightly, he said:

"I guess those big-bugs wish they had followed your advice now. Won't they feel sick when Cook and Wallace sue them? I think I shall go back to town and tell the fellows what a mare's nest has been found."

"Yes, that's right," said Warden; "get up a good crowd to laugh at them when they come in."

"I will see old Walker and Leitz," added Webster; "I guess they can get enough fellows to make it lively."

So saying Webster strolled through the house and passed out the front gate. As he passed the two gentlemen he said in a low voice:

"Don't give up now! Search the barn, and go over the house again. The goods are here, and I know it."

He hastened away before they had time to observe him closely, and, turning a corner, he was soon out of sight.

"That man is either one of Pinkerton's detectives or else he wants to get us into trouble," said Mr. Brown; "the voice was the same as that of the man who spoke to me before. Still he may be telling the truth, and we can soon find out by searching the barn."

"Yes; that is what we must do," said Mr. Lincoln. "I think there must be something wrong, for if not, why did the men run away?"

"'That's true; I think we had better make the whole job

complete. You can go into the barn and I will overhaul the house again. I don't believe they made a very thorough search," said Mr. Brown.

They therefore went back and told the Marshal that they wished him to search the barn. Warden again interposed, and said that Cook would bring double suits against them.

"All right," said Mr. Lincoln; "we may as well be hung for a sheep as a lamb. Come along, Marshal."

He led the way to the barn at once, followed by Binford and Warden, both of whom expostulated with him for continuing a useless search on the premises of honorable, law-abiding citizens. At length he became angry at their lack of zeal in the performance of their duty, and on reaching the barn he commenced searching the place himself. He had not been at work five minutes before he discovered a large quantity of the stolen goods concealed in a manger; and further careful investigation brought to light everything except a couple of bundles of silks and fine laces. These were found soon afterward in the house, in one of the rooms which Warden had searched. The latter was very much surprised at the disclosures, and was especially astonished that he should have overlooked anything.

Cook and Wallace were of course arrested and carried off to jail, and the goods were returned to Sanders & Co., who identified all the articles. Later in the day Warden engaged a lawyer to defend the prisoners, and he showed a great degree of interest in providing for their comfort. These circumstances led me to advise Webster not to lose sight of Mr. Warden, but to take a quiet interest in his habits ; for I began to suspect that he would soon be found engaged in some rascality himself.

The examination of the prisoners took place the next morning ; and at an early hour the whole town was alive with excited groups of farmers and merchants. In a place like Mariola, where the stores where not guarded at night, and where the locks and bolts on the doors were very frail, the arrest of any one for burglary was a very important matter. It was especially exciting at this time, since so many robberies had been committed, while no arrests had ever before been made. The news of the arrests, therefore, spread with great rapidity, and most of the best citizens in the whole township, together with all the loafers and hard characters, assembled in the vicinity of the Justice's court-room. When the doors were opened a general rush was made, and every foot of space was occupied by the eager throng.

The case was called at once, but it was necessary to clear a passage for the officers and their prisoners before the latter could be placed in the dock. At length all was ready, and the testimony was taken. Mr. Sanders testified that his store had been entered and a large quantity of valuable articles stolen ; that he afterwards found the goods in the barn and house occupied by the prisoners ; and that he was able to identify everything taken. The prisoners' lawyer tried to break down his testimony on cross-examination by asking a great many questions relative to the identification of the property ; but Mr. Sanders' answers were very conclusive, and the attempt to confuse him was a failure.

The remaining testimony was given by Marshal Binford

and several other citizens, all of whom testified to the circumstances attending the search, the flight of Cook and
Wallace, and their capture.   Neither Mr. Lincoln nor Mr.
Brown was called as a witness by the prosecution, since their
testimony was not necessary, and they did not wish to tell
whence they had received the information which induced
them to search the cottage.

On the conclusion of the hearing the prisoners' attorney
made a violent speech in favor of his clients, claiming that
they were honest citizens who had been made the victims
of a conspiracy.   He maintained that the goods found in
Cook's stable had not been conclusively shown to belong to
Sanders & Co. ; and even if the articles had been stolen, there
was no evidence to connect the prisoners with the theft ; the
goods might easily have been hidden where they were
found by some one else, in the absence of the two men
from home.   He said that it was a very significant fact that
the prosecution had not called as witnesses the men who
had been most active in dragging his clients ignominiously
to jail, against the remonstrances of many other good citizens.   He then moved that his clients be discharged on
the ground of insufficient evidence.   This being refused by
the Justices, he called several witnesses to prove that the prisoners had been away from home a great deal since the robbery, and others to prove the previous good character of
the accused ; he then rested his case.

Justice Green, after a short consultation with the two other
Justices sitting with him, announced that the prisoners
would be held to appear before the Grand Jury under bonds

of two thousand dollars each.   As this amount of bail was beyond their means to furnish, they were remanded to jail. The result of the preliminary examination was highly gratifying to the respectable portion of the community, though there was much dissatisfaction expressed among the loafer class at the large bail-bond required.   Webster had been cultivating Warden's acquaintance since he had witnessed the latter's actions during the search, and they stood together during the trial.   When the decision was announced Webster spoke up in a voice loud enough to be heard by several of the loafers around him :

"'That is an outrageous amount of bail to require from two poor men ; of course they cannot furnish it, and they will have to go to jail.   It is all the worse from the fact that the goods have been recovered, and I consider the decision an act of gross injustice."

" Well, what could you expect?" asked Warden.   "The big-bugs are down on them, and there is no justice here for a poor man."

"You are quite right," replied Webster, "and I think you have a very sensible idea of the way we are treated.   The only thing for us to do is to stick together as they do ; come, let's take a drink."

The invitation was promptly accepted, and in a short time Warden became quite pleased with Webster's style of conversation.   When they parted it was with the understanding that they should become better acquainted.

When the crowd passed out of the court-room Hays did not accompany Walker and Leitz immediately, as he wished to hear what was the general sentiment about Cook and Wallace. He found that nearly every one was convinced of their guilt, and that Mr. Lincoln was credited with having detected them himself; no one even suggested that any detectives were engaged in the affair. When most of the people had gone home, Hays went to Walker's restaurant and found the place crowded. He remained only a short time and then went to the Tremont House to dinner. In the evening he returned to the restaurant and found Walker in high good humor. His bar had been well patronized all day, and he had had over one hundred persons at dinner, so that his profits had been very large. He was delighted to see Hays, as he wished some one to talk to.

"I don't believe Cook stole those goods," he said; "but I know nothing about Wallace, and perhaps he did the job. I hope Leitz will come over this evening, for I want to have a good social talk with him. By the way, Hays, are you a mason?"

"No; I am not," replied Hays cautiously, uncertain how to reply. "I have been thinking of joining the order for some time, but I have been prevented in various ways. To tell the truth, I have been trying to find the right kind of a lodge, containing such men as you and Leitz; then I shall perhaps take the first degrees."

"You will be better off if you have nothing to do with the masons of any lodge. Men like Ben Leitz and me can keep our own secrets without taking a crowd into our confidence. It doesn't take me long to tell whom I can trust; and as I thought I could trust you I wanted to find out

I'll stick to you closer than a brother.—*p.* 71.

whether you were bound to any secret society. Now that I know you are not, I would be willing to tell you any of my secrets."

"I feel just that way toward you also," said Hays, "and I should like to tell you something about myself, so as to get your opinion and advice."

"Well, I shall be glad to hear it," answered Walker; "you can wait until after I shut up for the night and tell me your secret here."

Hays glanced around to see that he was not overheard by any one, and then said:

"All right, Walker; I feel that I can trust you. You must swear not to reveal the story, and I will tell you all. I want your advice very much, and I shall place my liberty and life in your hands."

Walker brought his clenched fist down on the bar with an oath, and added exultingly:

"Never fear me; I'll stick closer to you than a brother."

Hays then strolled over to one of the tables in the saloon and remained there all the evening gambling for small stakes. He won two or three dollars, and still further excited the admiration of the old *habitués* of the place by his expertness as a gambler. Leitz was playing at another table, and there were many customers present all the evening. They began to go away about ten o'clock, and at length Walker, Leitz, and Hays were left together. Walker locked his doors, pulled down the window-shades, and put out all the lights but one; then he drew Hays to one side and said:

"I wish you would take Leitz into your confidence, for we are old partners, and we always work together in everything. You needn't be afraid to trust him, for I would put myself into his hands without any hesitation. He can advise you better than I can, and he ought to know something about you, since, if you work with me, he will be more or less mixed up in it. What do you say?"

"Well, I have no objection," said Hays with great deliberation, at the same time rolling a huge chew of tobacco from one cheek to the other; "if you trust Mr. Leitz yourself, I do not ask any other guarantee."

"That's right, Hays; you stick to me and I'll help you to a good job," exclaimed Walker, delightedly. "Come, now, let's take a drink and go into the back room; we can talk there without fear of being disturbed."

They gathered around the stove in the back room, and Walker placed a large bottle of whiskey on a table close by. A few lemons, a bowl of sugar, several glasses, spoons, and a hot-water jug were at hand, and all the arrangements were completed to spend the night in talking and drinking together. Hays then commenced his story.

CHAPTER VIII

" I HAD been living in Cairo for some time previous to the events I am about to relate, and I had grown tired of working for nothing but a bare living. About six months ago I made the acquaintance of a man named Marsh, who owned quite a large brewery on the levee. He was doing a fair business, but he wanted to get into something which would pay better. He tried to sell out several times, but as he could not get any one to pay his price, he determined to sell out to an insurance company. For this purpose he insured the stock and buildings for a large amount, and then began to cultivate my acquaintance. At length he made a plain offer to give me one-fourth of what he received for insurance if I would set fire to his brewery. I thought there was no risk in it, and so I consented. He gave me a key to a side door, and said that he should go to St. Louis for a day or two, leaving his foreman in charge. During his absence I was to slip into the building and set fire to it near the furnace. Everything was arranged satisfactorily, and at the appointed time Mr. Marsh left town.

" As I was intending to burn it the next night, I was anxious to see how the place looked in the night-time; therefore I went down the levee about two o'clock in the morning. On approaching the brewery I found a large

4

barge alongside the levee, and a number of men were busily engaged in rolling kegs of beer into it. Every particle of stock was thus removed, and before daylight the barge cast off from the levee, and dropped down stream. I saw that his object, of course, was to get the insurance in full, while at the same time he would get the value of the stock by selling it in Kentucky or Missouri. The insurance companies would know nothing about the removal of the stock, hence they would pay the insurance upon it as if it had been destroyed. This did not concern me, except that I determined to get my share of the additional profit which he would make.

"The next night I went to my boarding-place about nine o'clock; I acted as if I was almost dead drunk, so that my friends carried me to my room and put me in bed. About midnight I dressed myself noiselessly, slipped out of the house, and went straight to the brewery. I found plenty of kindling stuff, and I made a large pile of it—too large, as I soon discovered. After lighting it I put a blanket over it to hide it until I should be far away. I then hurried out. The flames spread so rapidly, however, that the whole interior was in a light blaze before I could get off the levee, and the light instantly attracted the notice of the watchman at a neighboring warehouse. He caught sight of me at the same moment, and he immediately gave chase, shouting 'Stop thief!'

" He gained rapidly upon me, and his cries soon aroused a number of other people. By this time the flames were burning fiercely—as the brewery was very old and dry—and the light was so great that I feared being recognized by some one. I therefore dodged around a corner and waited for the watchman to come up. As he passed me under full headway I struck him a powerful blow with my fist, intending to stun him. He dropped instantly, and I escaped any further notice. I reached my boarding-house and got into bed without being seen or heard. The next morning the whole city was excited over the incendiarism and probable murder. The watchman had been struck on the jugular vein in the neck, and his condition was very serious. Several parties were arrested on suspicion, but they were discharged on examination. No one suspected me, but I learned that the case was to be put into the hands of Pinkerton, of Chicago, and then I decided to leave.

" When Marsh came back I asked him for my share of the insurance money. He said that I had done the job in such a bungling way that it was doubtful whether the companies would pay anything; moreover I had killed a man, and the result might be a hanging matter for me. He then said that he could give me only fifty dollars, and that I had better run away before I was arrested.

" He scared me a good deal, and I left there that night. Since then I have learned that the watchman has partly recovered, but his right side is wholly paralyzed, and he cannot move about. I have also learned that Marsh collected all his insurance without difficulty, since no one suspected him of having had anything to do with the fire. The fact is, he has played a pretty sharp trick on me, and I want to get even with him ; but I am afraid he will have me arrested if I make any fuss.   You see I have no hold on him at all.   He got twelve thousand dollars, and I ought to have one-fourth.   Now, gentlemen, I have put my safety in your hands, and have trusted you more than I ever trusted any one before ; but I have the utmost confidence in you and I wish you to give me your advice."

" Well, Hays, you're a trump," said old Walker, enthusiastically ; " I knew you were from the first—I am never mistaken in a man.   You did just right, and we will help you to get the money that fellow owes you, won't we, Leitz ? "

"Yes ; I think we can manage it," said Leitz, thoughtfully.   " As for the watchman, I would have served him the same myself."

"Ha! ha! ha! of course, you would," laughed old Walker.   " You *have* done the same scores of times. Come, let's have a good drink ; talking is dry work."

After drinking together they sat and discussed Hays' difficulty.   Leitz finally said that there was one way in which they might be able to squeeze the money out of Marsh : Hays might write to him that he knew all about the way in which the brewery was emptied of its stock the night before the fire ; that he knew how the insurance had been obtained on property which was not burned ; and that if Marsh still refused to pay . Hays the share agreed upon for setting fire to the brewery, the latter would get a friend to write a full account of the transaction to the insurance companies, so that they would arrest Marsh for arson and for fraud.

This plan was agreed upon as being the most feasible one, and they all drank success to the scheme. By this time both Leitz and Walker were somewhat under the influence of liquor, and their tongues were loosened to an unusual degree.

"Come, Leitz, tell Hays your story," said Walker; "he has placed confidence in us, and we ought to show the same trust in him."

"All right; I'm willing, though it isn't very interesting," replied Leitz, taking another drink.

He then gave a brief account of his early life, which was passed near Ogdensburgh, New York. He stated that he was a free-and-easy kind of a fellow until the time of the McKenzie rebellion in Canada, in 1838. He was then a young man of loose habits, and his mind was fired with the idea of becoming one of the liberators of Canada from British rule. When McKenzie organized his expedition on the Canada frontier, seized the steamer *Caroline*, and made his raid upon Toronto, Leitz joined the rebel forces, and entered the city among the first. They soon broke their ranks and began plundering the shop-keepers and other citizens. Leitz finally entered the house of a wealthy banker and demanded his money; on being told that there was only a small sum of money in the house, Leitz again insisted on receiving a large amount. By this time the Canadian volunteers were driving back the straggling bands of rebels, and Leitz told the gentleman that if at least one hundred guineas were not immediately produced, he would kill the whole family. At this some of the women rushed out screaming, and Leitz shot the old man dead. Before he had time to search for money he heard the approach of the Canadians in the street, and he was forced to escape by the back way. He succeeded in avoiding capture and reached the frontier in safety ; but the search became so hot for the murderer of the 'Toronto banker, that he thought best to leave that part of the country. He therefore travelled west and settled at Mariola, where he was joined by his wife, and where he had remained ever since.

".That shows you what a devil of a fellow Leitz is," said Walker. "Besides, he never goes back on his word, and he isn't afraid of anything. Now you shall hear my story : I was born in New York, where I grew up like a weed until I was about twenty-two years old. Then I was caught 'shoving the queer,'* and was 'sent up' for five years. Well, I served my time, and when I came out I went in with some friends of mine who were first-class 'coney' men.† I made a heap of money and secured it by putting all my property in my wife's name. Finally I was caught and was 'sent up' for ten years. I was pardoned out in six years, however, as I was rapidly dying of consumption."

Here he paused to laugh immoderately, as if he thought it was a good joke, and then continued :

" Well, I went at once to see my wife, but I found that she had obtained a divorce from me, and that she utterly

---

* Passing counterfeit money.

† Counterfeiters are called "coney" men or "coniackers," the terms being applied only to those who manufacture bogus coin for others to pass. They rarely handle it themselves.

repudiated me. I didn't mind losing her so much, but she had secure possession of all my hard earned savings, —— —— her.

Walker paused to take a drink, and the expression of his face plainly showed that he was disgusted with such a lack of honesty on the part of his wife. He actually felt that she had stolen from him all the money he had saved, and no honest mechanic, who had earned his living and saved money by the sweat of his brow, could have shown a greater degree of virtuous indignation than was depicted in the face of that hoary old scoundrel.

"When I found that my wife would not give up any of my money, I went to Texas in the hope of making a fortune in a new country. I kept the company of a wild crowd all the time, and a mistake about a horse caused me to leave Texas in some haste. I then started a restaurant in New Orleans, and succeeded very well; but I cannot endure slavery, and so I travelled north. Most abolitionists mix up a good deal of pious cant in their theories, but I am not one of that sort. Finally I settled here, and I have done well enough so far; but the teetotallers and pious people are persecuting me worse now than the Southern fire-eaters ever did in New Orleans for being an abolitionist. They are all fanatics, and they will not listen to reason; what with their praying and preaching they are determined to ruin my business and to prevent me from earning my living honestly. Well, I guess I'm about even with 'em; it ain't necessary to say anything about that," he continued, with a knowing wink at Leitz; "but they haven't as many churches as they once had. I was willing to cry quits with them after the churches burned, but they began to bring the subject up in the school. When the children passed me, they would point at me and cry: 'There goes the wicked rum-seller!' and then they would congregate around my saloon and sing temperance songs and such slush. I told them they had better leave me alone; but they kept it up, and now the children haven't any place to go to school, and they don't bother me any more. Ha! ha! ha! I guess I know how to protect myself."

"You served them just right," drawled Hays; "they had no right to intefere in your business."

"Of course not," said Leitz; " Walker has a legal license, and he has as good a right to sell liquor as they have to sell groceries or dry-goods."

"Are you doing anything in the 'coney' line now?" asked Hays.

"No; I have quit that business. I can make money fast enough by selling liquor, if these praying cusses will leave me alone. Besides, Leitz and I have a way of making money which we will tell you when the time comes."

"How do you suppose Cook and Wallace got those goods?" asked Hays.

"Well, I think they were working with Warden," said Leitz. "They aren't smart enough to have done the job alone. Do you like Warden, Walker?"

"No; I wouldn't trust him. He brags a good deal, but he would be sure to go back on any one that trusted him, if necessary to save himself."

"That is my opinion too," said Hays.

"Well, I must be going," said Leitz; "it is after one o'clock."

Walker went to the door with Lietz, and cautiously closed it after him. When he returned, Hays said:

"Leitz is a splendid fellow, but what do you think of Morgan?"

"Oh! he's well enough, only he's a little soft. He has been in the penitentiary twice," said Walker.

"Is it possible! What was it for?"

"Once for stealing, and the second time for passing coun terfeit money. He hasn't any grit, and he begged out each time."

"Do you think he fired the elevator the other night? I partly thought so myself; but, as you say, he doesn't seem to have the nerve to do such a thing."

"Oh! I dont know," said Walker, with a yawn; "I'll talk about that some other time."

Well, I must go," said Hays, taking the hint. "Good-night; I will see you again soon." So saying he departed.

4*

CHAPTER IX.

CLARK made good use of his time during Wolff's absence. By cultivating the friendship of Mrs. Black,
the housekeeper, he was able to learn, with no apparent
effort, all that she knew about the hotel-keeper and his
friends. It was Wolff's custom to go away nearly every
month for two or three days, and on his return he always
had plenty of money.

It was more than a week before he returned from his trip,
and he was in high spirits. Clark rendered a full account of
all that had occurred during his stewardship, and Wolff
showed perfect satisfaction with everything.

"Has Davis been here while I was away?" he asked,
finally.

"Oh! yes; he has been here nearly every day, and I had
to chalk down a great many drinks to him. He brought company several times, and they often took meals here, so that
the bill is quite large. Mrs. Black said that she thought it
was all right, and he told me that you let him have everything he wanted on credit, so I made no objection."

"Yes; that's all right; I meant to have told you about
him before I went, but I forgot it. We have dealings
together, and I guess he will be here soon to see me."

Davis was the watchmaker whose shop I had entered,

and who seemed so lazy and careless about getting a job. I had told Clark to make his acquaintance, as I suspected that he and Wolff were partners in some rascality.

In a day or two after Wolff's return, four men arrived at night and took the best rooms in the house. They had their meals in a separate room, and no one knew that they were there except the three regular inmates of the hotel. Davis came over every day, but he never stopped more than a few minutes. He would talk to Wolff for a moment, and then they would go up-stairs. After one drink at the bar he would hurry home, as if anxious to avoid observation.

One evening Clark and Wolff were sitting by the fire, when the former made some allusion to Davis, to which Wolff replied that Davis was one of his best friends.

" I hope he is doing well," said Clark, " but I am afraid his business doesn't pay very well just now."

" Oh ! yes it does," said Wolff, with a sly laugh ; " there are not many watchmakers in the country who are making money so fast as Davis. It takes a man of uncommon ability to turn out such work as this," he continued, taking a roll of counterfeit five-dollar gold pieces from his pocket.

Clark examined them carefully and exclaimed in admiration :

" Did he make these? they are the best I ever saw ! I am pretty well posted on this kind of work, but I believe I should have been fooled by these shiners myself."

At that moment footsteps were heard approaching, and Clark slipped the money into his pocket just as several customers entered the bar-room.

They remained until about nine o'clock, and on their departure Clark gave back the coin to Wolff, with the remark that he should like to get some like it.

"Well, I will see to that by-and-by," said Wolff; "but don't talk to Davis about it, for he is such a nervous, faint-hearted fellow that you might frighten him. While I was away I sold over twelve hundred dollars in bogus coin. I sell it as fast as Davis can make it, at fifty per cent. of its nominal value. Those four fellows up-stairs are waiting for a lot of it. They expected to have found it ready for them, for they don't usually come until I have a good supply; but Davis is lazy, and he will not work much while I'm away."

"I should think it would be to his interest to work steadily," said Clark.

"Yes; it is of course; but his work is very hard, as he has to do it at night in a very uncomfortable workshop. He has a fine set of tools and dies, however, and he can turn out a great deal in a short time. I must go up-stairs now to see my four customers; won't you come up and make their acquaintance?"

"You are sure they are all trustworthy?" asked Clark, cautiously.

"Oh! yes, indeed. Come along; they will be glad to know you."

Clark was introduced to them all by Wolff, who vouched for his character (or rather lack of character) in the most flattering terms. In fact, he whispered to one of the gang that Clark was one of the most skilful bank-robbers in the whole country; on receiving this information their respect for him was vastly increased, and they all showed a great anxiety to cultivate his friendship. They drank and played cards until a late hour, and it was nearly day-break before Clark went to bed. He remained up in order to write me an account of the discoveries he had made, as he feared the men would get their bogus coin next day. He did not sleep over two hours before it was time to take his letter to the depot in order to catch the early train.

On receiving his letter, I replied instantly, telling him to learn the route the men intended to take, and to telegraph to me the instant they started. I then called on the United States Marshal and told him that I had discovered a nest of counterfeiters, whom I desired to arrest myself at my own discretion, as I did not wish to expose my plans in another operation. At my request, therefore, the Marshal swore in George H. Bangs, my superintendent, as a Deputy Marshal. The latter then held himself in readiness to go at a moment's notice.

In two days Clark wrote that the men would start the following day. They had received about fourteen hundred dollars in ten and five-dollar gold pieces, and a large sum in silver fifty-cent pieces. They intended travelling rapidly to Tennessee, where the money could be passed without 'suspicion. Clark had previously sent an accurate description of the men, so that I anticipated no difficulty in capturing them. As I knew the road they were to take, I sent Bangs to intercept them at the junction of another road about twenty miles from Mariola. I also telegraphed to the sheriff of a county about one hundred miles further along on the same road, asking him to meet Bangs on the train at the depot of the principal town in that county. I told him that he would need several assistants, as there were four desperate men to be arrested.

The next day Clark telegraphed to me that the men had left, and I soon received a despatch from Bangs stating that he had discovered the quartet of counterfeit-passers, and that he should keep them in view until he reached the place where I had decided to arrest them.

Bangs found them occupying widely distant seats, acting as if they were total strangers to each other. He had no difficulty in recognizing them, however, and when the train reached the point agreed upon, where the sheriff came on board with three deputies, Bangs designated the four whom he wished arrested. The arrests were made at night, and the men offered no resistance. They were taken into a private room at the station, and were immediately searched. Over fifteen hundred dollars of counterfeit gold coin and about three hundred dollars in bogus silver coin were found upon their persons and in their satchels. They all gave fictitious names, but my warrants were good enough to hold them, especially in view of the discovery of the bogus coin. Bangs brought them immediately to Chicago, and United States Commissioner Meeker held them for trial under bonds of fifteen hundred dollars each.

CHAPTER X.

WHILE Webster was idling about town he chanced tc make the acquaintance of a farmer named James Curran. He was a good-natured, honest-looking, jolly Irishman, about fifty-five years of age, and he was known far and wide as "Jimmy." He lived on his farm about nine miles from Mariola, and his reputation was untarnished by even the suspicion of wrong-doing. His wife was a comely, contented German, and they had four children. His farm was quite small, but he seemed to work it to great advantage, as he sold a great deal of produce to Mariola merchants.

Webster was a remarkably keen observer, and he soon noticed that Jimmy came to town at least once a week, and sometimes oftener. His loads usually consisted of poultry, eggs, butter, lard, hides, etc., and the quantities of these articles were so great that Webster's attention was attracted. He thought that probably Jimmy was all right, but still there could be no harm in looking after him a little. He noticed that Jimmy always came to town in the forenoon, and after selling his load he spent the day in the saloons, though he never became drunk. Then he would get supper and start home a little after seven o'clock. This was rather peculiar, since by starting two hours earlier he would have daylight to travel by and would save the price of his supper.

Webster began to interest himself in Curran's movements, and he frequently met the farmer at saloons; after a time they became quite intimate, and Curran showed a great partiality for Webster's society. It was therefore easy for Webster to keep a good watch upon him without exciting suspicion.

The season was a very open one, and the water-fowl began to fly early; Webster was fond of hunting, and he determined to visit Curran's house while out on a shooting expedition, as he was anxious to learn something about the farm which was so enormously productive. In fact, by this time, he had reached the conclusion that Jimmy Curran was either a notorious thief or else the receiver of goods stolen by others. Accordingly he left Mariola early in the morning, and by good luck and skilful shooting he had a well-filled game-bag on arriving at Curran's house. Jimmy was very glad to see him, and so was Mrs. Curran, a plump, neat German. They stayed about the house until noon, when a fine dinner was served.

While indoors Webster was engaged in making a mental inventory of the contents of the house, though he did not appear to observe anything. He was particularly struck with the furniture, knick-knacks, modern conveniences, and ornaments which were scattered about in great profusion. When they sat down to dinner he noticed that the table-ware was of the finest quality, and there were several luxuries among the dishes which seemed quite out of place in such a household. After dinner they took a walk about the barn and the out-houses, where Webster observed a number of suspicious signs. In the tool-house he saw about four or five dozen axes, nearly as many saws, several kegs of nails, a dozen large grind-stones, and many other things in the same proportion. They were all new, and most of the articles were in their original packages, just as they were sold in the stores. The quantity of tools was so great that Webster came to the conclusion that Curran must be intending to start a country store of his own.

On returning to the house Curran said that he was obliged to go to see a neighbor for an hour or two, and that Webster must remain until his return, when he would take him part way to Mariola in his wagon. Webster was quite willing, and Jimmy started off. Mrs. Curran was busy with her children and with other household affairs, so that Webster had a fine opportunity to examine the barn, granary, hen-house, and tool-house without interruption. A more miscellaneous collection than the contents of these buildings can hardly be imagined. Under the hay were dry-goods, groceries, furniture, kitchen utensils, crockery, and hardware, while barrels of salt, whiskey, molasses, vinegar, and all varieties of wet groceries were neatly hidden in large grain bins ; these bins had false bottoms, with only a light layer of grain on top, and admittance to the space below was gained by a door at the back of each bin. Webster found such a vast collection of goods that he could not understand how they had been stolen. It was certainly impossible that they had been pilfered in broad daylight, since many of the articles were very bulky. He determined to solve the mystery at the earliest opportunity, and to have

Jimmy Curran arrested in the act of stealing, if possible
He did not await Curran's return, but started away after he
made his discoveries, telling Mrs. Curran that the shooting
was too good to lose and that he would return to Mariola
on foot.

After leaving the house he made quite a tour around the
country, stopping at all the farm-houses. He soon learned
that Curran was in the habit of selling all kinds of goods to
the neighboring farmers ; his prices were often lower than
those of the Mariola store-keepers, so that he was exten-
sively patronized. He did not profess to keep a store, but
he was able to furnish almost all kinds of merchandise ; he
accounted for his supply of goods by saying that he always
bought everything by wholesale for himself, and he could
afford to let his neighbors have it cheap if they wished to
save the journey to Mariola.

Webster returned to the city and awaited further developments. In a day or two Curran drove in with a load of
grain, which he sold at the building temporarily used for the
elevator. He then spent the day with Webster, and they
had such a jovial time at the saloons, that by eight o'clock
in the evening Webster seemed wholly intoxicated.
Curran had reached that happy stage where he

<blockquote>

" Wasna fu', but just had plenty."

</blockquote>

He left Webster in a maudlin condition in a low saloon
and went to get his horses at the stable where they had been
left. Webster staggered out shortly afterward, and by the
time Curran had harnessed up his team Webster was near

by in a miraculously sober condition. The night was quite dark, and Curran drove home at only a moderate gait, so that Webster had no difficulty in keeping up with him. On reaching an unsettled stretch of the road he drove very slowly, occasionally stopping as if to listen ; at length, turning out of the highway, he went about two hundred yards from the road and then stopped in a small grove of trees. Webster crept up close and saw that he had blanketed his horses and had rolled himself up in anothor blanket on some hay in his wagon.

The situation was anything but agreeable to Webster, who shivered and chattered in the raw night wind for over three hours before Curran made a movement. The horses stood perfectly still, without neighing or stamping, as if they were quite accustomed to their duties, and not a sound was heard except Jimmy's heavy snoring as he slept off the effects of the liquor he had drank.

About midnight, however, he awoke with a start, raised himself up to listen, and got out of the wagon. He cautiously lit a match to enable him to look at his watch, and he then uncovered his horses preparatory to making a start. As he drove back to the road Webster noticed that the wagon wheels ran almost noiselessly, and that there was no clicking of the harness. The phantom team turned back towards Mariola, with Webster close behind. Curran entered the town at a walk, and drove to a large, well-kept saloon. The whole town was wrapped in sleep, and no sound could be heard except the whistling of the wind and the creaking of signs and shutters ; the sky was overcast with heavy clouds and inky darkness shrouded everything, so that nothing could be distinguished at a distance of more than twenty feet.

Curran seemed to know his way intuitively, however, and passing to the rear of the saloon, he entered by a door which was left unlocked. He soon opened the front door and rolled out a barrel, which seemed quite heavy. He left it standing beside his wagon and returned to the saloon, but he came out again almost instantly and began to scrape the head of the barrel. Webster concluded that he was removing the names and marks, and it afterward proved that such was the case. Having scraped a few minutes, Curran returned to the saloon, closed and locked the front door, and came out as he had entered, leaving no trace of his visit except the absence of the barrel of liquor which he rolled into his wagon.

He then drove to a marble-cutter's yard, followed by the astonished Webster, who could not imagine what there was worth stealing in such a place. Jimmy thought differently, however, for he selected a fine marble slab and slid it up an inclined board into his wagon. A neat foot-stone was placed beside the other, and he then turned his horses' heads homeward. Webster followed him about two miles, and was about to turn back when Curran stopped near a large farm-house and cautiously crept up to the hen-roost. He soon returned with an armful of chickens, whose necks he had wrung so scientifically that not one of them had uttered a cackle or a squawk. He then resumed his journey, and Webster returned to town.

Stealing the Marble Slab.—*p. 92.*

On receiving Webster's report I wrote to Messrs. Brown and Lincoln that I would like them to keep a close watch upon a man named Jimmy Curran, who lived about nine miles from Mariola. I told them that he was in the habit of bringing large quantities of produce to town to sell, most of which was probably stolen from his neighbors; that he usu‑ally left town early in the evening, but that he went only a short distance and then hitched his horses in a grove until about midnight, at which time he returned to Mariola and stole anything he could lay his hands on. I advised them to follow him on horseback at the first opportunity, and then if he should act as I expected, they could capture him with full evidence of his guilt in his possession.

"Well, this *is* strange," said Mr. Brown to Mr. Lincoln on reading my letter; "we have known Jimmy Curran for several years, 'and have never had the slightest suspicion of him. I can hardly believe that Mr. Pinkerton's informa‑tion is correct; but still, you recollect how much we gained by following his instructions with regard to Cook and Wal‑lace, and so we had better obey him implicitly in this mat‑ter also."

"Yes; I agree with you," said Mr. Lincoln; "besides, now that I come to think about it, I recollect that Jimmy has sold me an immense quantity of produce. I have never given it a second thought until now, but it does seem odd how he could have raised such crops on that little farm. I guess we may as well follow Mr. Pinkerton's advice; so the next time Jimmy comes to town I will let you know, and we will follow him in the evening."

Two days later Jimmy drove up to Mr. Lincoln's store and sold a large amount of butter, eggs, and live poultry. He then spent the day with Webster in visiting the different saloons. At eight o'clock in the evening he took his departure for home, and Webster went to his boarding-place, knowing that his presence would not be required.

The night was not very dark, and Messrs. Brown and Lincoln did not dare to follow Curran very closely for fear of being seen by him. He drove off at a rapid gait, and the two gentlemen took the same road at a long distance in his rear. They had made all preparations for passing the night out-doors, and they decided to take their stations near the road, so as to make sure of seeing Curran on his return. They chose a spot just outside of the town, where a clump of trees gave them shelter, and there they awaited the events which the night might bring forth.

Shortly after midnight they saw a team coming toward Mariola; leaving their horses in the grove, they followed the noiseless wagon into the city. They knew that Curran would not dare to drive fast for fear of making a noise, and so they preferred to follow on foot, as they could watch him with less risk of discovery. He first stopped in front of a merchant tailor's shop, which he entered by raising a side window. He then brought out several bolts of cloth and placed them beneath the hay in the bottom of his wagon. A short distance further down the street he walked into a butcher's shop, the door of which was unlocked, and there he selected a number of fine roasts and steaks, which he put into a large market-basket; this he covered with hay as before, and then he stood two or three minutes in meditation. He seemed desirous of completing his marketing in good style, for, leaving his team standing, he went to a restaurant where Webster had treated him to oysters that day. He had a key which fitted a side-door, and he soon came out with a box of canned oysters on his shoulder. Finally he drove to a lumber-yard, where he took on a load of about three or four hundred feet of choice lumber.

The lumber-yard was so situated that Messrs. Lincoln and Brown were unable to approach close to Curran without being seen by him; hence they were some distance away when he again took his seat. They had decided to wait until he had completed his stealing before arresting him, but they had not expected that he would be so soon satisfied; therefore when they saw him turn towards home at a brisk trot they were not able to overtake him on foot, and they were obliged to hasten after him as rapidly as possible until they reached the spot where they had left their horses. Jimmy, however, had caught sight of them, and he was already far in advance, driving at a fast trot. The moment they gained their saddles they began the pursuit in earnest, and, although the fugitive urged his horses into a full gallop, there was no hope for his escape. As they gradually drew nearer and nearer, Jimmy became desperate, as he began to feel sure that they had seen him in the city, and that they intended to arrest him. On reaching a point where the road passed through a piece of thick woods a bright idea flashed into his mind: leaving his horses to gallop on without guidance, Jimmy sprang into the rear of his wagon, and commenced to throw out the goods he had stolen ; out went the lumber first of all, as it was the heaviest and the most conspicuous of all his plunder. Still the pursuers gained ; out went the oysters in a damaged heap by the roadside, and closely following went the choice cuts of meat in a confused mass of mud, basket, and hay ; last of all he flung out the bolts of cloth, throwing them as far as possible into the shrubbery on each side. Then, resuming his seat, he urged on his tired and panting horses ; but the latter were unable to keep the pace, and one of them at length stumbled and fell. The next moment Mr. Lincoln ranged up on one side and Mr. Brown on the other.

"Shure, an' is it you, Mr. Lincoln ?" asked Jimmy, as he recognized his pursuers. "'Troth, thin, but it's glad I am to see yez both. D'ye see, I've been radin' about the highwaymin in the ould counthry, an' I thought yez were a pair o' Claude Duvals, mebbe. Will yez help me up with me horse ? shure it's a divil of a fall he had."

The horse was much frightened and exhausted, but not hurt, and in a few minutes the team was in good condition again.

"Now, Jimmy," said Mr. Lincoln, "you are our prisoner, and you must go back to Mariola with us."

"Yer prisoner, is it ! Shure now, Misther Lincoln, ye wouldn't arrest a dacint, rispectable farmer for goin' on a bit of a shpray ? Och, I know I've taken a dhrop too much ; but let me go this time, gintlemin, an' you'll never see me dhrunk agin."

" It isn't on that account that we arrest you, Mr. Curran, as you well know," replied Mr. Brown.

"Well, ye see, Misther Brown, I must ha' bin ashlape whin me horses began to run so fast; I thought I was goin' home, but, be dad, I don't know whether I'm on the right road or not."

" No; I think not," said Mr. Lincoln; " you are on a very bad road, indeed. However, you must go back to Mariola with us, and we will pick up your load on the way."

Jimmy expressed entire ignorance of Mr. Lincoln's meaning, but, finding that he could not escape, he took his seat in the wagon with the remark :

" Oh ! well, Mr. Lincoln, ye will have yer joke, so I suppose I must go to satisfy ye."

Mr. Brown led Mr. Lincoln's horse, while Mr. Lincoln and Jimmy occupied the wagon seat. They made their prisoner assist in picking up the various stolen articles along the roadside, and as each new article was reached he expressed his unqualified wonder that he had not seen them as he drove by. On entering Mariola they placed the load in Mr. Lincoln's store, and then took their prisoner to Marshal Binford. The latter was aroused with much difficulty, and Mr. Brown told him that they had a prisoner to be locked up.

" All right," said the Marshal from his upper window ; " I'll be down presently. Did you arrest him on a warrant ? "

" No ; but we caught him in the act," said Mr. Brown. " He is another of the same kind of honest men as Cook

5

and Wallace ; you needn't be afraid that he'll sue you for false arrest, Marshal."

Binford drew in his head quickly, as if the retort were not pleasant to him ; in a short time he came down and gave Curran a room in the jail.

It was now nearly daylight, and Messrs. Lincoln and Brown ordered three or four large wagons to be made ready to go to Curran's farm, as I had written to them that several teams would be necessary to move all the stolen goods. They then roused up a magistrate and swore out a search-warrant to enable them to overhaul Curran's house, stables, etc. It was seven o'clock by the time they reached the farm, and Mrs. Curran had evidently been up several hours. Finding that her husband had not returned at the usual hour, she had suspected that something had been discovered to cause his arrest; she had therefore carefully hidden everything which could lead any one to imagine there was anything wrong about the place. There were a number of storekeepers and leading merchants of the town in the party, and Mrs. Curran received them so naturally and easily that some of them began to think there must be a mistake. They looked around the buildings for a few minutes while waiting for the arrival of Messrs. Brown and Lincoln, but they discovered no evidences of the presence of stolen goods, and they almost felt like dissuading Mr. Lincoln from searching the premises.

The two leaders had been detained some minutes later than the rest of the party; but on their arrival the search began in earnest, in spite of the cries and protestation of the whole Curran family. As nest after nest was discovered, the astonishment of the storekeepers was unbounded. They identified goods which they had missed months before, and there was not a single merchant present who failed to find a portion of his stock on the Curran premises. The whole forenoon was spent in moving the goods, and by the time the articles known to have been stolen had been removed, there was little left in the house.

Curran was brought before two Justices on the following day, and was then held for trial on six different counts for larceny. His bail was fixed at fifteen hundred dollars on each count, in default of which he was committed to the county jail.

During the next week there was a daily congregation of the Mariola storekeepers and the neighbors of Curran to examine the stolen goods; gradually the articles were identified and taken away, until only a few lots remained unclaimed, and these were eventually sold at auction.

CHAPTER XI.

WALKER, Morgan, Leitz, and Hays were drinking together early on the morning that the search was made at Curran's. They had heard of Curran's arrest, but they could not find out what was the charge against him. When the first wagon-load of goods came in they went together to hear the news. The story soon spread rapidly that Jimmy Curran had been arrested for stealing, and that his house had been found filled with stolen property. The quartette above mentioned having heard all there was to be told, returned to Walker's saloon and sat down together in the bar-room.

"Well, I thought I was a good judge of human nature," said Walker, "but this business completely upsets me. I never thought Jimmy Curran had enough sense to do a job so neatly as he has been doing."

"No; nor I either," said Leitz. "The beauty of his game was, that it was so simple."

"Yes; that showed his shrewdness," said Hays; "it is not always the most cunning trick that succeeds the best."

"That is all very true," said Morgan in a boasting manner; "but if I had been smart enough to steal all those goods, I should have hidden them so they could not be found. Do you suppose I would have been caught as Jimmy was ? No, siree !"

"You don't know what you're talking about, Morgan," replied Walker. "Do you think that Lincoln and Brown caught Jimmy Curran without anybody else's help ? They are reasonably smart, but they aren't smart enough for that. No, sir ; they have had detectives at work—I am sure of it."

"You don't think so !" exclaimed Morgan, turning very white.

"Yes ; I do think so," replied the old man.

"So do I," said Leitz ; "the more I think about it the more I know that Walker is right."

"Well, then, we must find out who they are," said Hays.

"Yes ; that ought to be done the first thing," said Walker. "They will soon begin to blow about their success in capturing Cook, Wallace, and Curran, and then we shall easily find out who are engaged in spying 'round."

"I'm not afraid of 'em anyhow," Leitz remarked in a low tone ; "I never trust any one with my secrets, and so I have no cause to fear the best detective that ever lived."

"You can't keep everything to yourself," replied Walker ; "you must have some one to confide in. Why, it is only lately that you and I told our secrets to Hays."

"That is an entirely different thing," argued Leitz. "We have Hays in our power, for we know enough about him to settle him for life if he should attempt to inform upon us. You see, we are all three tied together ; if one should try to sell out the other two, he would have only his word against both of the others'; besides, the other two could easily prove that the other was a criminal, and thus they would get their revenge."

"That's a fact," said Walker; "you are always right, Leitz. But, now, who is it that is helping Lincoln and Brown? We must find out right away."

A crowd came in just at this time, full of excitement about Curran's arrest, and Hays helped Walker serve out drinks. They were quite busy for some time, but at last Hays had a chance to speak to Walker quietly, though Morgan and Leitz were not far away, and several others were in the saloon.

"Walker, I want to speak to you alone," said Hays, in a very low tone.

"What's up now?" asked Walker.

"Never mind," replied Hays; "get rid of Morgan if you can, for I don't want any one to hear except you and Leitz."

"All right," said Walker; then walking to the other end of the bar he spoke to Morgan: "I wish you would go over to the Globe Hotel, Morgan, and hear what Wolff thinks about this arrest. I don't like Wolff myself, but he is a shrewd fellow, and he may know something more about the case than we do."

"I was just thinking of that," answered Morgan, ever ready to do anything for the "old man."

"Well, find out what he knows and thinks about it," said Walker, handing Morgan a parting drink.

When Morgan had left the saloon, Walker nodded to

Leitz, and the two men joined Hays at one end of the bar. Hays had an immense chew of tobacco in his mouth, and by the rapidity with which he chewed he showed that he was somewhat excited. The two older men had noticed that this was the only way in which Hays ever showed haste or excitement, and so they waited several minutes for him to speak.

"Well, what is it, Hays?" asked Walker. "I see you have something on your mind."

"Walker, you know I trust you and Leitz perfectly," finally drawled out Hays; "but I have my ideas about a certain other person, and I was sorry you talked so plainly this morning about our secrets. It may be that I am too suspicious, but I tell you I—don't—like—Morgan. Now he may be all right; but there is something that looks bad: he was the first man to know anything about Curran's arrest, and he knew more than anybody else. I am afraid that he is the man that gave Curran away. Anyhow, whether that is true or not, I don't like to trust him."

"I don't know but that you are right," replied Leitz, thoughtfully; "yet I can hardly see how he did it. He was here playing cards until after one o'clock, and it was about that time that the chase commenced. He might have seen Curran on his way home, and then informed Lincoln and Brown."

"No; it was all planned beforehand," said Walker. "Morgan may have seen Curran before, and if so he could have told Lincoln and Brown to be ready the next time Jimmy came to town. Still, I don't feel sure about it, and so I'll tell you what we'll do: we will watch Morgan all the time—never allow him to go anywhere except with us or watched by one of us. I tell you, if he should blow on us we should be in a bad fix."

"All right," said Hays; "we will never lose sight of him, and if he shows any signs of going back on us—well, I guess something will happen to him."

The three men looked at each other a moment, nodded significantly, and then the conference broke up.

Meantime everything went along quietly at the Globe Hotel. Clark was a great favorite with Wolff, and his intimacy with the handsome housekeeper progressed most satisfactorily. They paid no attention to the arrest of Jimmy Curran, since that was a kind of knavery which they did not countenance. The news of the arrest of the four counterfeiters reached them after some delay, and they were all much alarmed for a time. Wolff, Clark, and Davis held several consultations on the subject, and they tried to reason out a theory to account for the arrest of the four men. On learning of this I caused a brief paragraph to be inserted in the daily newspapers, to the effect that four men had passed counterfeit money in payment for railroad tickets, and they had finally been arrested on the railroad train with a large quantity of bogus coin in their possession. This paragraph was seen by Wolff, and he immediately showed it to Clark and Davis.

"There, that accounts for the arrest," he said. "You know that they changed cars about twenty miles south of here and bought tickets on the other road. I should have supposed that they would have had better sense than to pay out any of the stuff in these parts. Probably the ticket agent recollected them and telegraphed to have them arrested."

"Well, I'm mighty glad that we've found out how they were caught, for I began tô be afraid that there had been detectives at work," said Davis.

"Yes; I feel much easier about the matter now," said Clark.

"I must acknowledge I was rather nervous myself," said Wolff, "especially as I wanted to start off again to sell some more of the shiners. How long will it take you to make me about two thousand dollars, Davis?"

"I don't know whether I care to do it just now," replied Davis. "You see, if they caught you they would be sure to catch me too."

"Oh! I can fix that safe enough," Wolff argued "Clark and I will manage it together. I will go ahead and make the arrangements, while Clark follows me with the money. He will simply deliver the bogus and receive the genuine money, and the purchasers will not know whence he comes nor whither he goes. We will each have a horse and buggy, and all deliveries shall be made at specified points on the roadside, so that there will be no danger to either of us."

"Yes; that will be a good plan, and I will commence to make the coin to-night," said Davis. "It will take me about three weeks to make two thousand dollars, and I must get to work as soon as possible."

5*

" Is the work very hard ? " asked Clark.

" Not very, except that I have to do much of it at night. I have excavated a room underneath my house, where I can work without the least danger.   There is a trap-door in my sitting-room, and it fits so closely that it would never be noticed even if the floor were bare ; but I keep it always covered by a large rug, and no one could possibly suspect its presence.   I have a set of simple signals with my wife, and she tells me when to come out and when I must keep quiet."

" Well, you must work as fast as you can," said Wolff, " so you had better begin at once."

" All right ; I'm not afraid, now that I know those fellows were captured by their own carelessness.   You must come over and see my place, Clark ; it is as good a shop as you ever saw, I fancy."

" I will drop in soon," replied Clark ; " but I will let you know beforehand.   Well, good-day."

After Davis had gone, Wolff laid out a plan of operations with Clark, and all the details were fully settled.

" By the way, we must find some one to take charge of the bar," said Wolff.   " Do you know of a suitable man ? "

" No, not just now," said Clark ; " but it seems to me that it would be well to hire a man who is a comparative stranger in the town."

" That's a good idea," said Wolff, " and we will look around for some such fellow."

When I received Clark's report of this conversation I sent him instructions to make Webster's acquaintance, and to introduce Wolff and Webster to each other as soon as possible. I wrote to Webster at the same time to cultivate Wolff's friendship in order to get installed as bar-keeper during the absence of Wolff and Clark.

In a day or two Clark paid his promised visit to Davis. He was introduced to Mrs. Davis, and the three sat together talking until a neighbor's child who was present went home. Then Davis took a hasty glance up and down the street, pulled the rug to one side, and then went to the side of the room. Clark was able, on close examination, to perceive the outline of a trap-door about two feet square, but he saw no means of raising it.

"How do you get it up?" he asked.

"That's the prettiest thing about it," said Davis, chuckling at his own ingenuity.

He then pointed to a knob on the floor which was apparently intended to keep the front door from striking the wall when opened wide; on pulling a small iron bolt out of the side, and stepping on the knob, it yielded to his weight, while at the same instant one side of the trap-door raised up sufficiently to permit it to be lifted off without difficulty.

"You see," said Davis, "there is a lever under the floor which is worked by this knob. There is no danger of lifting the trap-door by accident, for when this bolt is in place the knob will not go down. Ain't that a pretty clever piece of work?"

"It is, indeed," replied Clark; "it beats anything I ever saw."

They then descended into the secret cellar, and Mrs.

Davis closed the door above them. Davis quickly lit a lamp, and Clark had a good view of the whole place. The room was about nine feet high, and twelve feet wide by fifteen feet long. The floor was covered by boards laid on the earth, so that there was no rumbling noise made by stepping on them. They were also protected by a rag carpet to prevent sound, and Davis, as an additional precaution, pulled off his boots. There were two good apertures for ventilation, and the air of the room was fresh and comfortably warm. The workshop was completely furnished with every necessity for melting, moulding, filing, and cutting metals, and all the tools were of the best character. A large battery and trough in one corner showed the means by which the bogus money was made to appear so much like the genuine article, and indeed all the appliances were such as are used by only the most scientific counterfeiters.

When they were ready to come out, Davis made a sound like the gnawing of a rat, and Mrs. Davis immediately let them out. After an explanation of the signals which Mrs. Davis used to warn him of the approach of strangers and their departure, Davis gave a practical illustration of the way in which he worked. When engaged in the noisiest part of the process of manufacture, no sound could be heard outside the house, and only a faint clinking could be distinguished indoors. At a simple signal from Mrs. Davis everything was silent as the grave, while a second signal was instantly followed by the resumption of work below. Clark acknowledged that Davis had a perfect workshop and an unsurpassed system of labor; having seen all there was, he returned to the hotel.

On receiving Clark's report I wrote to the Secretary of the Treasury describing this secret laboratory, and asking authority to arrest the members of the partnership at my own discreton. He sent me a document addressed to the United States Marshal, ordering him to assist me when called upon, but to wait for the completion of my plans before making any move. I gave this order to Harry Wilton, the United States Marshal for Illinois, and he agreed to give me all the assistance necessary when I was ready to make the arrests.

CHAPTER XII.

WEBSTER had become well acquainted with almost every one in town during his stay there, and he was generally regarded as a lazy loafer; yet he was so good-humored that no one seemed to think ill of him. Among his casual acquaintances was a young fellow named William Condon, who had about the same reputation as Webster's. He was a jack-of-all-trades, earning his living by farm-work in the mild weather, and by odd jobs in town during the winter. His distinguishing characteristic was his appetite, which was simply enormous; it was uncontrolled by any considerations of time, place, or quantity provided, and the principal objects of Condon's life seemed to be to work as little and to eat as much as possible.

One evening the weather suddenly turned very cold, and the loafers found it necessary to congregate in the saloons to keep warm. Webster was seated alone in a small saloon when Condon joined him. After the usual greetings, Condon leaned over confidentially, and said:

"Webster, do you like oysters?"

"Yes, indeed; I used to live on Long Island Sound, where we had oysters all the year round."

"Well, would you like to get some to-night?" again queried Condon.

"Of course I should," replied Webster; "but they cost too much for me."

"They needn't cost you a cent," said Condon; "if you will come along with me I will show you where we can get all we want for nothing."

"I'm your man," said Webster. "Just show me that place and I sha'n't ask any questions as to who pays for the feast."

The two men passed out of the saloon and walked down the principal street until they came in sight of a large grocery store. In front of the store was a large case of canned oysters exposed for sale, and Condon called Webster's attention to them.

"There, do you see them cans?" he asked, smacking his lips in anticipation of a feast. "They leave that case out all night, and if you'll help me, we can take the whole lot. My wife will cook 'em up in splendid style, and for once I shall have enough oysters for a meal."

"You can depend upon me for all the help I can give." said Webster; "but I strained my back yesterday, and I don't know whether I can lift much."

"Never mind about that," said Condon; "I can carry the whole box, but I want you to keep watch while I take it."

Having agreed to meet at a certain spot about midnight, they separated for the evening. Webster soon returned to the grocery store and dropped in to buy some crackers.

"Are the oysters good at this season?" he asked.

"Oh! yes; they are better than usual, owing to this cold snap," replied the proprietor.

" Do you think it is safe to leave them out-doors ?" Webster asked, pointing to the case on the sidewalk.

"What ! do you think I would leave them out there ? They would spoil in no time.   That box in front is my sign ; I have plenty of empty cans, and I fill them with water, solder them up, and arrange them neatly in a case, as if they were really full cans of oysters. I have lots of fun, for every little while some fellow steals a can, and runs off as if he thought he had a prize."

"That is a mighty good sell," said Webster, and he laughed heartily at the manner in which Condon would be taken in.

He soon went out and spent the evening in Wolff's bar-room, where he had begun to make frequent visits.   At the appointed time and place he met Condon, and they walked quietly to the grocery store.   It was agreed that Condon should walk off with the box, while Webster followed to keep watch ; then they were to have their feast at supper-time next evening.   Accordingly Condon listened a few minutes, to be sure that no one was coming, and, being sat-isfied, he hurried across the street.   He was a very powerful man, but it took all his strength to raise the box to his shoulder.   He succeeded, however, and as he staggered off toward his home, Webster sat down on a door-step and rolled over with suppressed laughter, as he thought of Con-don's disappointment on opening the case.

The next evening Webster went to Condon's house at seven o'clock, and walked in without ceremony. Condon did not appear very glad to see him, but they conversed

Do you see anything green in my eye?—*p.* 113.

together about the weather and other topics for some min-utes. At length Webster said :

"Come, Condon, what are you waiting for ? Let's have some oysters."

The expression that came into Condon's face at this remark was almost too much for Webster's equanimity. It was a compound of longing, disappointment, disgust, and mortification, such as nearly drove him to distraction, and he blurted out :

"Oysters be —— ! There wasn't a single one in the whole case, and I nearly broke my back in lugging home a lot of cans full of frozen water."

"Oh ! see here now," replied Webster, incredulously, " I want fair play. I don't mind letting you have all you can eat, but I don't want to be cheated out of the whole lot. Come, give me enough for one supper, and you can eat the rest whenever you feel like it. There ought to be enough there to last even you two or three meals."

"I tell you there wasn't an oyster in the whole case ; the cans were only dummies filled with water. You can bet that I'm as much disappointed as you are."

Webster drew down his left eyelid with one finger, and said in a most aggravating way :

"Do you see anything green in my eye ? Fetch out one stew, and then you can eat the rest yourself."

"I swear I am telling you the truth : there was nothing in the cans but water," replied the exasperated gourmand ; "see, there are the empty cans in the woodshed."

"Well, if you are such a hog as to keep all the plunder

yourself, after getting me out on a cold night to help you steal it, I don't want anything more to do with you. I believe you've eaten the whole lot already."

So saying, Webster grabbed his hat and left the house. Having had enough fun out of Condon to satisfy him, he did not care to keep up his acquaintance. He knew now, however, that Condon would steal if he had a chance, and so he decided to watch him carefully.

As he hurried away from Condon's house he met Warden, the braggart Deputy Marshal, coming away from the depot with a travelling-bag in his hand. They greeted each other very warmly, as Warden had been away for some days. From the time they had become acquainted at the preliminary examination of Cook and Wallace, they had been much together, and Warden had formed quite an attachment for Webster ; hence they met like old chums.

" You are just the man I want to see," said Warden, shaking hands with Webster warmly; " come along to old Walker's and tell me the news."

They were soon seated at a quiet table, and Webster told all about Curran's arrest and such other matters as had occurred in Warden's absence.

"So Jimmy Curran was running a country store without paying for his stock, was he ? " said Warden, musingly. " I wish I had known it, for I could have helped him off with every bit of his plunder, and we would have made a good speculation out of it. Have Cook and Wallace got bail yet ? "

" No; they do not seem to have any friends," said Webster.

"Well, I would like to help them, for they are good men. I gave their lawyer a small retainer, but I am afraid he will not work very hard unless I can raise some more. If I had a couple of good men I could make a big haul," said Warden, looking at Webster significantly.

"Speak right out if you feel like it," answered Webster. "You ought to know by this time that I'm ready for anything to make money."

"Well, I thought so," said Warden, looking much pleased; "now, if you'll help me, we can make a couple of thousand apiece. Down at Bromfield there is a large jewelry store owned by a man named Bliss. I have inspected his stock, and I am satisfied that he carries a stock of not less than eight thousand dollars in value. The train-hands are changed at Bromfield, and so he finds it profitable to keep a large stock of good watches, while his miscellaneous jewelry is quite valuable also. Now, I think we can help ourselves there without any trouble at all."

"How is the place situated, and how much of a safe has he?" asked Webster.

"The store is in a business block, and no one sleeps anywhere near it except Bliss's journeyman watch-mender. He is a mild-spoken German, and he could be overpowered easily. He sleeps in the back part of the store, and he drinks so much beer every evening that he must sleep pretty sound."

"How would you proceed in the affair?"

"Well, we should need three men—one to stand outside and watch, while the other two forced open the safe. There would be little difficulty in doing that, since it is a mere iron chest, and I could force it open in ten minutes. After making the haul we would go to Mrs. Vreeland's tavern at Winchester, on the canal. We could remain there in safety until the fuss about the robbery had blown over, and then take a canal-boat down to Bordertown; from there we could go to any point we pleased to dispose of our plunder."

"Who is Mrs. Vreeland?" asked Webster.

"She is a smart tavern-keeper at Winchester, and she can be trusted more than most men. She has kept me safely hidden two or three times, and we are the best of friends. Well, what do you think about it: will you go in?"

"I think it is a first-class chance to make a good haul, and of course I'll go in," replied Webster; "but who will be the third man?"

"Well, I think I can get a fellow named Condon—oh! you know him?"

"I should say I did," said Webster, "and if he ain't a fox I don't know anybody who is."

"Why, what has he been doing?" asked Warden.

"Oh! it wasn't much of a job, but he got me to help him steal a whole case of canned oysters last night, and when I went around this evening to get my share the hog had eaten the whole lot——"

"What! a whole case of oysters in one day!" exclaimed Warden.

"Yes, sir, every one; he never gave me even a taste. I saw him carry off the whole box of full cans last night, and this evening he showed me the empty cans and tried to make me believe there hadn't been an oyster in them. I have no objection to him as a partner in this job, for he is as strong as an ox; but I won't consent to let him carry the plunder away, for if he does we shall not get one penny's worth for our share."

" Well, well; I never thought he was that kind of a fellow; but we can prevent him from handling the jewelry until we give him his share."

" All right; I didn't really expect to have any great amount of trouble with him, but I thought best to warn you of his trickiness."

" Well, I will see him to-morrow," said Warden, "and if he is willing to join us we will make our arrangements for the first dark night."

The next day Warden met Webster and said that Condon was willing to help them for one-fifth of the value of the goods obtained, the other two dividing the remainder equally. They went to Condon's house that evening and arranged the details of their plan. There would be no moon for several nights, and the appearance of the weather indicated a storm of two or three days' duration; they therefore fixed the second night following for the time of committing the robbery. Warden took Webster to his room, and there produced a " jimmy," several fine steel wedges a small pair of bellows for blowing powder into the key-hole of the safe, and several other necessary articles. When they parted they agreed to meet at Bromfield at ten o'clock on the night fixed upon.

Webster immediately sent me a telegram in cipher,

giving all the particulars of the intended burglary.   His own part in the affair was to be that of watchman outside, while Warden and Condon were to enter the store, gag the German who slept there, and blow open the safe.   I replied by a telegram, also in cipher, instructing him to allow them to carry out their plan in full, since I wished to break up the den at Mrs. Vreeland's, and I therefore preferred to capture them in her house.   I ordered Webster to take no part in entering the store, but to remain outside all the time ; also to take none of the stolen goods, but to suggest that they had better separate after the burglary had been accomplished.

The night agreed upon was very dark, though not rainy, and everything appeared auspicious for the success of their scheme.   They took passage by the evening train, keeping apart from each other : the train being very crowded, they had no fear of being noticed.   Condon carried the tools in a large carpet-bag, and Warden took a key which he thought would fit the lock of the outside door.   They did not get off at the depot in Bromfield, as they did not want to appear in such a public place ; accordingly when the train began to slacken its speed they sprang off, and walked a short distance out of town. They obtained a comfortable shelter in a straw-stack until about midnight, and then they started for the jewelry store.   At the outskirts of the town they again separated, and went by different routes to their destination.

On arriving at the store Webster immediately took a position to watch and listen, while Warden and Condon tried to open the door.   Warden had observed that the lock was a very common one, the same kind apparently being in use in a number of other stores ; he had therefore obtained a key which he had found by experiment would fit several of these locks. On applying it here, however, it failed to turn the bolt the full distance, there being a slight difference in the arrangment of this particular lock. This was a totally unexpected obstacle to their success, and Warden stood disconsolate for several minutes.

"Never mind," said Condon ; "I will push the door in by main force.

So saying he applied his shoulder and gave a tremendous thrust ; the weak fastening yielded instantly to the enormous pressure, and the door flew open. For two minutes not a movement nor a sound was made by the burglars : the stillness was so complete that the snoring of the German in the back part of the store was the only audible sound about the whole building. Being thus satisfied that no one had been aroused by the noise of forcing the door, Warden and Condon stole in noiselessly, closed the door, and opened their dark lantern. They slipt cautiously to the German's bedside, and Condon grasped him by the throat, at the same time sitting down on his body. He had evidently been nearly stupefied with liquor before going to bed, and he now merely opened his mouth to gasp. Warden instantly slipped in a large gag, tied it fast behind his head, and then rolled him face downward on the pillow. Having secured his arms and legs, they left him perfectly helpless and unable even to cry out.

They then went to the safe, the outer door of which was

easily forced open; but they found that the inner door resisted both the jimmy and the wedges. They therefore blew a quantity of fine rifle-powder into the key-hole, covered the safe with a couple of blankets taken from the German's bed, and, applying a fuse, they exploded the powder. There was a muffled shock, a smothered puff, and a great gush of smoke, but the noise was very slight. On removing the blankets it was found that the inner door was blown completely open, and the valuable contents of the safe were now at their disposal. They immediately emptied the carpet-sack of its contents and refilled it with the least bulky and most valuable articles of jewelry. They obtained over twenty gold watches, more than double the number of silver ones, and a very large collection of rings, bracelets, necklaces, watch-chains, etc.

Webster meantime was quietly keeping watch outside, and, as he made no danger signal, they worked on without any interruption. The two workmen inside the store would have been terribly frightened if they had known what was taking place outside. I had given the charge of this particular operation to my superintendent, Mr. George H. Bangs, and he was already on the scene of action when the burglars arrived there. As soon as Warden and Condon entered the store, Bangs slipped over silently to Webster's side. He had a double object in being there : he wished to learn from Webster whether there had been any change of plan since Webster's telegram had been sent ; secondly, he wished to be able to testify that Webster had had nothing to do with the robbery except as a detective. After a short conference with Webster, Bangs returned to his hiding-place to watch for the reappearance of the other two.

When Warden had selected everything worth taking, he gave the sack to Condon to carry, and they went to the front door together. Finding that the coast was clear outside, they came out and carefully closed the door. They then joined Webster and started for the country at a rapid pace. As soon as they had cleared the town Webster left them, according to their previous agreement. Webster was to remain around Mariola for a week, and then join the other two at Bordertown, where the spoil was to be divided.

The moment that the burglars had passed out of sight Bangs hurried into the jewelry store to make an inspection of the place. Hearing a series of grunts and moans from the unfortunate German, he released him from his disagreeable situation, and laid him out in a more comfortable position. Having noted the position of the safe and the appearance of the whole interior, he hastened after the thieves. He took the high road to Winchester, and soon was close behind them; having followed them about five miles, he felt convinced that they were going straight to Winchester, and he therefore let them proceed alone.

Returning to Bromfield, he went to Morengo, the county seat, and called upon the Sheriff. He stated that, in the course of another operation, Mr. Pinkerton had learned that a burglary would be committed at Bromfield; that he had been sent to attend to the case, and that he had witnessed the whole affair. He gave the Sheriff the full particulars—with the exception of Webster's action in the matter—and

6

told the Sheriff that he knew where the burglars were con-cealed.   Hardly had he finished speaking when a messen-ger arrived in hot haste from Bromfield, bringing a corrobo-ration of the story of the robbery and a request for the Sheriff to visit the scene of action at once.

Sheriff Arkwright immediately sent a deputy to Bromfield and called three other deputies to assist in arresting the criminals; the party then started for Winchester in carriages. They reached the village about noon, and without delay they drove to Mrs. Vreeland's tavern.   To Bang's aston-ishment the first person he met in the hall was Clark, who was last heard from at the Globe Hotel in Mariola.   Of course they did not show any signs of recognition, and Bangs paid no attention to Clark's presence, well-knowing that he must be there on some other operation.

Mrs. Vreeland was well acquainted with the Sheriff and his deputies, and she received them with great cordiality, saying that they were just in time for dinner.

"Thank you, Mrs. Vreeland, I dont know whether we shall have time to stay for dinner," said Mr. Arkwright. "What people have stopped here lately?"

"Well, not many; you see the roads are so bad that very few people are travelling about the county just now. There was one gentleman spent the day here yesterday, leaving in the evening, and two men arrived last night, but they went away early this morning.   Then Mr. Clark and Mrs. Black, of the Globe Hotel in Mariola, arrived this morning, and are here yet.   Whom are you looking for, Sheriff?"

Mrs. Vreeland was very handsome, and she smiled upon the Sheriff most bewitchingly, but he was intent on business, and he heeded not her arts and blandishments; he replied therefore :

"Well, to tell the truth, Mrs. Vreeland, I have a warrant to search your house."

"What nonsense ! You know that you have searched my house forty times, and you have always found everything just as I have told you. Why, it would be impossible for any one to hide here without my knowledge."

"That makes no difference," replied the Sheriff, "I must search the place again."

"Oh ! then you suspect me of hiding somebody, do you ?" she asked, with great dignity. "Very well, if that is the case I have no more to say ; go on with your search."

"I think I will walk down to the canal," said Clark, putting on his hat.

"You will stay where you are," said the Sheriff. "Mrs. Vreeland, you will accompany us around the house."

One deputy was left in the sitting-room with the other occupants of the house, and a second deputy was sent to search the barn and outhouses. Bangs, Sheriff Arkwright, and the other deputies then made a thorough search of the whole tavern, ransacking every nook and corner. This search was conducted with great care, although Bangs knew that the men were concealed in a room beneath the house, similar to the one which Davis had in Mariola; but he did not wish to expose Webster's connection with the case, and so he proceeded as if he knew nothing about the house. When the tavern had been overhauled from the first floor to the garret, the Sheriff was quite disappointed at the failure to discover anything.

"I thought you were certain those men were here," he said to Bangs in a whisper.

"So I am," replied Bangs; "now let us examine the floors of the rooms down-stairs."

"Are you sure, Mrs. Vreeland, that you have no one concealed about the house?" asked the Sheriff.

"I have told you already that there were no other persons here except those whom you see," she replied. "You know I always tell the truth, and now I hope you are satisfied. I should think, Sheriff, that you would refuse to listen to every idle tale you hear. My house is as respectable as any, and if I should know of any improper characters coming here, I should be as anxious to give them up to you as you would be to capture them. Now that you have seen everything, I suppose you will let us go and attend to our work, won't you?"

"I am sorry to refuse you," said the Sheriff, politely, "but we must first take a look at your floors."

As he said this Mrs. Vreeland turned very pale, but she recovered herself in a moment and answered:

"Oh! by all means; and then you may as well lift the roof off—anything to oblige you."

"Well, let us take up this carpet first," said the Sheriff; "handle it carefully, boys."

The furniture was passed out quickly, and the carpet was pulled up; but nothing was discovered.

"Now let us take a hasty glance at this little room," said Bangs, well knowing that there he would find the trap-door.

"You needn't trouble that room," said Mrs Vreeland, "for I slept there myself last night. You aren't going to insult me by supposing that I admitted any one to my bedroom, I hope."

"Oh! no, indeed, Mrs. Vreeland," said Bangs in his most sympathizing tones; "such an idea never entered my head; but I think you must be mistaken about having slept here, for there is scarcely any furniture in the room."

In fact, the room contained only two or three chairs and a table, which were quickly carried out while Bangs was speaking. It was then found that the carpet was not tacked down, and on rolling it back a large trap-door was seen in the centre of the floor. Mrs. Vreeland was very much agitated as she looked on, but she had nothing to say.

"Dear me!" exclaimed the Sheriff, "I wonder where that door leads to. I guess we shall need a candle to investigate that place."

"Here is one," said Bangs, taking one from his pocket and lighting it.

"Well, you are a walking store-house," said the Sheriff; "I never ask you for anything without finding that you have it instantly ready for use."

The trap-door was immediately lifted, revealing a dark chamber below, and simultaneously with the opening of the door two pistol shots were fired up into the room above. Fortunately no one was hit, and the fire was returned by all the officers present. Before the smoke cleared away, Bangs sprang into the hole, followed by the Sheriff and a deputy. They found Warden and Condon in the underground chamber, the former wounded in the head. The prisoners were quickly secured and hoisted to the floor above. The search was then continued for the stolen property, as only a few watches and jewels were found on the persons of the men.   On being questioned closely, however, Condon acknowledged that he had been engaged in the robbery, and that they had brought all the plunder to Mrs. Vreeland's tavern, in the hope of getting away quietly some night by canal boat.

"What have you done with the jewelry?" asked Bangs.

"It is hidden in the room where you found us," replied Condon.   "Warden hid it by scratching a hole in the soft earth deep enough to hide the carpet-sack and its contents."

"Did Mrs. Vreeland know what you came for?" asked Bangs.

"Oh! yes; she agreed to hide us and get a canal boat to take us away, for a watch and some rings."

Bangs soon unearthed the carpet-sack, and the Sheriff took charge of it after they had made a joint inventory of all the recovered goods.   A doctor meanwhile was engaged in dressing Warden's wound, which was painful but not at all dangerous.   He was kept in irons all the time, as it was evident that he was a dangerous man, who would not hesitate to risk his life to escape.

After consulting together, Bangs and the Sheriff decided not to arrest Mrs. Vreeland, since it was doubtful whether she could be convicted. As her character was now clearly shown, Bangs advised the Sheriff to keep a careful watch upon her house, and possibly she might be detected in aiding some plan of rascality more definitely than in this case, and then she would receive a severe sentence, as she could not plead previous good character. .

The two prisoners were taken to 'Bromfield, where, in default of bail, they were placed in jail to await trial, and the property was returned to the jeweller to whom it belonged.

After the officers had left the house, Clark, Mrs. Black, and Mrs. Vreeland held a consultation together. The two former were especially sorry that the detectives had seen them under such circumstances, for they feared that they would now be watched as suspicious characters. They decided to return to Mariola at once, to inform Wolff of the unfortunate termination of their visit.

When the news of the robbery reached Mariola every one was much excited thereat, and the general opinion was that the gang would soon recommence operations in that city. The speedy capture of the burglars consoled the frightened villagers somewhat, but they were greatly surprised to think that Warden and Condon should have set out as thieves. The City Marshal was often joked about his favorite deputy, who had turned out to be a desperate burglar.

Clark, Wolff, and Davis held a meeting soon after Clark's return from Mrs. Vreeland's. Wolff was not much disturbed by the arrests, though he was sorry that Clark and Mrs. Black should have been seen by the officers under such circumstances. Every one would be on the look-out for thieves, and the excitement on that score would divert attention from any other form of rascality.

"Still we must be very cautious," said Wolff, "and when we are ready to get off some more of the stuff, I think it can be easily managed."

"Oh! yes," said Davis, "I am perfectly safe at my work, for no person could ever suspect anything about my underground workshop."

"You forget," said Wolff, "that they found the trap-door in Mrs. Vreeland's house."

"I know that, but they did not find it until they had pulled up the carpets in two or three rooms. Besides, no one would know I had a trap-door, even if they did pull up the carpet, for it fits just like the rest of the floor."

"Well, we need not be alarmed yet," said Wolff, "for no one has had any reason to suspect us. Hereafter, we will be doubly careful."

CHAPTER XIII

OLD man Walker was much disturbed at the news of the arrest of Warden and Condon, because he believed that detectives were at work in the affair. Hays, Leitz, and Walker were talking the matter over one evening, and the latter said that he was afraid they would be forced to act very cautiously thereafter in everything they might undertake, owing to the probable presence of detectives.

"Oh, pshaw! I ain't afraid," said Leitz, "and I don't think detectives had anything to do about these arrests. It was a rough job all the way through, and it is every way likely that they were seen in Bromfield and tracked to Mrs. Vreeland's. The Sheriff would naturally go to her place anyhow."

Just then Morgan came in and said that he had stepped into the Methodist prayer-meeting for a little while, and that it was full of red-hot teetotal abstinence advocates, who were working themselves up into a fine state of excitement.

"What's the special grievance now?" asked Leitz.

"Oh! they say that all these robberies and burglaries are caused by the saloon-keepers, and that if the saloons were not shut up there would soon be no safety for decent people. The women particularly became greatly excited,

. 6*

and one of them wanted to lead a mob to destroy all the saloons and all the liquor in the place ; but more moderate counsel prevailed for the time, and the meeting broke up without taking any action. There is a great feeling over the matter, however," continued Morgan, "and I should not be surprised some day if they attempted to carry out their threat."

"What do you think about it, Walker?" asked Leitz. "Don't you think it would be well to ship your stock of liquor away, keeping a small supply on hand for immediate use?"

"No, never!" thundered the old man, drawing up his spare figure to his full height and shaking his fist at his imaginary foes. "Let them molest me if they dare. This is my property and I will defend it. I have a license good for five months, and I have a better right to my business than other men, for I have paid for the privilege of carrying it on. If they try to destroy me, I will show them that two can play at that game. I will——"

Leitz caught the old man's eye, made a gesture of caution, and said :

"Yes, indeed ; you can call upon the Sheriff to protect you. Come, let's drink."

"All right," said Walker, " I'll treat you all this time and then shut up, for it's getting late. I guess there's no use in being scared yet awhile, and when anything does happen, it will be time enough to talk about what we'll do."

As they passed out after drinking together, Walker whispered to Hays to come back after he had parted from

Morgan. Accordingly, after leaving the latter at his house, Hays slipped back to the rear door of Walker's saloon, and was quickly admitted by the old man. As he expected, Hays found Leitz there also, and the three sat down together.

"Hays," said Leitz, "we have all confidence in you, and we have decided to take you into our plan. Morgan is a pretty good man to go 'round and pick up news, but he has no nerve, and we want a man to lead him. We might get other saloon-keepers to join us, but it is too risky to trust ourselves in the power of such men. Now we are all three bound together so that we dare not betray each other, and we can do the work with, perhaps, Morgan's help. The old man has a plan which he will tell you himself."

"Yes, I have a plan for revenge on these canting hypocrites and on the railroad company," hissed out old Walker. "The town depends on the railroad for its very life, and if we can drive the company away the town will fade out like a puff of smoke. Now I propose to go over to the embankment some dark night just before the fast train arrives, and draw the spikes of one or two rails, so that the train will be thrown off the track. The stoves in the cars will certainly set them afire, and the whole train will be destroyed. At the same time we will place some kindling-wood soaked in oil under the old meeting-house alongside of a keg of gunpowder, and will set it off by a long fuse. Then when the train and the church are burning and blowing up together, the folks will receive a lesson to mind their own affairs."

As the old wretch spoke, or rather hissed out these words, he looked a personification of Satan himself, and the others listened attentively without moving a muscle. For several seconds not a word was spoken ; then Walker strode over to Leitz and held out his right hand, which Leitz grasped.

"Dare you do it?" Walker said to Hays, holding out his left hand.

"I dare anything with you," replied Hays, taking the proffered hand.

"Then swear!" said Walker.

"I swear to carry out your wishes and to be faithful to you till death," said Leitz solemnly.

Hays repeated a similar oath, and Walker swore to do nothing without their advice and to be faithful to them forever. Then he raised a bottle of whiskey to his lips, drank heavily, and passed it 'round.

"Now I am captain," said Walker, "and I will tell you my whole plan. We must wait until the court meets, when we can determine what steps our enemies are going to take. Meantime we must get the powder and fuse."

"Lucy and I will attend to that," said Leitz. "She can buy the fuse in Chicago when she goes there next week, and we can buy the powder here in small quantities without attracting attention."

"We must be very careful, however," said Hays slowly. "We must be sure to have no failure in the working of our plan, and to leave no clues for detection."

"Yes, we must watch every one," said Walker, approvingly.

" Shall you tell Morgan ? " asked Hays.

" No, not just now," replied Walker. " We shall probably need him when the time comes, but there is no need of telling him until then."

The party then broke up and left old Walker alone.

As the time for holding court approached, the excitement was very great, and many of the citizens of Mariola went over to Columbia, the county seat, while the grand jury was sitting. At the conclusion of the session it was announced that the jury had found indictments against Curran on twenty different counts, and against Cook and Wallace on three counts each. Curran was playing the insane dodge, but he showed a remarkable amount of common-sense in his management of his property ; fearing that civil actions to recover the value of goods stolen by him might be brought against him, he deeded all his property to a brother, on the ground that this brother had lent him the money to buy his farm, etc. Besides the indictments above mentioned, the jury brought indictments against Walker, Wolff, and all the other saloon-keepers in Mariola, for selling liquor on Sunday. All these cases were continued until the next term of court, to give the accused time to prepare their defence, and the judge then went to the adjoining county, where Warden was in jail. In like manner their cases were continued, and the excitement temporarily abated.

In a few days Clark went over to see Warden in jail, and found him pale and weak, but determined to escape. He asked Clark to get Wolff to smuggle in to him a steel saw and a revolver, for he only needed to cut a few bars to en able him to reach the outside. Once free, with a revolver to defend himself, he declared that he would not be retaken alive. Clark promised to do all in his power to aid him, and then returned to Mariola.

Wolff was the only man upon whom the prisoners could depend, and he was frequently obliged to pay out money on their account. First, the four counterfeiters sent to him for enough to pay a lawyer to defend them; then Esquire Harvey, who had been retained by all the Mariola criminals, applied for a large retaining fee, and in addition to these demands Davis was continually asking for money for materials and for his own use. Wolff paid all these expenses, but he grumbled about it, and declared that if the prisoners did not escape before trial they would have to shift for themselves, as he could not afford to pay all their lawyers' fees, etc.

Meantime Davis worked steadily in his subterranean workshop, and by the end of April he had finished $3,200 in gold and $1,000 in silver coin. It was of nearly the exact weight, size, and appearance of the genuine article, and few persons could have detected its counterfeit character, except by cutting.

Webster had become so intimate with Wolff, that the latter had appointed him to act as clerk while Clark and Wolff were away getting rid of the counterfeit money. When their plans had all been arranged, Clark wrote to me exactly how they were to proceed, and I immediately arranged for their capture. Bangs obtained warrants from the United States Commissioner, and then went quietly with three assistants to Winchester, where they appeared at the Airy House as stock-drovers. Here they awaited the arrival of their game.

On the night determined upon, Clark and Wolff prepared for their journey. They each had a fine riding horse saddled, and Clark started off at ten o'clock with all the counterfeit gold coin in a pair of saddle-bags. The silver coin was left behind, on account of its weight, and Davis took it back to his workshop for safe keeping.

About midnight Wolff followed Clark, taking a slightly different route. About day-break Clark reached Winchester, after a slow ride, and went directly to Mrs. Vreeland's tavern. After putting his horse in the stable, he walked into the house, with his saddle-bags over his arm, as carelessly as if they contained nothing but rubbish. Mrs. Vreeland greeted him warmly, and said that she would take care of his saddle-bags, as she supposed they contained valuable articles which it would not be safe to leave around carelessly. Clark told her that she was quite right, and that she must find a safe place. Accordingly she carried them to her own room and hid them underneath her dresses hanging up in her closet. In a few hours Wolff arrived, he having gone to several places to let the men know that they could get the counterfeit money by calling at the tavern that night. He paid no attention to Clark, and no one seeing them would have supposed them to be acquainted with each other ; but they succeeded in meeting in Mrs. Vreeland's room and arranging their plans. The day passed quietly, and shortly after dark the purchasers of the "coney" money began to drop in. There were only four in all, but they took a good deal of time to count, weigh, and test the coin. When they had gone, Wolff gave Mrs. Vreeland $200, which she was to pay for when she had disposed of it.

After Wolff had retired Clark joined Mrs. Vreeland in the sitting-room, and they chatted together for some time,—indeed he made love to her quite furiously. He suggested that she would have to be very careful about handling the bogus coin, and that she ought to have a safe place to hide the bulk of it while she was disposing of it piece by piece, since she would be in a bad predicament if the whole quantity should be discovered. She laughed and said that there was no danger, for she had hidden the money where no one would ever look for it ; then taking hold of the edge of her balmoral skirt, she showed him that she had quilted in each piece of coin in a separate tuck.

Meantime Bangs was carefully watching the house, and as each purchaser of the bogus money came out he was followed to his home by the assistants whom Bangs had with him. When all was quiet and the lights in the tavern put out, Bangs commenced active operations. A man named Gardner was the first of the counterfeit purchasers to be visited, and after arresting him they found about $600 of the coin hidden away between two mattrasses. The next victim was a well-to-do farmer, owning a large and valuable place of eighty acres. The remaining two were soon captured. The money found at each place was counted, sealed up, and marked, and the prisoners were all taken to the Airy House. Leaving them under a strong guard, and placing the bogus coin in the safe of the hotel, Bangs prepared to descend upon the more important criminals at Mrs. Vreeland's tavern. On arriving there, he stationed his men so as to prevent the possibility of any one escaping, and then he boldly knocked at the main door. In a few minutes Mrs. Vreeland called out :

" Who is there ? "

" Jim Styles and two friends," responded Bangs.

" All right, Jim, I'll be down directly," and she soon appeared at the door.

Bangs instantly seized her hands and slipped a pair of handcuffs on her wrists before she had time to say a word or make a motion. She had evidently expected a very different style of visitor, and had merely put on her balmoral skirt and a loose sack. Bangs noticed the skirt with much pleasure, for Clark had slipped out after leaving Mrs. Vreeland, and had told him where she had hidden her money.

Leaving Mrs. Vreeland in charge of a detective, Bangs hastened up to Wolff's room, and without any ceremony proceeded to kick the door open. As he reached the bedside, he found Wolff just springing up and rushing toward the window. On finding that he was caught, however, Wolff sullenly inquired what was the matter.

" Well, I shall have to ask you to go with me for a short trip, so put on your clothes as quickly as possible," said Bangs.

" What do you want of me ? " asked Wolff. " I have done nothing."

" I did not say you had done anything," replied Bangs,

cooly ; " but I have orders to arrest every one found in this house, and so you may as well come without making any trouble."

Before Bangs allowed Wolff to dress, however, he took the precaution to search his clothes, being rewarded by the discovery of two revolvers, a dirk knife, and two rolls of bogus coin. Then the saddle-bags were found stowed under the bolster, and they contained such a quantity of counter-feit money that Wolff had nothing further to say.

" This is a remarkably good imitation of the genuine article," said Bangs, as he looked at some of the money before sealing it up ; " who made this for you ? "

Wolff maintained a dogged silence, but he plainly showed that he was completely overwhelmed by his misfortune. When he was dressed, Bangs put handcuffs on his wrists and gave him in charge of an assistant to take down-stairs. An idea seemed to strike Wolff's mind at this moment, and he said :

" I wish I could send word to Mrs. Black in Mariola, for I shall want her to get bail for me."

" Well, I guess you can get a messenger," said Bangs, " but there is no one about the hotel now that can go. If you have any friends in Winchester I have no objection to letting you see them."

" There is a man stopping here who used to board at my hotel occasionally," said Wolff, " and I guess he would take a message for me. He is right in the next room."

" Another man stopping here ? " queried Bangs, as if greatly surprised. " I shall have to see about that."

So saying he went to Clark's door, quickly forced it open, and told Clark to consider himself under arrest. The room was then thoroughly searched, while Clark was put into Wolff's room to dress ; but as no counterfeit coin was found, and as Clark protested that he was an innocent traveller, Bangs was forced to let him go, though he pretended that he did it very unwillingly.

"You may be all right," said Bangs, "but you are in mighty bad company, and I've a good notion to hold you anyhow."

"You have no kind of proof against me at all," said Clark. "I merely happened to stop at this tavern yesterday because it was convenient, and I don't know anything about these folks."

"This man Wolff says he knows you," replied Bangs.

"Well, what of that?" asked Clark; "I have travelled a good deal through this part of the country, and I have stopped a few times at his hotel. That's all I know about him."

"Then you pretend to say that you didn't come here to meet him?"

"Of course I didn't ; but even if I did, what right have you to arrest me? Where is your warrant?"

Bangs was obliged to admit that he had no warrant.

"Well, then, if you dare to arrest me I'll have you indicted for false arrest," said Clark in high wrath. "I'll show you that you can't arrest honest travellers for nothing."

"Don't you get impudent," replied Bangs, "or I will take you on general suspicion. I don't believe you would care to try any suit against me.   However, I have no warrant for you, and I guess I will let you go ; but I shall keep you here until I am ready to go away myself."

Clark aquiesced with a bad grace, as if he thought himself very unjustly treated ; but he had no alternative, and so he and Wolff were taken down to the sitting-room, where all the other inmates of the house were confined.   Meantime all the rooms had been thoroughly searched by Bangs' assistants, except Mrs. Vreeland's bed-chamber, and Bangs said :

"Mrs. Vreeland, I am going to search your room and your clothing, and you can go up with us while we do so."

"You ought to be ashamed of yourself to keep me here with these irons on," replied the indignant hostess.   "If you had not told me a lie by claiming to be Jim Styles, I would not have let you in."

"Well, it can't be helped now," replied Bangs, good-humoredly ; "so come along and let us see what you have hidden in your room."

"Well, what are you looking after this time ?" she asked.

"I guess you know well enough," said Bangs, "and if you want any further information I will give it to you after I have finished the search."

It took nearly an hour to search Mrs. Vreeland's room and all her dresses, for each article was carefully investigated in every part, until there was not a place left unexamined which would hold a mouse ; but no bogus coin was found, and Mrs. Vreeland's spirits evidently rose very high, though she said nothing.

After every nook and corner had been examined, Bangs stood a moment and thought. Then he remarked, as if soliloquizing :

"Well, I guess we have captured all they had, for we have searched every inch of the house and all the clothes of all the inmates."

"Then you'll let me go, won't you?" asked Mrs. Vreeland eagerly.

"I guess so," said Bangs, "for we haven't found any of the counterfeit money in your possession."

"Counterfeit money! You don't suppose that I would pass counterfeit money, do you?" exclaimed the virtuous Mrs. Vreeland.

"Oh! we have to suspect everybody, madam," replied Bangs politely; "and that reminds me—I haven't searched the clothes you have on. I guess we shall have to do that simply as a matter of form, you know,—only a matter of form."

"You ought to be ashamed of yourself," stammered Mrs. Vreeland, turning ghastly pale ; "you might have some respect for my sex if you have none for my word."

"Really I am very sorry," said Bangs, "but my duty must be done, and I shall have to ask you for that shawl and skirt. Here are others that you can change them for."

"Oh! for shame, you wretch! have you no regard for my modesty? Think how you would like to have your wife, your sister, or your mother treated in this brutal manner ! Have you no decency, man?"

"Madam," replied Bangs, with some acerbity, "if my

wife or sister or mother kept a resort for thieves and counterfeiters, she would have to take the consequences of her own unlawful actions. I don't wish to shock you nor shame your sense of decency, *but your clothing I must have,* and the sooner you change it the better it will be for your comfort."

"Never! never!" she shrieked hysterically. "I will die first, but you shall not expose my person on pretence of searching my clothing."

"There is no need to do so," answered Bangs; "you can slip one skirt over your head and let the other drop after the first is fastened."

"No, sir; I will not. This is an outrage—I will not submit——"

"Well, Jake," said Bangs, tired of parleying with a woman whose pretensions to modesty were only a cloak to hide her from a different kind of exposure, "you put this skirt over her head and I will drop the other,"

As they approached her, Mrs. Vreeland saw that resistance would be useless, and therefore quieted down and sullenly agreed to make the change herself. On receiving the skirt, the wily Bangs carefully felt of it until he came to one of the coins, which he cut out. He took out several others to identify them, and then made up the skirt in a sealed package to be used as testimony on the trial. Having secured the objects of his search without betraying Clark's share in the arrests, Bangs allowed Mrs. Vreeland to enter her room alone to dress, and then put all the prisoners in the sitting-room until daylight, which soon came.   He then marched them all to the Airy House, where they had breakfast before leaving for Chicago.   On taking the early train for that city, Bangs gave Clark his liberty, saying that he ought to be more careful of his associates in future.

Bangs soon delivered his prisoners to the United States Marshal and immediately started for Mariola, arriving just before Clark, who rode over from Winchester.   The first place that Bangs visited was the house of Davis the watch-maker. and he had no difficulty in obtaining complete evidence of his guilt.   On being told that there was a war-rant for his arrest, Davis broke down completely, and sat in a sort of stupor after being placed in irons, taking no interest in the search of his house.   Bangs quickly found the trap-door, but he professed to be unable to get it open except by using an axe.   Entrance was soon obtained, and in a short time all the implements of counterfeiting were passed out and boxed up to be used on the trial.   In addition to the moulds, dies, etc., the detectives found the rolls of fifty-cent piéces which Wolff had sent back. They next searched Wolff's tavern, much to Mrs. Black's alarm, but nothing was found there.   Immediately on learn-ing that Wolff had been arrested, Mrs. Black took complete charge of the tavern and managed it for her own benefit, as there was no one to call her to account.   She did not seem greatly afflicted at Wolff's enforced absence, but welcomed Clark back with the utmost cordiality.

Bangs had proceeded so quietly that his object in visiting Mariola was not suspected until he had arrested Davis and was preparing to return to Chicago with him. Then the excitement became intense, and every one in the town turned out to see the prisoner and the detectives. People gathered on every street corner to discuss the great topic, and to congratulate each other that the gang of counterfeiters had been broken up. They generally agreed in attributing to these men all the acts of crime the detection of which had so baffled their efforts theretofore ; and in this view my detectives, according to my instructions, seemed to coincide. Thus there was great rejoicing, for it was universally believed that the whole gang of scoundrels who had been engaged in plundering and injuring Mariola were now safely locked up.

In a few days the counterfeiters were arraigned before the United States commissioner, and were held for trial, Wolff and Davis in the sum of $3,000 each, and the others in the sum of $1,000 each. Failing in obtaining bondsmen, they were all sent to jail to await trial.

CHAPTER XIV.

M ORGAN was one of the first men in Mariola to hear of the arrest of Wolff, Davis, and the others, and he immediately began a conversation with one of the detectives. Having learned all that he could, he hurried to Walker's restaurant to tell the news. Hays was already there and Leitz soon dropped in. Morgan related all that he had learned, and drew upon his imagination for a great deal more. He said that the detectives assured him that there would be no more danger of robberies and fires, for the last of the criminals of the town had been captured. King was then sent out to learn the current talk among the townspeople, and the three men sat down to discuss the situation.

"Now is our time to strike a blow," said old Walker. "They are flushed with success and think that there is no one left here to do them any injury. Ha! ha! we'll show them the biggest scheme yet. They are thrown off their guard now; they have no suspicions of any one, and if we act at once they will suppose our actions were done out of revenge for Wolff's arrest. They will instantly suspect his friends—those fe lows Clark and Webster—and we shall have our revenge without any danger to ourselves."

"Yes, I agree with you," said Leitz, "especially after

7

hearing what that detective told Morgan. They are all a set of blowhards, and the minute they succeed in the least thing they begin to brag about it. How they will open their eyes when we blow up the old meeting-house ! "

"That's so," echoed Hays; "I don't think we could choose a better time. They will give up watching for any-thing unusual, and our scheme will strike them like a thunder-clap out of a clear sky."

" I think we have been mistaken about Morgan," said Walker reflectively. " He has always told us the truth so far as I know, and he came straight to us with the story about Wolff and Davis. Don't you think we can trust him to take part in this affair, Leitz ? "

"Well, I think we can. I don't consider that he is worth anything as a planner, but I think he would work faithfully under proper control. What do you think, Hays ? "

" I suppose I may have been mistaken," said Hays, " and if you and Walker believe that Morgan is a good man, I shall have no objection to him. You have both known him longer than I, and, as Walker says, he seems to have told the truth ; so whenever you are ready, old man, lay out the work and I will do my share of it."

"'That's the talk," said the old reprobate delightedly ; " now listen to my plan : I propose that two of us shall go to the meeting-house, taking the shavings, oil, fuse, and gun-powder. At the same time the other two will go to the railroad track at the curve on the bluff. When they have drawn the spikes and taken up the outer rail, they can come away and leave the train to its fate. It will get in a little before three o'clock, and my idea is to fire the church about half past two o'clock, so as to give the passengers a fine scene before they make their great flying leap. Won't it be glorious ? "

The expression on the face of the old wretch was perfectly devilish, and one might have supposed him crazy, were it not that his plans were laid with such carefulness as to show him to be perfectly sane.

The three men then drank succsss to their scheme, and Walker proceeded to give his plan in detail.

" I think, Hays, that as you and Morgan are the youngest," he said, " you had better attend to the railroad, while Leitz and I will fix the church. I have a claw-bar with which you can draw the spikes; and I have also all the kindling-wood, oil, powder, and fuse with which we can send the whole affair to kingdom come. We must be careful to finish our work and be at home in bed in time to avoid detection. I will fix the Marshal all right by giving him a heavy dose of whiskey early in the evening. Then when he is roused up, he will be too stupid to take any decided action, and half the wrath of the church hypocrites will be expended on him for not catching us."

" At what time shall we start out ? " asked Hays.

" Well, I will see Morgan to-morrow," replied Walker, "and then we will decide upon some day next week."

" Are you sure that Morgan will go in ? " said Hays.

" Oh ! yes, he will do anything I tell him, and will be glad to be taken into our confidence. Now let us break up, for we must be very careful not to attract any especial attention to ourselves before the affair takes place."

The next day Walker told Leitz and Hays that he had decided to carry out their scheme the following Friday night, and a meeting of the four men was held that evening to arrange all the details of the plan. Nothing now remained to be done until the eventful night.

As the reader has probably already surmised, Hays was one of my detectives, and every movement of the precious trio with whom he was associated was instantly reported to me. On learning the full particulars of their fiendish design I made arrangements to defeat them. I first wrote to Mr. Lincoln an account of the plot, and cautioned him not to frustrate my plans by being too hasty, but to follow out my instructions to the letter. One man with a red signal light was to be stationed about a quarter of a mile down the track to stop the incoming train; several others were to hide themselves close to the spot where the rail was to be removed; still another party was to be hidden around the church, and others near Walker's and Leitz's houses.

Then when Hays and Morgan had fairly removed the rail they were to be captured instantly by the men in ambush. In like manner, after Walker and Leitz had placed the kindling wood, the powder, and the fuse, and had lighted the latter, the citizens were to spring upon them, disconnect the fuse, and take the men prisoners. In case they escaped at first, they would nevertheless fall into the hands of the other guards watching the houses.

In compliance with Mr. Lincoln's earnest entreaty, I went

to Mariola myself to superintend the counterplot, and when the night came everything was in readiness. I posted myself where I could see Walker's house, and early in the evening I saw the three men assemble there. The hours passed very slowly, but at length the time approached when the attempt should be made, and we were all alert to see the first move in the affair. But no one emerged from Walker's house and I began to feel nervous. At length I saw Hays and Morgan come out together, and the latter immediately went home. Hays took the direction of a spot where I had agreed to meet him in case of any change of programme, and I therefore went there at once.

He then explained that old Walker had had a very severe attack of cholera morbus, and they had been afraid he would die. He had recovered, however, and Leitz was sitting up with him. In consequence of this accident the attacks on the railroad and on the church had been postponed indefinitely, but they were resolved to carry them out as soon as Walker recovered. I instantly sent a messenger to call in the man with the signal lantern, and also the other parties, and after cautioning them not to mention their night's work to any one, we all went to our respective beds.

It was three days before Walker felt able to undertake the job he had planned, but Tuesday was finally selected for its execution. He was nerved up to a state of feverish anxiety, and his eyes were even more snaky and restless than usual. In the afternoon Leitz came over and borrowed a suit of clothes of Walker, as the night was likely to be rainy and he had only one suit. Of course it would not do to get that suit wet, for in case of a search of his house after the "accidents" had occurred, the wet clothes would betray him.

I had returned to Chicago Saturday morning, and my business was so pressing that I was unable to be present Tuesday night; but I had given Messrs. Lincoln and Brown such minute instructions that I felt sure nothing could go wrong.

The three men met as before at Walker's saloon early in the evening, and spent the time until after midnight in drinking and playing cards. They were careful not to drink enough to intoxicate, but only to enliven their spirits, The night was very dark and stormy, the rain falling in torrents, but about one o'clock Hays and Morgan started out. They soon reached the curve and began work. Hays had the claw-bar, but he handled it so clumsily that Morgan snatched it from him and soon drew the first spike. The others followed in quick succession, and in a few minutes the work was done—no train could reach that point without going over the steep embankment.

Meanwhile Walker and Leitz left the saloon, each carrying a portion of the incendiary articles. They proceeded with great caution, but they soon reached the church, the door of which Walker kicked open with little effort. Having arranged everything satisfactorily, they stretched out the fuse, lit it, and hurried home. The fuse could not be extinguished by water, and it burned steadily on, spitting and hissing as the water occasionally retarded the combustion somewhat, yet never stopping nor going out. From the

gate through the yard the fire ran, then up the steps and on through the vestibule; up the broad aisle it hastened more rapidly, being dry, and finally the kindling was reached. The oil-soaked sticks quickly blazed up and created an intense heat; then the whole interior was ablaze, a terrible explosion followed, and the Methodist church was a thing of the past. The incoming passengers saw from the car windows a bright light reaching to and reddening the heavy clouds hanging over Mariola; and at the same time they were rushing on toward the bluff where the rail was gone.

But the man with the red light was on hand, the danger signal waved on the track soon caused the engineer to bring the train to a stop, and he then moved slowly along until the break was reached. Here the frightened passengers first learned the terrible danger they had so narrowly escaped, and also found a group of men guarding two desperate-looking fellows who had been captured in the act of removing a second rail. The track was quickly repaired and the train proceeded on its journey.

CHAPTER XV.

THE question naturally arises : Where were the men who had been stationed to watch the church when Walker and Leitz broke into it ? Why did they prove faithless to their trust ? Well, they were well-meaning men, and they were highly anxious to save their church and to catch its would-be destroyers ; but, alas ! they could not bear the discomfort of getting wet, and so when the rain came and the storm blew they took shelter in a dry place at the rear of the building. No proper comprehension of the importance of their trust seemed to have occurred to them, and the first intimation they had of the presence of the villains was the flames inside lighting up the whole building; then knowing that there was a keg of powder in the middle of that flame, they stood not upon the order of their going, but scattered like a flock of sheep. Hence, long before the explosion took place, Walker and Leitz were safely hidden away in their beds, and no one had seen them in the vicinity of the burning building.

The explosion and the glare of the fire aroused the whole town, and the streets were soon filled with an excited crowd. Webster was among the earliest arrivals on the scene, and Lincoln and Brown were only a few minutes later. Webster saw that something must be done instantly, so he hurried up to these gentlemen and told them to arrest both Leitz and Walker without delay, and to search their premises thoroughly to find their wet clothes. It was evident that nothing could be done to save the church, and so Lincoln went to Leitz's house and Brown to Walker's. Both the men were found in bed with perfectly dry clothes close at hand; but Walker's long locks were found to be very damp, and a careful search finally revealed the wet clothing of each of them.

Walker showed fight when the party entered his house, first springing to a drawer to get a revolver and then a knife. Fortunately he did not succeed, and after being forced to dress he was placed in irons and taken to the town jail, where the other prisoners were also placed. A strict guard was placed over them, and no possible means of escape was permitted to them.

The examination of all four of the men took place next day, and on the testimony of the men who made the arrests they were all held to await the action of the grand jury. Walker and Leitz were held in the sum of $10,000 each, Morgan $3,000, and Hays $1,000, in default of which they were all sent to the county jail. The grand jury met soon afterward, and indictments were found against them all.

The excitement over these two diabolical attempts, one of which had so fully succeeded, was intense, and but for a strong guard around the jail for the first week or two after their arrest, the prisoners might have experienced the attentions of "Judge Lynch," without even the form of a trial. At length, however, the first flush of popular fury faded out,

and people contented themselves with discussing the proba
ble result of the various trials.   It was generally admitted
that Curran, Warden, Condon, Wolff, Mrs. Vreeland, Hays,
and Morgan would certainly be convicted on their respective indictments; but there was not the same certainty in
the case of Walker and Leitz.   While nearly every one was
convinced of their guilt, the known evidence was very slight,
and it was greatly feared that a sharp lawyer like 'Squire
Harvey would succeed in obtaining their acquittal.   Of
course the presence of Hays as a detective was not suspected by any one.

The trial of Wolff, Davis, Mrs. Vreeland, and the eight
men charged with passing counterfeit money took place
before the United States Court in Chicago in due time, and
conviction followed as a matter of course, without Clark's
testimony.   Wolff, being the leader and organizer of the
gang, received the heaviest sentence,—ten years in the
penitentiary.   Davis was given five years, and the others one
year each.   Clark left Mariola just before the trial, promising Mrs. Black to return ; but it was not convenient for him
to keep his promise, and she was soon left to run the tavern
alone, as Webster strayed away one day and never returned.

The trial of Curran, Cook, Wallace, Warden, and Condon
took place next in the adjoining county, the three first named
having obtained a change of venue.   All the cases were
vigorously defended by 'Squire Harvey, but it was impossible to obtain the acquittal of any one of them, in the face of
the evidence given.   Cook and Wallace each received three

years in the penitentiary. Curran strove hard to appear crazy, but the jury decided that there was too much method in his madness, and he was found guilty on five counts, receiving a sentence of one year in the penitentiary on each count. Warden and Condon were the last victims, and their guilt was also conclusively shown. As in Wolff's case, I did not consider it necessary to call Webster; since I never put my detectives in the witness-box when it is possible to avoid it. Warden was sentenced to ten years and Condon to two years in the penitentiary.

As the time drew near for the trial of the four conspirators, Walker, Leitz, Hays, and Morgan, the excitement began to revive, and when the day arrived the town was crowded, many people having driven twenty miles to be present. Walker and Leitz were in good spirits, and they felt so confident of a speedy acquittal that no motion was made for a change of venue on their part, while Morgan knew there would be no difference in the result wherever he was tried, and so no change was asked by him.

The first case was that of Hays and Morgan, and they were brought in heavily ironed. Before any pleas were asked, the prosecuting attorney arose and stated to the Court that he wished to enter a *nolle prosequi* in the case of Hays, who was a detective in my employ, and who would be the principal witness for the prosecution. He presented the affidavits of Messrs. Brown and Lincoln and myself, showing that it was due to the information given by Hays that the plot was discovered and frustrated. The judge at once ordered the clerk to make the proper entry on the records, and Hays was released.   Morgan, seeing that there was not the slightest hope to escape, pleaded guilty and was remanded for sentence.

When Walker and Leitz were brought in, all eyes were turned upon them, and as the old man calmly walked into the dock he bore the appearance of a deeply injured man. When he had taken his seat 'Squire Harvey leaned over and said :

" Hays has turned State's evidence and he will be the principal witness against you."

" I'm not afraid of that," replied Walker calmly ; " he won't dare to testify against me.   Why, I can hang him for murder, if I choose to tell what I know about him.   He killed a man and set fire to a distillery down in Cairo last year."

" Well, they say now that he is a detective," said 'Squire Harvey, "and he is standing over yonder with Pinkerton now."

" Let · me speak to him," said Walker with a marked change of manner ; " can't you call him over here ? "

" Oh ! he won't come."

" Try him ; I must speak to him.   I can't believe that he would betray me.   I am perfectly calm ; there is no danger that I will disturb the Court."

'Squire Harvey came to Hays and said :

" The old man wants to talk to you for a few mo-ments."

" He cannot go," I replied ; " I cannot let my man talk to a prisoner until the case has been tried."

'Squire Harvey conveyed my answer to Walker, and the latter looked keenly at me a moment, and then said:

"Well, ask Pinkerton to come himself."

I immediately complied with his request.

"Are you Pinkerton, the detective?" he asked as I stepped forward.

"Yes," I replied.

"Is Hays one of your men?"

"He is."

"What do you know about him?"

"I know that he is honest, truthful, and in every way reliable," I answered.

"Do you know that he killed a man down in Cairo, and that I can have him convicted of arson and murder?" said Walker, as if he thought his revelation would astonish me.

"No, I do not know it; but, on the contrary, I know just where he has been for two years, and he has been constantly in my employ. I told him to invent a story to gain your confidence, and he told you about an imaginary murder, to make you think he was a criminal. There was no truth in it whatever."

The old man seemed dazed for a moment; and Leitz, who was listening, dropped into his chair without a word. Finally old Walker said:

"Well, he got my confidence, and now I shall pay the penalty of my own folly. I believe you, Mr. Pinkerton. I see it all now, and I have nothing more to say. Leitz, it is useless to make any defence; that man knows everything, and he is a Pinkerton detective. 'Squire Harvey, I will not trouble you to make any defence." Then rising to his feet he calmly addressed the Court. "May it please your honor, I plead guilty as charged in the indictment. I can make no defence, and I must go to prison in my old age. When the doors of the penitentiary close upon me the world will see me no more. Before my sentence expires I shall be carried to a felon's grave. I have nothing more to say—I plead guilty."

When he sat down, not a murmur nor sound was heard in the court-room. Hardened sinner though he was, his calm and dignified manner had touched the feelings of every one present, and there were many who felt really sorry for the old reprobate and thought he might not be so very bad after all.

Leitz was completely broken down, and he allowed a plea of guilty to be entered, without appearing to care what the result might be. Both prisoners were then remanded until next morning, and the Court adjourned. As the throng moved out of the court-room there was a general hum of congratulation that this trio of scoundrels were now in a fair way to receive their just punishment, and the only regretful expression heard was that they had not been prevented from destroying the Methodist church.

I received a great many thanks and good words for my share in bringing the villains to justice, and Hays was also warmly treated. When he had dressed himself in a neat business suit, people wondered that they had ever thought him to be such a vicious-looking fellow.

The following day the prisoners were brought up for

sentence, Morgan receiving five, Leitz twelve, and Walker eighteen years in the penitentiary. They were soon re moved to the State's Prison, and Mariola was left compara tively free from hard characters. So effectual had been the lesson, that for several years no serious crimes were committed in the vicinity, the rogues being impressed with the idea that it was full of detectives, and that any crime would be sure to bring me on their track. It thus became noted as a very moral locality, and was frequently spoken of in no sarcastic sense as "The Model Town."

THE END.

BYRON
AS A DETECTIVE.

BYRON AS A DETECTIVE

IN the year 1854 I was summoned to Washington by the Hon. James Guthrie, Postmaster-General, who informed me that he required my services, and requested that I should devote my whole time and attention to the business with which he was about to entrust me. He said that the matter would require skill, patience, and perseverance, and he had no one at that time in his employ who knew much of a detective's duties. He had plenty of politicians in his service at this time, but he could not rely on them; and said that he wanted the services of just such a man as I was reported to be, being assured that I would keep aloof from politics and political schemes, and devote my energies to the development of matters to be placed in my hands.

I thanked him for his kind opinion of me, feeling flattered that so prominent a personage should have heard of my humble efforts towards reforming society, and assured him that I would endeavor to merit his good opinion of myself.

The Postmaster-General then proceeded to give me the

facts of the case he wished me to undertake. He said that for some time back the mails had been robbed of a large amount of money. The stealing was principally on the line of the Michigan Southern and Northern Indiana Railroad, and lately the amount abstracted was enormous; and in reposing confidence in my ability to ferret out the matter he would request me to let no one know anything about it but himself and Mr. Oakford, his chief clerk, trusting that I would realize all or more than he had heard reported about me. I might rely upon the coöperation and support of the Department in all my proceedings. He then turned me over to Mr. Oakford, and as soon as my instructions were made out I left Washington and returned home by Toledo.

Western railroads were then in their incipiency, and projectors often encountered serious difficulties from the ignorance and prejudices of settlers through whose lands the roads ran.

The "right of way" for these great public enterprises was then but little understood or respected by the farmers, who waxed morose and indignant because the arbitrators appointed to appraise the lands required for railroad purposes sometimes put them at a figure which the owners thought too low.

A good deal of ill-feeling was thereby engendered against railroad corporations, and the frequency of the obstructions placed upon many of the lines caused suspicion to fall upon these dissatisfied parties.

There were, however, other theories regarding the obstructions; one of which was they might have been the preconcerted work of regularly organized robbers, or of individuals who had no connection with the disaffected settlers, and whose ulterior object was the plunder of the mails.

At first I was not decided which of these theories to accept as the most probable, although I strongly inclined to the last, for the reason that there were great temptations for these mail robberies.

The express system, which now takes in the whole of the United States, did not then extend further west than Chicago ; and the consequence was that all the money sent to and from points West, Northwest, and part of the Southwest, embracing Wisconsin, Illinois, Iowa, Missouri, and a portion of the Territories, including Minnesota, was carried by mail. These were facts which expert thieves would be very apt to take advantage of; and, reasoning from this data alone, I concluded that the robberies in question were the result of plans which were devised upon the spot where they occurred, in conjunction with intelligence received from confederates in the East, who were probably connected with the Post-office Department. I strongly inclined to this view of the case, and the sequel proved that I was right.

It so happened that, about a year before the present investigation took place, there had been a collision between the Michigan Southern and Northern Indiana Railroad train with that of the Michigan Central, about nine miles east of Chicago, where the tracks cross nearly at right angles, one train running entirely through the other, killing and wounding a great number of persons. The mails of both

the collided trains were found to be robbed after the
collision

Here, then, was a case where there could have been no
premeditation by thieves, as no one could have calculated
that the trains would come in contact at that time and place.
The presumption therefore was that the robbery was perpe-
trated by transient thieves, who were upon the trains when
the accident occurred.

I was on the ground after the collision, but I could not
determine the persons who committed the robbery and outrage.   They were not suspected at the time, and made their
escape without discovery ; but whilst I was proceeding with
my investigation on the Michigan Southern Railroad, under
the sanction of the Government, I discovered that two
young men, Scotchmen, had been passengers on that train ;
and that when they arrived in the United States they had
considerable money in their possession, which they squan-
dered in the West, and were returning East, *en route* for
Scotland, when this accident took place.

They were both young men of good address and pleasing
manners.   One called himself Augustus Stuart Byron, and
claimed to be a natural son of Lord Byron the poet ; and
the other represented himself to be the nephew of Admiral
Napier, at that time commander of the Baltic British Naval
Squadron.   Taking advantage of the confusion and terror
of the passengers who were aiding the railway officials to
remove the dead from the ruins, these young men conceived
the idea of robbing the mail, which they accomplished and
escaped to Europe with their booty.

The amount stolen was about fourteen thousand dollars; but in this, as in all similar cases, where money comes easily it was spent lavishly, and finding themselves reduced to the last two or three hundred dollars they resolved to return to the scene of their former success.

None of these facts were known when I began this investigation, nor was I then aware of the existence of these young men.

Had I known these facts at the time, much trouble, suspicion, and anxiety would have been obviated. They were merely remembered as old visitors, and were favorites with their associates, but not a breath of suspicion had ever rested upon them.

They are here introduced at this early stage of the narrative because they strike the key-note to the whole history we are about to narrate.

I had to conduct my inquiries with the greatest circumspection, whilst I spread out my *tentacula* in all directions, hoping and believing that sooner or later I would solve the mystery.

To facilitate operations I took lodgings at Adrian, Michigan, the head-quarters of the chief officers of the railroad company, to whom it was necessary I should now make myself known, in order to secure their coöperation.

The General Superintendent, Joseph H. Moore, Esq., well known as a man of high character and ability, was the first person to whom I introduced myself and exhibited my credentials.

He was fully alive to the importance of the mission I had

undertaken, and manifested every disposition to give me all the aid in his power. He introduced me to Mr. Baker, counsel of the company at Adrian, and Mr. Emmons, now Judge of United States Court in Detroit, the acting counsel for the company, who also expressed themselves pleased that my services were secured on behalf of the Government; but remarked that they had already employed a detective to act for the railway company, who represented that he had been approached by certain members of a gang of theives, the real obstructionists, who desired him to join their organization.

My suspicions were aroused on hearing this extraordinary proposition, which seemed to me like a very stale expedient to extort money, and perhaps hiding a much deeper design; but I kept my surmises to myself.

Mr. Moore handed me a letter for my perusal which the so-called detective had written, offering his services to the company, and which read as follows:

"ADRIAN, March 27, 1854.

"Jos. H. MOORE, ESQ.—Sir: I have for the past few days written five or six notes to send you, but as often I have changed my mind and concluded to let the information that I wished to convey to you lie buried in obscurity.

"But the late act of villainy that was committed, I may say, within sight of our city, forces me to disclose to you information that I received a few days since of the formation of a gang of rascals who have combined together to commit, I may say, wholesale murder and other criminal acts by obstructing the passage of trains and endangering the same on the M. S. & N. I. R. R. This gang of villains are under the management of two men who are known to me. The subject came to my knowledge by an offer from those men of a large sum of money, providing I would take part with them in their intended villainy.

" This I refused, and scornfully rejected their proposals, or to have anything to do with them. I further threatened to expose them should they attempt at any time to carry their intentions into effect, whereupon one of them said if I should ever disclose to any one their intentions it would be certain death to me. I cannot in this note explain to you the information that I wish to convey in full, but should you answer this note by dropping a line in the post-office to me, I will, if you wish, disclose to you the names of the parties; in fact, I will give you all the information that I have of the parties and their intended plot, on condition that you will give a liberal reward. I would be able to point them out or describe them, that they might be arrested. I am satisfied that one of them has in his trunk documents that could disclose the whole matter.

" I hope you will keep this subject dark, as I am exposing myself to great danger by disclosing this to you, and would also expose the interest of the road by disclosing this subject to the public; yes, such would make the road a terror to all.

" As I cannot write to any satisfaction, should you wish to know further about the matter, let me know, and I will go to your office any evening that may be convenient to you.

"For the present I remain, yours and others,

"A. STUART."

This letter did not by any means allay my suspicions. The author seemed to know too much of the doings of the obstructionists, and to be too wide awake to his own interests for an honest man. Were it otherwise, and he in possession of such information as he claimed to be able to give, he would not probably have asked the company for a reward.

I, however, said nothing of this to the Directors, but simply inquired if they knew anything about the present occupation and associates of Stuart, or of his antecedents.

They informed me that he occasionally added M.D. to his signature, and sometimes signed himself as Augustus Stuart Byron; that he claimed, as before stated, to be the natural son of Lord Byron, and was at present engaged as a compositor on the *Michigan Expositor*, and was a person of irregular habits, given to night wanderings, etc.

This was precisely the kind of man I had pictured in my own mind, and as it was of importance for me to know something of his antecedents, I sent a detective to get in with him, who learned the following, although I am not certain of its truth.

He pretended to be a natural son of Lord Byron, and in childhood to have been thus recognized by the gallant Lord; that his mother, whose maiden name was Mary

Stuart, afterward married a man named McDonald; was born in Edinburgh, May 24th, 1817; entered the British service as assistant surgeon in Woolwich Naval Hospital in 1835; came to Quebec in 1836; returned to England in 1840, and from thence went to China, and in 1841 came to his country,—his mother then residing east of Kingston, Upper Canada. In 1844 he went to Holland; returned to Montreal in 1845, and during this year his mother died. After the commencement of our war with Mexico, he was in New Orleans, and joined the army that went to the City of Mexico as First Lieutenant of Dragoons, under Captain Drew, St. Louis. In 1848 he came back to Canada, and in 1850 returned to London from Montreal with goods for the World's Fair. Subsequently visited Glasgow and Edinburgh, and in 1852 returned to New York, thence to Buffalo and to Detroit, where he worked in the *Free Press* office, having somewhere picked up a knowledge of printing.

He afterwards visited Chicago, St. Louis, Memphis, and New Orleans, thence back to Milwankee with the body of a man who had died in New Orleans; stayed awhile in Chicago, and again visited New Orleans.

In August, 1853, he returned to St. Louis, and afterwards was employed on the Fort Wayne Railroad. In January, 1854, he strayed back to Detroit and other places in that vicinity.

I had thus gathered all the facts regarding *the detective* who was so anxious to sell his information to the railway company, and I determined that henceforth I would be the secret invisible shadow of this man, and never leave him until I had satisfied myself of the justice of my suspicions concerning him.

The disclosures above mentioned confirmed me in my previous belief that the late obstructions on the Michigan Southern and Northern Indiana Railroads had not been placed there by the farmers, but either by a gang of thieves living in the immediate neighborhood, or by some one or more persons well acquainted with the localities and having an accomplice in the Post-office Department in the East.

By a strange coincidence, and in a quarter where I least expected to receive intelligence upon the subject, I discovered a clue to the robbery, and determined to follow it up.

CHAPTER II.

A S soon as my conference with the railroad officials
was over, I strolled down the railroad track and
carefully examined the different places where the late so-
called accidents had occurred, in the forlorn hope of
making discoveries which would assist my investigations.
I conversed with the engineers and firemen who had been
on the ill-fated trains, and ascertained from them that the
character of the obstructions varied from time to time.
Now a switch had been reversed and the train run into a
gravel pit. Then one end of an iron " T " rail had been
placed under the tie so that the other end was struck by the
engine. At one time the spikes had been drawn out of the
rails, and these so moved as to form a switch on which the
whole train was whirled off. At another time a rail had
been altogether removed, and in this manner the programme of destruction had been changed so that the engineers were at a loss what to be on the look-out for as a
warning of danger.

There were, however, two coincident facts connected with
the cases. The first was that no attempt had ever been
made to obstruct any other than the night train going west-
ward and carrying the heavy through mails ; and the second
was, that in no instance had more than the foot-prints of two

persons been discovered when the trains had been thrown from the tracks.

These two insignificant facts strongly impressed my mind and started me on the trail of fresh suspicions, every one of which pointed toward Byron, or Stuart, as he now called himself.

I now felt sure this man was implicated in the transactions. Slowly and obscurely there began to appear to my mind the skeleton of a device by means of which I might perchance bring this man's crime home to him. I had heard, and in two instances seen with my own eyes, that about the scene of the railroad catastrophe there was always one foot-print more prominent than the other, and this was very clearly made by a boot not manufactured in the West, the soles being well covered with round-headed nails in double rows along the top and down the sides and heels, whilst in the centre the same description of nails were arranged in the diagram of a heart. It was, in fact, an English boot, no workmanship of that kind being turned out of the shops in this country at that time.

Here, then, was an important clue to the mystery, indicating that the owner of the boots was a foreigner. Again the image of Stuart arose in my mind, and I had a strong desire to see the man who so boldly pushed himself forward in his special business. Although at present the evidence against him did not amount to much, still I felt certain I was on the right track.

Shortly afterwards I returned to Adrian and had another interview with the officers of the company. I this time met Mr. Sinclair, the company's train agent, a very discreet and intelligent man. I arranged with him and Mr. Moore that my operations should be kept a profound secret from their detective, and that an order should be privately issued to all the conductors, engineers, and employees, that if another accident occurred they should proceed at once to the point and thoroughly examine the foot-marks before they could be obliterated by the passengers of the train, who would naturally rush to the spot out of curiosity to see what had brought about the calamity. I also suggested that the locality should be carefully guarded until one of the officials could arrive upon the ground and make a personal inspection. I did not tell them what my motive was, nor was it necessary. They were now very anxious that I should see their detective ; and happening later in the day to be in the office of Mr. Baker, the solicitor of the company, I also urged the same thing, they being desirous of hearing my opinion of him. An interview was arranged at Baker's office. I appeared at the appointed hour, and shortly afterwards Byron entered the front gate, giving me barely time to step into an adjoining room, before he entered the office and seated himself with his back to the door, which enabled me to hold it slightly ajar and hear all that was said.

Byron at once opened the conversation by remarking that two men named Dean and Napier would place an obstruction upon the track that night, but he was not positive as to the exact spot where it was to be done, and he asked Baker's advice as to whether he should accompany them or not. He expressed great indignation against the men, in terms indicative of an educated man ; but it seemed to me that he was more anxious to elicit than to communicate information.

The interview concluded by Baker telling him he must consult Mr. Moore, the superintendent, before he could answer his question as to whether he should accompany the men when they proceeded to obstruct the track.

Directly after this, Byron left, followed by me, who made a detour around a block and met him upon the sidewalk; and as he had not before seen me, it gave me a good opportunity to take the measure of this man, who was about five feet eight inches in height, probably about thirty-three or four years of age, rather stout, and with dark hair which hung in profusion over his shoulders, large projecting black eyes, nose slightly retrousé, and his complexion tanned to nearly an olive color. I also noticed that his eyes had a keen restless, penetrating appearance; that his posture was firm, but that he walked with a slight stoop of the shoulders.

Byron paid no special attention to me, as my dress and appearance were similar to those of the people of the town.

When the scrutiny was completed, I returned to Baker's office, where, in consultation with the general superintendent, it was decided that Byron, instead of accompanying the men who were to obstruct the track, should be directed to follow them and watch their movements, while at the same time I resolved to shadow him all through. I did not make this known to the officials, who as yet placed implicit confidence in *their detective.*

Accordingly, as the evening approached, I went out in search of Byron with the intention of following him until he should meet the conspirators, and soon discovered him walking slowly through the streets, occasionally stopping at a store, as if to consume the time until the hour for the arrival of the doomed train.

About nine o'clock he left the village in a westerly direction, which made it difficult for me to follow him, as the night was very dark. I was, however, by the peculiar squeaking of the man's boots, enabled to follow him until he crossed the railroad track, where he was met by somebody with whom he commenced talking in a low but earnest tone of voice. I crawled along under the fence as near them as possible, but could not distinguish what they were saying.

Soon after the voices were hushed, and I heard their feet strike the iron rails as they crossed the road. After this I heard nothing more, although I continued listening attentively for some time for a sound that would indicate their whereabouts, but in vain.

During this time my feelings were wrought up to the highest pitch of anxiety and apprehension. The train was due at Adrian in a short time, and unless something was done at once to avert it a terrible catastrophe was inevitable. I was certain that the conspirators either had already or would soon place an obstruction upon the track that would hurl a large number cf people to destruction and death. What was I to do? If I left my hiding-place to follow them, the train might pass me on the road, and I could give no warning to the engineer, as he hurried on to his doom.

The town of Adrian was not far off, and if I went rapidly on the rail line I might arrive at the station in time to give

8*

the alarm.   In an instant I was over the fence and on the track, and running towards the light of Adrian station.   Almost breathless I arrived, and sprang over the platform to the office, where Mr. Moore was in waiting; told him what I had discovered, and advised him to start a hand car down the line as quickly as possible to remove the obstruction, carrying with them the proper signal lights and torpedos. The car was promptly dispatched, and I returned to my hiding-place behind the fence.   Happily for the passengers and the company, the obstruction was quickly discovered.   It was a tie that had been placed on the track about a mile west of the place where I had been concealed, but of this I was not aware at the time.

After waiting in my lair about twenty minutes, I saw a man cross the railroad and go towards the town, whom I took to be Byron, and immediately followed him.   After walking a short distance, the man hesitated, as if in doubt which way he should go.   He was then directly opposite the city cemetery, a beautifully sheltered and retired spot, laid out with walks and shrubs and decorated with flower-beds.

> " Beneath those rugged elms, that yew-tree's shade,
>   Where heaves the turf in many a mouldering heap,
> Each in his narrow cell forever laid,
>   The rude forefathers of the hamlet sleep."

But what Byron had to do with sacred enclosures I was at a loss to conjecture, and could scarcely believe my eyes when I saw him suddenly turn aside from the main road and climb over the churchyard fence.   I have often since im

Running down the track to Adrian.—*p.* 178.

agined that Byron might have inherited from his father the morbid feeling which then induced him to go to the city of the dead for sympathy and relief. It seemed to me a strong evidence of his being the son of the moody poet.

It was this saturnine propensity that animated Manfred and Cain, as well as others, desperate lovers, in Byron's morbid love stories. Besides, all know what ghastly companionship he sought at Newstead Abbey in his drinking bouts; how he made a wine-cup out of an old monk's skull; what a mania he at times evinced for solitude, and how fond he was when at Harrow of reading in the old graveyard as he lay outstretched upon the marble lid of a sarcophagus.

The young man wandered about among the silent graves for some time without any apparent aim, and finally seated himself upon a tombstone. He remained in apparently deep meditation until he heard the train—which was fifteen minutes late—leave Adrian. He started up as he heard the shrill whistle of the locomotive pierce the air, with his eyes directed towards the cars, as they tore over the road after the ponderous engine, and in an instant passed them with a mighty blast and vanished into the darkness. Byron followed it with his eyes starting from their sockets; every moment expecting to hear a tremendous crash. Still the train rolled onwards, and there was nothing as yet to indicate that any accident had happened. The feelings of both the men were at that moment wrought up to the highest pitch of excitement and anxiety, as the train with its freight of living souls was hurrying on to what might be certain destruction; and here, in the presence of the dead, and in close proximity to each other, were the criminal who perpetrated the diabolical deed and the detective lying in wait to bring him to justice.

To the latter it was an unspeakable relief the moment he felt that the train was out of danger, and from that moment he was sure of his victim. He had crawled under a tombstone, where he could plainly see Byron, but was completely concealed himself. Byron remained standing for some time upon a gravestone, apparently waiting for the smash. It seemed to me a very long time, and although persuaded that the train was safe, I still kept listening for the anticipated disaster.

When he had satisfied myself that there would be no tragedy that night, Byron came down from his platform, and, winding his way slowly among the graves, passed so near the spot where I lay concealed, that I could have touched him with my hand ; but I remained quiet until he passed, then followed him to the town, where he entered a saloon and took a drink of whiskey, still deeply absorbed in his own thoughts and replying morosely to those who ventured to converse with him. After repeating his drink he left the place and slowly walked to his hotel.

CHAPTER III.

ON the following day he reported to Mr. Baker that according to instructions he had declined accompanying the obstructionists, but had followed them until they turned upon him with curses and imprecations and drove him back. He however made no mention of his visit to the graveyard, nor did I then enlighten them upon that matter : my plans were not then sufficiently matured to permit my doing so.

Thus matters went on for some time. I was chiefly occupied keeping track of Byron, in intercourse with railroad officers, and in trips to various points along the line of road, one of which I had extended to Chicago ; and, while there, I was startled by the receipt of a telegram from Mr. Baker informing me that a train had been thrown off the track about three quarters of a mile east of Adrian by a "T" rail having been placed across the track, and that the locomotive and several cars were destroyed and the engineer killed.

I hurried off to Adrian by the next train, where I met Mr. Sinclair, who had carried out his instructions to the letter, and showed marked sagacity and intelligence throughout the entire conduct of the affair.

The distance between Adrian and the place of the acci

dent was so short, that Mr. Sinclair, who was on duty at the time, heard the shrill whistle of the locomotive which the unfortunate engineer gave for the brakeman to put on the brakes; too late, however, to avert the danger, for the next moment the poor fellow was in eternity, the ponderous locomotive having fallen upon him. He found that the train had stopped immediately after the whistle. Sinclair instantly ordered out a hand-car, and rushed to the spot where the train lay in a promiscuous ruin. He immediately stationed the employees around the place where the obsructions were laid, with instructions to allow no one to disturb the ground until daylight, when he could examine it carefully. This he did and discovered the same old boot-tracks with the marks of round nails, .with the identical heart upon the soles, which I discovered on the spot where the last accident occurred.

The tell-tale earth being particularly soft on this occasion related the whole story as plainly as if it had been revealed in letter-press. Heavy "T" rail had been thrown across the track by a single person, and the marks of the boots told how that person had contrived to place it. Thus, he had lifted up one end until it was fairly in place, and in doing this his heels sank deep in the soft soil. He had then raised the other end in the same manner, and with a like result. Furthermore, the foot-prints showed how many times the man had passed from side to side before the work was completed.

It was the story of a great crime told in picture symbols upon the earth's surface.

This, in my mind, settled the question as to the guilty party. It was true that the mails had not been robbed, but it was also true that no opportunity was afforded for this exploit, the train having been too well watched and guarded through the forethought of Mr. Sinclair, who was perfectly satisfied that the farmers had no hand in the obstruction; that it was not the work of organized robbers, but of one in-dividual, and that individual was doubtless the owner of the boots.

The inquiry was thus reduced to a very narrow com-pass, the only question remaining to be solved being the ownership of the boots.

On the day of my arrival in Adrian to investigate this last sad catastrophe, Byron called upon Mr. Baker, and informed him that he had reason for believing that Napier had perpe-trated the deed; that as he had been unsuccessful in getting at the mails, and fearing pursuit, he had started to New York, where Napier and Dean had a friend engaged in that Depart-ment of the Post-office where the mails were made up for the West, and that this position enabled him to advise them when large money packages were sent through to the West; that he was undoubtedly in the habit of doing this, and when heavy amounts were about to be transmitted he could tele-graph them, sending his messages to Toledo, this giving them twenty-four hours' notice, which enabled them to cal-culate with accuracy at what time the packages would reach the Michigan Sou'hern and Northern Indiana road, and be due at Adrian.

This statement looked plausible, and in fact I believed it.

Byron further stated that he should write to Napier in New York under the assumed name of Crawford. Whereupon I resolved to secure that letter when it reached its destination and have the person who called for it secured and kept under surveillance. This was easy for me to do, on account of my position as special agent of the Post-office Department.

I accordingly wrote to James Holbrook, Esq., then the able special agent of the Post-office Department in New York, and afterwards author of *Ten Years Among the Mail Bags*, telling him what I wanted done in case such a letter should reach that office, which it did in due course of time, and Mr. Holbrook arranged everything very skilfully to meet my wishes. The letter was not called for, however, but it disappeared out of the post-office and no one could tell how or by what agency. There was no clerk by name of MacDonald in the New York Post-office, but there was a young Scotchman there whom Mr. Holbrook suspected to be the incognito, as he was employed in putting up mails for the West; but he had no access to the delivery department in that office, and the delivery clerks declared that he had not been near that department during the whole time the letter lay there.

Whilst this examination was progressing in New York I continued my investigations at Adrian, examining the foot-tracks in the town, and also in the neighborhood of the railroad, hoping to find the person who wore those peculiar boots; and at the same time I kept track of Byron.

Many were the anxious hours and days I spent walking the streets and railroads in search of the tracks.

While on one of these tours of inspection I was overtaken by a violent thunderstorm, which forced me to retreat to my hotel.

As soon as the storm subsided, I hurried to Baker's office, keeping my eyes intently fixed on the ground the whole way. Suddenly I stopped as if petrified, directly before me was the identical impression I was in search of. There were the double rows of round-headed nails in the soles and heels, and there too the identical heart in the centre. Long and earnestly had I looked for this revelation by night and by day, and such vast interests were involved that I well might be excused for becoming faint and giddy. This passing weakness lasted but a moment however, and the next I was myself again ; all the old activities of mind and body returned to me with fresh energy.

I had struck a "hot" trail at last. I was near Baker's garden gate when the 'foot-prints attracted my attention, and here they stopped.

It was evident the man who made them had walked towards the gate and probably gone to the office. I opened the gate. The path had been newly strewn with a fine sandy gravel which would have taken the impress of a dime, and there were the suspicious footsteps leading in a direct line up to the very door. They corresponded exactly with the diagram made on the morning of the last catastrophe. Every nail was distinctly visible, with the vacant spaces between them.

As it was yet daylight, I did not stop to examine them very closely, lest I might attract attention. I saw enough however, to convince me that the footsteps were the same I had seen before, and I now felt sure of my victim.

I found Baker in his office, and was informed that Byron had just been there with intelligence that his correspondent Napier had received his letter in New York, and that he had replied cautioning him not to send any more communications, as the last one had been watched. This news perplexed me not a little at the time, and I asked Mr. Baker if he noticed what kind of boots Byron wore when he called.

He said he usually wore fine boots, but he remarked that on this occasion he had on a pair of heavy coarse boots, with his pantaloons inside the legs.

I then told him what I had discovered, and on whom my suspicion rested, at which Mr. Baker was greatly astonished.

We then went out into the garden, creeping cautiously between the bushes and examining carefully the foot-prints, which corresponded exactly with the diagram, which convinced Baker that I was on the right track, and that Byron had been vid ently playing the double character of villain and detective.

That evening I found Byron, and followed him around for some time. He still wore the same coarse boots. The sidewalks were wet and soft, so that the impression would not lie, as fox-hunters say, of the scent on a frosty morning.

He was evidently unsettled and nervous, and drank freely

of whiskey at the various saloons where he called. He
wandered up and down the streets in an aimless way and
I was growing weary of following him, when suddenly, as if
struck by some powerful impulse, he turned on the street
which led to the graveyard, and once more betook himself
to that sacred enclosure.

What induced him to carry there the burden of his crime
I could not imagine, unless he acted in obedience to the
theory before alluded to. It will be remembered that when
Lord Byron found himself tormented by evil moods, he
generally rushed into dark and dismal scenes. He found
no relief in society for his sufferings, but banished himself
from his native land from a morbid love of notoriety, and
haunted wild scenery and lonely ruins because these
accorded with his gloomy thoughts and imaginings. That
this wild waif who had drifted into the West, far away from
his birth-place, and might have ended his life as a good
citizen instead of a thief and a murderer; that this son of
the noble poet inherited the worst part of his father's nature
and his morbid temperament, is evident from his conduct
all through the investigation and especially in his love for
that graveyard.

No ordinary criminal would have sought the companionship of the dead in his moments of gloom and despondency;
he would rather have rushed into scenes of dissipation and
riot, and have sought to deaden the pangs of his conscience.

I followed him a second time to the graveyard. He
seemed very much excited, and this may have been his

usual place of resort on the special occasions of his evil possession.

On this occasion he walked to the centre of the holy ground, and once more sat down on the same tombstone he had previously occupied. His mind was terribly disturbed and he talked aloud to the raging of the winds. What he said I could not distinctly hear, as I was afraid of advancing too near him. It was evident, however, that superstition, so far as the dead was concerned, gave him no apprehension. My belief was and is, that he retired to that lonely spot to relieve his mind of the great burden which oppressed it, as Eugene Aram did in the relation of his own story, according to Thomas Hood's poem, to those innocent, happy school-boys on the village green.

It was a wild night of wind, rain and darkness, but every now and then the moon appeared for an instant, and revealed the dark figure of the guilty man as he raved among the tombs.

I was hidden under a gravestone where I crawled for shelter while listening to Byron's declaiming, and became almost chilled with rain.

At the end of half an hour, Byron rose and stalked wildly over the graves towards the railroad track, going east, passing through the depot grounds, and continuing an easterly course until he came to the spot where the train was wrecked and the engineer killed. Here he stood in gloomy meditation, muttering to himself, and occasionally speaking aloud. If at this moment I had walked boldly up to him through the darkness, arrested him, and accused him of his

Byron in the Graveyard.—_p._ 188.

crime, I would in all probability have brought him at once to confession; but I hesitated, I thought I had not yet sufficient legal evidence against him to convict him.

Byron then left the spot, and went across a field to the highway which led to Adrian, where, as usual, the first thing he did was to take a drink.

At daybreak next morning I was up and retraced the whole of the ground over which Byron had led me the night before, and examined the foot-prints at every place where he had stopped. They were everywhere clear enough to trace him from the grave down the railway track, over the depot ground, and at the place of the train wreck. I then followed them, with more or less distinctness, across the field and on the road until I reached Adrian.

After breakfast I called on Mr. Baker and related to him my new adventures and discoveries. Baker was perfectly satisfied, but thought it would be safest to wait for further evidence before arresting the man.

They then agreed to wait for the next stormy night; and, as soon as the rain came, Baker was to provide himself with sufficent new soil, mixed with sand, to cover the walk from the wicket gate in front to the office door. Sinclair and others were to be summoned as witnesses, taking good care that they did not tread on the gravel walk.

Then Byron was to be sent for, and the probability was that, owing to the mud and wet, he would wear the same boots which had made the foot-prints previously referred to; if so, there would be abundant witnesses of the fact, and there need be no more delay in arresting the criminal.

As the weather was now unsettled, they had not long to wait for another storm, which indeed came on the follow-. ing day. The pathway was prepared, Messrs. Sinclair and Moore were called in, and Byron sent for. The two men and I remained in the adjoining room while Mr. Baker talked with Byron, and as the interview was a mere pretence, it was also made a very short one.

When Byron left, they all felt that his doom was sealed. I had felt and known it long before, but I postponed action to oblige these gentlemen who had been so invariably courteous to him.

CHAPTER IV.

THE whole party immediately went out and examined the foot-marks, comparing them as before with the diagram, and all agreed that they were identical. Still, as the case then stood, I had not such satisfactory and conclusive evidence against him as would convince a jury. It was absolute enough as far as it went, but I felt that I must have more and stronger proof before I could be sure of a verdict, as the law stood. Although capital punishment was abolished in Michigan, Byron would, if convicted, be immured within four stone walls for the term of his natural life. It was a fearful punishment, infinitely more to be feared than death, which is only a momentary pang, and more dreadful in thought than in reality. But to a sensitive mind the perpetual confinement—with no break, no relief to it, no visitation of friendly faces, neither books nor writing materials allowed, and no occupation of any sort; the criminal doomed never more to see the face of his fellow-man; his very bread and water thrust to him through a hole in the wall, with no accompanying voice even to curse him—is a punishment than which the human intellect, with all its resources, can invent none more dreadful. Time to a man in this condition has no longer any relation to thought or feeling. It cannot be marked or measured; it swells its moments into eternities. From meal to meal is a period of immeasurable duration. The mind, so fertile in presence of objects, living or dead, now in the absence of both sinks at last into hopeless idiocy.

Then by night and by day, which are all one recordless vacancy to this dreadful sufferer, the four black pitiless walls of his narrow cell resound with the cries, yells, and ravings of madness. Still no one takes compassion on him, no one comes to him ; he raves himself to sleep, and dreams perchance of green fields and babbling brooks, and the bright sunshine and the song of birds,—dreams that he is free and happy with those whom he loves, and wakes to retrace only the empty cell, the bare walls, and the iron bars which admit the air of heaven to visit him, and occasionally a gleam, perhaps, of sunshine. Then his mind sinks into despair; then reaction follows, and once more the walls resound with his yells, oaths, and blas-phemies, until he dies blaspheming his Maker. This was the fate in reserve for Byron in case he was convicted ; and a jury, knowing this, would naturally and rightly demand ample evidence, which I was equally anxious to furnish ; but there was only one way of procuring this, so far as I could see, and that was by inducing or compelling him to confess, and this I determined to venture upon.

Byron was frequently in the habit of going to Chicago, and I thought it would be safest to await one of these trips ; accordingly I arranged with the Sheriff of Chicago to place Byron in arrest in a cell by himself, or with a person of my selection. For this purpose I visited an officer named

Black, in an adjoining county, in whom I had the greatest confidence, explained to him my desire that he should come to Chicago and await Byron's arrival there, when, immediately prior to the arrest, he was to be locked up in the cell which was reserved for Byron. He was to assume the name of Grover, and to pretend that he had been arrested by me for a heavy express robbery, but that there was not sufficient evidence against him to convict him, and therefore he would soon have to be discharged.

The object in securing Black's services was that he might induce Byron to confess his crime, as criminals locked up together in the same cell frequently do, as a relief to their perturbance.

As soon as I had arranged this business to my satisfaction, I returned to Adrian, where I ascertained that Byron was anxious to go to New York, to communicate with his friends the obstructionists. I informed Mr. Baker that I heard of Dean in Chicago, and that it would aid my plans if he would send Byron to Chicago to obtain an interview with him. This Byron readily consented to.

On the following day I had the satisfaction, while standing on the steps of his Hotel, to see Byron's trunk, with the identical boots strapped on the outside, put on the omnibus, while Byron took an inside seat and I mounted the box with the driver. Arriving at the depot Byron checked his trunk and the train started. I was well known to all the employees on the train, and having the right to enter the baggage car by virtue of my office, I took advantage of the stoppage of the train at White Pigeon, where twenty minutes were allowed for dinner, and after I had seen Byron enter the dining-room, unstrapped the boots, and carried them off to the passenger car, where I stowed them away under my seat.

On arriving at Chicago, Byron had his trunk sent to the Garden City House, where he first discovered the absence of his boots, and immediately began to curse the thief that took them, and next day he wrote to Mr. Moore complaining of his loss and claiming damages.

It was now midsummer, and the time having come for action, I had Grover locked up in the cell, having taken the precaution to make a handsome *douceur* to the jailor and his attachés to keep the secret.

Shortly after this I met Byron on Clark street, directly opposite the jail. There was scarcely a human being in sight, so intense was the heat at the time. I walked up, collared him, and telling him who he was, informed him that he was a prisoner.

Byron was greatly astonished; without a word went with me, and in three minutes from his arrest was safely locked up with Grover, who pretended to be unable to give him any information as to the cause of his arrest. The turnkey could give him no information, except that he had been arrested by me, special agent of the Post-office Department. Matters remained in this state until about the third day, Byron being exceedingly reticent in respect to his companion, evidently regarding him as a vulgar person far beneath his notice. He then asked to see me, and inquired why he was arrested ; when told, he of course stoutly denied

Stealing Byron's Boots.—*p.* 194.

the charge. I then fairly and honestly detailed to him all the evidence I had against him, reserving the abstraction of the boots to come in hereafter as an episode, when it would best serve my purpose. He still maintained that he was innocent. Thus matters stood for about five weeks, varied by occasional interviews between me and the prisoner, and then I was no nearer my aim than on the day of the arrest.

Byron continued to treat Grover with the same reserve he had manifested at the first; he would talk to him, however, now and then, on casual subjects, but very seldom about his own arrest, and when he did, he invariably asserted his innocence.

All this time Grover was doing his best to pass for a very astute burglar who could not be held much longer in durance, for want of sufficient evidence to convict him. He expected to get out every day, when he would certainly make some rich citizen suffer for the wrong that had been done him by his imprisonment. And he continued to insinuate that he was a man of great daring, resources, and desperation, and that anything which he had set his mind upon he was certain to accomplish; nobody could escape him, and he was equal to any emergency.

About this time Mr. Moore came to Chicago at the earnest request of Byron. Called on me first of all, and was advised by me to tell Byron that I said there could be no doubt of his guilt, as I had a diagram made of the localities where the train was thrown off the track, and the footprints discovered on the ground; that these corresponded in every particular with the boots which Byron had been in the habit of wearing, and with which he made the tracks in Baker's garden. I further desired him to say that I had good reason to believe that the boots which Byron had lost and which he claimed compensation for were now in my possession. This Mr. Moore did very faithfully during the interview which he had with Byron. At first he was struck dumb by the appalling array of evidence against him, especially that which the boots afforded. He quickly rallied however, and said the boots he had lost were not those I had found,—that they were coarse ones, while his boots were made of fine calf-skin. Mr. Moore assured him that I was firm in the belief of convicting him. At Byron's request, Mr. Moore had another interview with me, and again called to see the prisoner in his cell, and told him that he could do nothing for him, and that I, acting under the orders of the Government, had power transmitted to me.

Byron was much excited on hearing this, and the moment Mr. Moore left him he turned upon Grover, whom he supposed was about to be liberated in a day or two, and said:

"Grover, you say you are a great man, and that whatever you take in hand is sure to succeed. You are going to be set at liberty in a few days, will you serve me?"

Mr. Grover, who had been waiting for six or seven weeks to hear these words, and had begun to think that all his efforts were useless, answered that he would be delighted to do any thing he could for him.

"I am in great distress," said Byron.

"Yes, I perceive you are," said the other dryly; "what is the matter?"

"Matter enough," was the rejoinder; "I want you to help me."

"I am willing," said Grover; "but how can I help you if you are innocent?"

"But," said Byron, "what if I am not innocent? We all get on the wrong track sometimes, and are only sorry for it when we are thrown off. Here am I in a dungeon for a crime not proven. Will you help me out?"

Grover replied with apparent warmth that he would be out in a few days, and that if Byron could show him how to serve him, he would move heaven and earth to do so.

"Then you're my man," exclaimed the delighted Byron, "and I will make a clean breast of it to you."

This he did with a precision and accuracy as to facts which were surprising. He drew out a chart of the whole neighborhood, marking the railroad depot, and then the various points east and west of it where the trains were wrecked. He seemed familiar with every object around the site where the last obstruction had been placed. Here was the track. Here was the "T" rail which he had lifted, end after end, until he accomplished his purpose. Here the locomotive first struck, and here the engineer was killed, his body in such and such a position, and partly covered by the engine. Then he described the road by which he had returned to Adrian after he had laid his traps.

The boots were his greatest trouble. All would be well without them; but if I had them, all was up with him unless he could prove an *alibi*, or contrive to get the boots on another man's legs for that night.   Now he wanted Grover to swear that he had been in Adrian for several days before the accident happened ; that he had become acquainted with a man at the hotel who invited him, on the night in question, to go with him for the purpose of stealing or burglary ; that the man had returned with him early in the evening to his room, and that he shortly afterwards stepped out into the hall, and on his return brought with him a pair of boots, which he carried in his hands; that he (Grover) examined them and knew they were Byron's ; that he accompanied this man to the railroad and saw him put the rail on the track. He then asked Grover if he would do this service for him. Grover replied that he might be induced to do this, and inquired :

"What am I to make by running this risk for you ? "

"Oh !" said he, "you only swear to that and get me clear, and when I am once at liberty I will do the handsome thing by you.   I am in the confidence of the railway people, and shall keep it up if I get clear.   Then I will introduce you to some good fellows who do nothing but jobs of this character, and can put you in a position where you can help yourself."

The terms were agreed upon ; and Byron, to impress more strongly upon the mind of Grover what he wanted him to swear on the trial, made a memorandum of it and handed it to his friend, with an injunction to be very careful not to let it go out of his hands.

Grover was released the next day, after bidding Byron

a very affectionate adieu; at the same time he pondered over the remarkable fact that the son of a man who had set the whole world ablaze with his genius should be immured in Chicago jail on a charge of destroying trains and killing engineers.

It must be acknowledged that Grover played his part remarkably well. It certainly was no joke to spend so many hot days in a prison heated like an oven, whilst the cholera was raging throughout the city.

This was a part of the duty of a detective's life, however, and he had to endure it.

Byron was very much elated at the prospect. He now felt certain of Grover's aid, and that he would be able to regain the confidence of the railroad officials.

ABOUT the 2nd of August, Byron wrote to Mr. Baker requesting him to use his influence to have him tried at Adrian instead of Chicago, informing that gentleman that although he understood he had been threatened by the railway employees with lynch law in case they caught him, he had no fear of them, being innocent, and that he would be able to clear himself of all suspicion, besides prove to the railroad officials and all concerned that he was their true friend, and had been so throughout these calamitous events. He assured him he was most anxious for a speedy trial, relying of course upon Grover to prove an *alibi*.

Baker at once communicated the contents of the letter to me, who was also desirous to have the trial take place at Adrian without having recourse to the slow process of obtaining a requisition from the Governor of Michigan to the Governor of Illinois to effect this object, which would have been necessary had I determined on removing the prisoner. I therefore very cordially agreed to Byron's proposal, and he was removed to Adrian jail, where the Attorney–General of the State, who was well versed in the practice of criminal law, was retained for the defence.

We must now leave Byron for a while to his own private meditations and go back a little in this history.

After Byron had been lodged as a prisoner in Chicago jail, it became necessary for me to go to New York and endeavor to hunt up Napier, who had been Byron's coadjutor in crime from the commencement. It was evident to me that there was some employee in the New York Post-office who was also connected with them, and who from time to time gave them information when they might expect a train which it would be worth while to attack; and it was reasonable to suppose that, whoever this person was, he would be very-likely to know Napier's whereabouts.

As I was known in New York Post-office, I found no difficulty in making the necessary investigations. I ascertained that there was a young Scotchman there who bore in his whole aspect the marks of a dissipated life.. This man I caused to be watched, and was not long in learning that he frequented a fashionable saloon in Hudson street, a favorite resort both for Scotchmen and Englishmen. I went there immediately, and being a Scotchman myself, was not long in making the acquaintance of a good many of my countrymen who were habitués of the place. The house was frequented by respectable merchants, clerks, tradesmen, and others; and among my new acquaintances was a harness-maker who had a shop near, where he was doing good business, and bore an excellent character. I found out that this man knew Napier, and he spoke in terms of the highest praise of him, but said he had not seen him for some time, nor could he tell where he boarded or lodged.

He had formerly visited the saloon every day, but lately he had missed him, and was afraid he was sick. The frank

9*

and credulous harness-maker was evidently proud of knowing the nephew of an English admiral, and intimated that
he was on the best terms with him.

To account for my seeming interest in Napier, I told
him, I had met him some years ago in the old country and
would like to see him again ; although it was very likely, if I
were to meet him, I should not at first recognize him.

The harness-maker seemed delighted, and offered to make
inquiries for him, and I learned through him, that Napier
was living in a respectable boarding-house on MacDougal
street. Upon calling there, I found that the landlady was not
only from Scotland but from my own native town. She
knew nothing of Napier, however, as he left her house about
a week previous and had gone, as she surmised, to Europe.
He had certainly received money from England to enable
him to do so, and had paid his board bill up to the time of
leaving. This accounted for my detention in New York,
and was a capital one for me. So, after thanking the lady for
her courtesy, I parted with her on the best of terms, and set
off at once to visit the various steam-ship offices, where I
examined the passenger register of the ships that had
lately sailed for England.

At the Cunard line office I met the purser of the steam-
ship "Britannia," who told me that he was on board the
'Asia" the day before she sailed, then about ten days previous, and that he saw there a young man whom he recognized as Napier from the fact that he came out about a twelve-
month previous on the "Britannia." Being quite confident
in his own mind that he was the same man, the purser

accosted him, when Napier told him he was mistaken ; and denied that he was ever aboard the " Britannia." The purser was completely nonplussed at this, but was still more astonished when, standing by the gangway just previous to the sailing of the " Asia," he saw Napier, who had already paid his passage money, go ashore carrying a heavy satchel in his hand. The purser further remarked that he remained there until the " Asia" left, and that he was certain Napier was not aboard.

Satisfied upon this point, I visited the various other steamboat offices from which vessels had sailed for Europe since the departure of the "Asia," and searched the passenger lists, but in vain, and concluded that he had taken his passage under an assumed name. If so, this would account for his leaving the " Asia " when he saw he was recognized by the purser of the " Britannia." Requesting the purser to keep a good look-out for him, and promising to call upon him the next day before he sailed, I next went to the offices of the sailing vessels. This investigation continued for three days. Meanwhile I had again called upon the purser, but, as I anticipated, Napier had not appeared. On calling however at the office of Tapscott sailing vessels, he found that a ship named the Martha Washington had sailed a day after the departure of the " Asia," and that Napier had left on her ; for to his utter astonishment he beheld his name recorded in full upon the books of the company. This was soon explained by one of the clerks, in reply to some questions asked him in respect to the missing man, who said that one of the captains of Tapscott's vessels had recognized the man when he entered the office, and accosted him by name.   This was after he had paid his passage money, but prior to his securing his berth and recording his name.

The opportunity for securing this wily rogue was now ended, and nothing remained for me but to return to Chicago and look after Byron.

As the time for the sitting of the Lewanee Circuit Court at Adrian approached, I went there and had an interview with Mr. Hart, special agent of the Post-office Department, and consulted with him as to the chances of bringing on Byron's trial at the first term of court.   Mr. Hart was on friendly terms with Byron's counsel, Judge Morey, and I learned from him that it was his intention to apply for a continuance of the case at the approaching term of the court. I regarded this as the ordinary course of lawyers when they have no valid defence, to endeavor to clear their client by wearing out the prosecution, and by causing the witnesses all the annoyance in their power.   I therefore determined to frustrate the design.   Accordingly, I made secret arrangements with Mr. Hart; and as the court was to meet on the following Monday, I sent Grover at once to Chicago to visit Byron, and directed him, during my conversation with him to say that he hoped his trial would come off as early in the week as possible, because he (Grover) had a big job to do ; and if it were successful he might leave the States for a long time. I knew Byron relied entirely upon Grover's evidence, and that he would do anything rather than lose it,—indeed if he failed him his last hope was gone.   This, then, was what I did to thwart the lawyers.

I did not appear in Adrian on the first day of the court, but two bills of indictment were found against Byron. On the second day, I telegraphed from Chicago to Mr. Hart, in accordance with our previous arrangement, asking him to have Byron's case continued until next term ; adding that I had just received a telegram from the Postmaster-General ordering me to come to Washington, and that I should leave Chicago by the first train, which indeed I did ; but went to Adrian instead of Washington. I arrived there in the night, and getting quietly off at the rear of the train where I met Mr. Sinclair, and without being noticed by any one else, went direct to that gentleman's house, where a private room had been prepared for me. No one here saw me, except Mr. Hart and Mr. Moore, who called to tell me that Judge Morey had swallowed the bait ; and that in his argument before the court that morning he had vehemently protested against any continuance in the case, urging that it was no duty of his to disregard the rights of his client by postponing the trial until next court, because I chose to be absent ; and especially since that man was no witness but a mere representative of the Government. He also urged that Byron would suffer irreparable injury, as his principal and most important witness, a very respectable man named Grover, would not be able to attend during the next term of court, owing to important business which would compel his presence in a distant State.

The counsel for the prosecution pleaded for the ' continuance of course, although he was not very eloquent upon the subject. But Judge Wing decided that the case must go

to trial; and thus far my plans succeeded to my entire satisfaction.

Being informed of these particulars, and that the case was
now progressing well, I walked down to the court; and
when I entered, the prosecuting attorney had finished his
opening speech, and Judge Morey was addressing the
court, informing the jury what he meant to prove through
Grover by way of defence. He expatiated largely upon
the illustrious parentage of the prisoner. Lord Byron, he
said, was a name emblazoned upon the scrolls of fame all
the world over. His poems were the pride and boast of all
who spoke the great English language. He had rendered
incalculable service to the literature of his country; and he
should prove to him that the name of the father was not
more spotless than that of the son.

As he concluded and sat down, my eyes met his, and I
made him a polite bow, at which Judge Morey appeared
completely taken by surprise. He could hardly believe that
I was there *in propria persona.* He removed the specta
cles from his nose, and tried the naked eye, then wiped and
placed the glasses in their position; during the whole of
which performance the counsel for the prosecution and I
were the observed of all observers. Desirous of relieving
Mr. Morey's mind of its uncertainty respecting my identity, I advanced and held out my hand to him. Mr.
Morey started to his feet and demanded in not the most
refined language where I came from; adding, " I understood, sir, that you were in Washington. How—came you
here ? "

The Surprised Lawyer.—*p.* 206.

I replied that, owing to some stupidity on the part of the government officials, the dispatch which I had received came to the wrong man ; so that, instead of going to Washington I had come to Adrian.

I then congratulated the Judge on the eloquent speech he had made ; but the compliment was treated with supreme contempt, Mr. Morey turning round and addressing Byron— who sat by his side—in an audible voice said : "I'm d——d, Byron, if old Pinkerton has not sold us !"

The trial proceeded. The witnesses for the prosecution were nearly all examined, and Mr. Morey cherished the idea that a very weak case had been made out, and that there was a fair chance of victory being upon his side.

As regards the boots, I was confident I could explain that to the satisfaction of the Judge and Jury, while by means of Grover's evidence an *alibi* would be proven. He was so satisfied that he would establish the innocence of his client by the testimony of this witness that he actually ceased any longer to pay particular attention to the trial.

At this juncture the evidence of the prosecution was drawing rapidly to a close. Only another witness remained to be examined. He was soon summoned by the officer of the court, and John Black was no sooner called than he was in the witness-box. Then began a series of questions which were answered as rapidly as they were put, like a running fire all along the lines. Neither Morey nor Byron lifted up their heads to honor the witness with a glance. They doubtless heard the name "John Black" called ; but as he did not, as they supposed, in any way concern them, they went on

with a pleasant and private *tête-à-tête*, as if nothing par
ticular was about to happen.

"What is your name, sir?" said the prosecuting counsel.

"John Black," was the reply.

"Where do you reside?"

"In Chicago."

"In whose employ are you?"

"Allan Pinkerton's."

"What are your duties?"

"I am a detective, sir."

"Where did you become acquainted with the prisoner
Byron?"

"In Chicago jail."

"Well, sir, tell us what you have to say about him."

At this moment the greatest silence reigned throughout the
court Judge Morey and Byron raised their heads, and gazed
with-astonishment upon the scene before them. Byron's
face changed in a moment from vivid life to ashy paleness of
death. His eyes seemed to dilate as if they would burst
from their sockets.

He could hardly believe that the witness was the same per·
son on whom he had so faithfully relied, and who was to come
into court and swear as he had instructed him; but as the
witness proceeded the awful truth gradually took possession
of his mind that he must pay the penalty for his crime,
and an expression of utter horror and despair settled upon
his face. Indeed he looked like a lost soul, shivering with
terror on the margin of eternity.

In a moment Mr. Morey apprehended the scene. There,

in the person of Black, stood bold and upright in the witness-box the Mr. Grover by whose testimony he had expected to prove the prisoner's innocence.

His great bald head, his round, full-moon face, steamed with perspiration ; his eyes rolled and flashed in agonies of rage to find himself so absolutely baffled and cheated. Off and on went the spectacles in rapid succession. He shifted and twisted about in his seat, crushed his brief in his hands, and tore it to pieces, bit by bit, as the imperturbable Black went on with his straightforward story. When he came to relate how he had been employed by me to induce Byron to make a confession, the Judge could bear no more. He bounded from his chair, capsizing it as he went, with both hands on the top of his head, he stalked hurriedly up and down the open space in the hall before the bar, his face bathed with perspiration and his mouth foaming with half inarticulate imprecations. Then he suddenly confronted Byron, and in a voice choking with excitement said: " Is this your witness Grover ?" Byron made no reply, but. stared at him with the vacant eyes of an idiot. Again he approached Byron and repeated the question : " Is this your witness Grover ?" Byron, utterly bewildered, muttered "Yes." After telling Byron that he (Byron) had no longer any need of his services, he added aloud, so that all the court heard him : " We are sold, sir ! I repeat it, sir, we are sold by that d——d old Pinkerton !"

Then seizing his hat he rushed from the court-room before the presiding Judge was able to censure him for his con tempt of court.

The remainder of the story is soon told.   Black went on
with his evidence in spite of the ludicrous scene which has
just been described, and the jury, without retiring from their
seats, found Byron guilty of the two indictments preferred
against him.

Judge Wing, in summing up the case before passing sentence, spoke of the heinousness of the prisoner's crime, and
regretted that capital punishment was not in force in Michigan.   He sentenced him, however, only upon one of the
indictments, and sent him to Jackson Penitentiary for
ninety-nine years ; adding that at this present time he thought
this would be enough for him, and satisfy the claims of
justice.   "When the prisoner," continued the learned and
somewhat facetious Judge, "has served the period prescribed
by this sentence, I shall be happy, if I am spared till then,
to sentence him on the remaining indictment."

Byron was then taken from the court-house to the jail.
The fearful revulsion of feeling produced by his suddenly
altered circumstances, from the prospect and hope of immediate liberty to a doom of solitary imprisonment for life,
utterly prostrated him.

On a warm, bright, and sunny morning, a few days after the
trial, while I was enjoying a walk and admiring the beautiful
scenery around the pretty city of Adrian, I met Sheriff Ben-
nett, who had Byron in charge heavily ironed and strongly
guarded on his way to Jackson.   Byron at once recognized
me, and suddenly sprang to his feet with all the fury and
malice of hell in his eyes and on his tongue.

There he stood, in spite of the efforts of the guard to

thrust him down, and cursed me with the most horrible oaths and imprecations. This was the last time I saw Byron, who died in about three years afterwards, but not before he had sent for Mr. Baker and acknowledged that it was he and Napier who had robbed the mails at the time the collision occurred between the Michigan Central and Michigan Southern trains when about ten miles from Chicago, alluded to at the commencement of this narration.

Byron said that it was the easy manner in which they robbed the mails on that fearful occasion, thereby putting them into possession of a large sum of money at little risk, that instigated him and his comrade to the perpetration of the succeeding outrages.

THE END.

THE

HARD LIFE OF THE DETECTIVE.

The Hard Life

of

THE DETECTIVE.

CHAPTER I.

EVERY person who may have survived the experience has undoubtedly a lively recollection of the wild groups of people which the building of the Union and Central Pacific railroads brought together from all directions, and from all causes.

There were millions upon millions of dollars to be expended; and as the points of construction neared each other, and the twin bands of iron crept along the earth's surface like two huge serpents, spanning mighty rivers, penetrating vast mountains, and trailing through majestic forests, creeping slowly but surely towards each other, there was always the greatest dread at the most advanced points, which, like the heads, of serpents, always contained danger and death; and the vast cities of a day that then sprang into existence, and melted away like school-children's snow-houses, were the points where such wild scenes were enacted as will probably never again occur in the history of railroad building.

Everything contributed to make these places typical of Babelbic confusion or Pandemoniac contention. Foreigners were told of the exhaustless work, and the exhaustless wealth, of this new country which was being so rapidly developed, and they came; men,—brave men, too,—who had been on the wrong side during the late irritation, and who had lost all, having staked all on the result of the war, saw a possible opportunity of retrieving their fortunes rapidly, and they came; the big-headed youth of the village whose smattering of books at the academy, or the seminary, had enlarged his brain and contracted his sense so that he was too good for the common duties and everyday drudgeries which, with patience, lead to success, learned of the glory and grandeur of that new land, and he came; the speculating shirk and the peculating clerk came; the almond-eyed sons of the Orient in herds—herds of quick-witted, patient, plodding beings who could be beaten, starved, even murdered — came; the forger, the bruiser, the counterfeiter, the gambler, the garroter, the prostitute, the robber, and the murderer, each and every, came; there was adventure for the adventurous, gold for the thief, waiting throats for the murderer; while the few respectable people quickly became discouraged and fell into the general looseness of habits that the loose life engendered, and gradually grew reckless as the most reckless, or quickly acquiesced in the wild orgies or startling crimes which were of common occurrence. In fact, as in the human system, when any portion of it becomes diseased and all the poison in the blood flows to it, further corrupting and diseasing it until arrested by a gradual purification of the whole body, or by some severe treatment, so from every portion of the country flowed these streams of morally corrupt people, until nearly every town west of the Missouri, or east of the mountains, along these lines, became a terror to honest people, and continued so until an irresistible conflict compelled a moral revulsion, sometimes so sweeping and violent as to cause an application of that unwritten, though often exceedingly just law, the execution of which leaves offenders dangling to limbs of trees, lamp-posts, and other convenient points of suspension.

As a rule, in these places every man, whatever his business and condition, was thoroughly armed, the question of self-defence being a permanent one, from the fact that laws which governed older communities were completely a dead letter ; and the law of might, in a few instances made somewhat respectable by a faint outline of ruffianly honor, alone prevailed, until advancing civilization and altered conditions brought about a better state of society ; so that in these reckless crowds which pushed after the constantly changing termini of the approaching roads, any instrument of bloodshed was considered valuable, and stores where arms and ammunition could be secured did quite as large a trade as those devoted to any other branch of business ; while so outrageous was the price extorted for these instruments of aggression or defence, that they have often been known to sell for their weight in gold ; and just as, during the war, the army was followed by enterprising traders who turned many an honest penny trafficking at the heels of the weary soldiers, so the same class of people were not slow to take advantage of such opportunities for gigantic profits which, though often lessened by the many risks run in such trading, were still heavy enough to prove peculiarly attractive.

As a consequence, there were many firms engaged in this particular business, but probably the heaviest was that of Kuhn and Bro's., who were reported to be worth upwards of one hundred thousand dollars, which had principally been made along the line of the road, and who, with headquarters at Cheyenne, had established various "stores" at different points as the Union Pacific was pushed on, always keeping the largest stock at the most advanced point, and withdrawing stocks from the paper cities which had been left behind, though only in those towns which had not been altogether destroyed by the periodical exodus occasioned by each change of terminus.

For this reason the firms were obliged to entrust their business to the honesty of many different employés, who were subject to the vitiating influences and temptations, which were unusual and severe under the circumstances already mentioned, while the distances between the points, and the scarcity of secure means of safely keeping the large sums of money which would occasionally unavoidably accrue at certain points, left Kuhn and Bros., in many instances, really dependent on those dependent on them.

In this condition of affairs, and after a slight defalcation had occurred at one of their smaller stores in the spring of 1867, the firm were seeking a man whom they could place in actual charge of one or two of their establishments at the larger towns, and give a sort of general supervision over the others, when the senior member of the firm being in Laramie, casually met a young gentleman, who happened to be able to do him so great a favor that the incident led to a close friendship and ultimate business relations, eventually resulting in this narrative of facts.

It was a pleasant May evening, and Mr. Kuhn had decided to returned to Cheyenne in order to secure a proper man for the superintendency nearer home. He was to have left Laramie for the East at a late hour of the evening, and, being at a loss how to pass the intervening time, strolled out from the hotel with no particular destination in view, and his mind fully occupied with the cares of his business, only occasionally noticing some peculiarity or strange sight more than usually striking among the thousands of weired things, to which his frontier business had compelled him to become accustomed, when suddenly he found himself in front of a mammoth dance-house, and, yielding to a momentary impulse of curiosity, turned into the place with the stream of gamblers, adventurers, greasers ; and, in fact, everybody respectable or otherwise, who, so far from civilization, found such a place peculiarly attractive.

The dance-house was a sort of hell's bazaar, if the term may be allowed—and it is certainly the one most befitting it,—and was really no " house " at all, being merely a very large board enclosure covered with a gigantic tent or series of tents, bedecked with flags and gaudy streamers. The entrance fee to this elegant place of amusement was one dollar, and you had only paid an initiatory fee when you had gained admission.

On either side as you entered were immense bars built of the roughest of boards, where every kind of liquid poison was dispensed at the moderate sum of twenty-five cents a drink, five-cent cigars selling at the same price, and the united efforts of a half-dozen murderous looking bar-tenders at each side were required to assuage the thirst of the quite as murderous-looking crowd that swayed back and forth within the space evidently prepared for that purpose.

Beyond this point, and to either side, as also down the centre for some distance, could be found almost every known game of chance, dealt, of course, " by the house," while surrounding the lay-outs were every description of men crazed with drink, flushed with success, or deathly pale from sudden ruin ; while everywhere the revolver or the bowie intimated with what terrible swiftness and certainty any trifling dispute, rankling grudge, or violent insult would be settled, one way or the other, and to be marked by the mere pitching of an inanimate form into the street !

After these attractions came a stout partition which had evidently been found necessary, for beyond it there was the strikingly strange heaven of a mushroom city—a vast department where there were music and women ; and it seemed that the " management " of this grand robbers' roost had shrewdly calculated on the fact that if a poor fool had not been swindled out of every dollar he might have had before he reached this point, those two elements, all powerful for good or evil the world over, would wring the last penny from him.

Here was another but a finer bar, where more time was

taken to prepare a drink and drug a man with some show of artistic excellence, and where a half dollar was changed for a single measure of poison; women,—shrewd, devilish women who could shoot or cut, if occasion required, with the nicety and effect of a man,—" steering " every person giving token of having money in his possession to the more genteelly gotten up " lay-outs," and acting in the same capacity, only with far more successful results, as the ordinary "ropers-in" of any large city ; a wild, discordant orchestra that would have been hooted out of the lowest of " varieties" east of the Missouri ; but in this place, and to these ears, so long unused to the music of the far-away homes beyond the Mississippi, producing the very perfection of enchanting harmonies ; but above all, and the crowning attraction before which every other thing paled and dwindled to insignificance, a score of abandoned women, dancing and ogling with every manner of man, robbing them while embracing, cheering and drinking with them, and in every way bedeviling them ; the whole forming a scene viler than imagination or the pen of man can conceive or picture; grouping of wild orgies and terrible debaucheries, such as would put Luciefer to a blush. and compel a revolution in the lowest depths of Hades.

Kuhn had strolled through the place, and now, out of compliment to general custom, purchased a cigar and was just turning to depart, when he suddenly found himself being hustled back and forth among several hard-looking fellows, who, evident'y knowing his business, and surmising that he carried large sums of money upon his person, had determined to provoke him to resistance; when there would according to the social codes then in existence at Laramie, have been a just cause for either robbing and beating him, or murdering him outright and robbing him afterwards; when a tall, finely-formed man suddenly stepped into the crowd, and in a very decided tone of voice said:

"I say, gentlemen, that won't do. You must stand back!"

Then taking the terror-stricken ammunition dealer by the coat collar with his left hand, but keeping his right hand free for quick use and certain work, if necessary, he trotted him through the now excited throng and out into the open air, hastily telling him to "cut for the hotel," which were quite unnecessary instructions, as he made for that point at as lively a gait as his rather dumpy legs could carry him.

The person who had thus prevented the merchant's being robbed, and had also possibly saved his life, was a tall, comely young man of about twenty-eight years of age, and with a complexion as fair as a woman's, pleasant, though determined, blue eyes, and a long, reddish, luxuriant beard, all of which, with a decidedly military cut to his grey, woollen garments, and long fair hair falling upon his shoulders—the whole crowned, or rather slouched over, by a white hat of extraordinary width of brim, gave him the appearance of an ex-Confederate officer, and right good fellow, as the term goes, perfectly capable of caring for himself wherever his fortune, or misfortune, might lead him; which proved the case as he turned and confronted the desperadoes, who had immediately followed him in a threatening manner, and whom he stood ready to receive with a navy revolver half as long as his arm, mysteriously whipped from some hiding-place, in each steady hand.

A critical examination of the man as he stood there, and a very casual survey of him, for that matter, would have instantly suggested the fact to an ordinary observer that a very cool man at the rear ends of two navy revolvers huge enough to have been mounted for light artillery service, was something well calculated to check the mounting ambition on the part of most anybody to punish him for the character of the interference shown; and the leader of the gang contented himself with remarking, "See here, Captain Harry, if it was'nt you, there'd be a reck'ning here; lively, too, I'm tellin' ye!"

"Well, but it *is* me; and so there won't be any reck-'ning. Will there, now, eh?"

The ruffians made no answer, but sullenly returned to the dance-house, when Captain Harry, as he had been called, rammed the two huge revolvers into his boot legs, which action displayed a smaller weapon of the same kind upon each hip; after which he nodded a pleasant "good night" to the bystanders, and walked away leisurely in the direction Mr. Kuhn had taken, pleasantly whistling "The Bonnie Blue Flag," or "The Star Spangled Banner," as best suited him.

The moment that Mr. Kuhn's protector appeared at the hotel, the former gentleman expressed his liveliest thanks for the opportune assistance he had been rendered, and introduced himself to the captain, who already knew of him, and who in return gave his name as " Harry G. Taylor, the man from somewhere," as he himself expressed it with a pleasant laugh.

It was easy to be seen that there was a stroke of business in Mr. Kuhn's eye, which his escape from the dance-house had suggested, as he told Taylor that he had intended to return to Cheyenne that night ; but he further stated that as he had so unexpectedly been befriended, he should certainly be obliged to remain another day in order to secure a further acquaintance with the man to whom he already owed so much.

Mr. Kuhn then produced some choice cigars, and the gentlemen secured a retired place upon the hotel-porch, at once entering into a general conversation which, from the merchant's evident unusual curiosity, and Taylor's quite as evident good humored, devil-may-care disposition, caused it to drift into the Captain's account of himself.

He told Mr. Kuhn that his family resided at that time in Philadelphia, where they had moved after his father had failed in business at Raleigh, N. C., but had taken so honorable a name with him to the former city that he had been able to retrieve his fortunes to some extent. The captain was born at Raleigh, and had received his education in the South, and, being unable to share in his father's regard for the North, even as a portion of the country best adapted for doing business, sought out some of his old college friends in Louisville, Atlanta, and New Orleans, who had been able to secure him a fine business position at Atlanta, where by care and economy in 1860, though but a mere boy yet, he had accumulated property that would have satisfied many a man twenty years his senior.

Being impulsive, and a warm admirer of Southern institutions, he was one of the first men to join the Confederate army at Atlanta, and fought in a Georgia Regiment under Johnson and Hood during the entire war, at Jonesville and Rough-and-ready Station seeing the smoke ascend above the ruins of the once beautiful city, and realizing that the most of his earthly possessions had disappeared when the flames died away.

Having been promoted to a captaincy, he had fought as bravely as he could against the "blue-coats," like a man acknowledging their bravery as well as that of his comrades; and at the close of the war, which of course terminated disadvantageously to his interests, he had sold his lots at Atlanta for whatever he could get for them, and with thousands of others in like circumstances, had come West and taken his chances at retrieving his fortunes.

This was told in a frank straightforward way, which seemed to completely captivate Mr. Kuhn, for he at once spoke to Taylor concerning his business in Laramie, and bluntly asked him, in the event of mutual and satisfactory references being exchanged, whether he would accept the engagement as superintendent of his business over that portion of the road, and take actual charge of the store in that place, and the one about to be established at Benton City.

The result of the evening's interview was the engagement of Taylor by the firm at a large salary; his immediately taking supervision of the business without bonds or any security whatever; and for a time his management and habits were so able and irreproachable that, with the gratitude for his protection of Mr. Kuhn at Lamarie still fresh and sincere, the firm felt that they had been most fortunate in their selection of an utter stranger, and were in every way gratified with the turn events had taken.

D URING the early morning of a blustering December day of the same year, I was quite annoyed by the persistence of a gentleman to see me, on what he insisted, in the business office of my Chicago agency, on terming "important business."

It was not later than half past eight o'clock; and, as I have made it a life-long practice to get at business at an early hour, get ahead of it, and keep ahead of it during the day, I was elbow-deep in the mass of letters, telegrams, and 'communications of a different nature which in my business invariably accumulates during the night, and felt anxious to wade through it before taking up any other matter.

The gentleman, who gave the name of Kuhn, seemed very anxious to see me, however and letting drop the statements that he greatly desired to take the morning train for Cheyenne, where he resided; might not be able to be in Chicago again for some time; felt very desirous of seeing me personally; and would require but a few moments to explain his business, which he agreed to make explicit; I concluded to drop everything else and see him.

On being ushered into my private apartments, he at once hastily gave me an outline of the facts related in the previous chapter, adding a new series of incidents which occasioned his visit, and to the effect that the firm had made the necessary arrangements for increasing their business under their new superintendent, having added largely to their stock at Laramie, and placed about twenty thousand dollars worth of goods at Benton City.

According to the agreement, he was required to forward money whenever the sales had reached a stated sum at each point, and was given authority to take charge of goods or moneys on hand at any of the less important stations, when convinced that things were being run loosely, or whenever it in any way appeared for the interests of the firm for him to do so.

It will be seen that under this arrangement, which was in every respect injudicious, no security having been given by Taylor, he immediately became possessed of great responsibility, as well as power; but appeared to appreciate the unusual confidence reposed in him, and conducted the business of Kuhn Bros. with unusual profit to them and credit to himself. Matters progressed in this way for some time, when suddenly, about the first of October, the firm at Cheyenne began to receive dispatches from different employés along the road, inquiring when Taylor was to return from Cheyenne, and intimating that business was greatly suffering from his absence. The members of the firm were astonished. They knew nothing of Taylor's being in Cheyenne. On the contrary, their last advices from him were to the affect that he should be at their city on the tenth of that month, with large collections; and the announcement was accompanied with glowing accounts of the prosperity of their business under his careful management.

After the startling intelligence of Taylor's unaccountable absence, a member of the firm immediately left for Laramie, Benton City, and other points, to ascertain the true condition of affairs, still unable to believe that the handsome, chivalrous captain had wronged them, and that everything would be found right' upon examination of matters which was immediately and searchingly entered upon ; but the first glance at affairs showed conclusively that they had been swindled, and it was soon discovered that he had gathered together at the stores under his own charge, and at different points along the line, under various pretexts, fully fourteen thousand dollars, and had been given two weeks in which to escape.

Mr. Kuhn did not desire to give the case into my hands on that morning ; but explained that he had returned from a fruitless trip to Philadelphia in search of his former superintendent, and had been advised by a telegram from his brothers to lay the case before me and request my advice about the matter; at the same time securing information about the probable pecuniary outlay necessary for further prosecution of the search, and such other items of information as would enable him to counsel with the remainder of the firm concerning the case, and be able to give the case into my hands, should they decide to do so, without further delay.

This was given him ; and I, in turn, secured from Mr. Kuhn all the information possible concerning Taylor, which was scant indeed, as they had seen very little of him, could give but a very general description of the man, and here they had injudiciously given him over two months start, during which time he might have safely got to the other side of the world.

Only one item of information had been developed by which a clue to his whereabouts could by any possibility be imagined. He had often spoken to Mr. Kuhn in the most glowing terms of life in both Texas and Mexico, as he had passed, so he had said, a portion of a year in that part of America, since the close of the war, and in connection with the subject, he had stated that he should have remained there had he been supplied with sufficient·capital to have enabled him to begin business.

This was all; and I dismissed the swindled merchant with little encouragement as to the result of a chase for a thief who had got so much the advantage; or, rather, intimated to him that though I had no doubts of being able to eventually catch him, it would be rather a poor investment for the firm to expend the amount of money which might be necessary to effect his capture, unless, in looking into the matter further, I should be able to see opportunities for securing much better knowledge as to his present whereabouts, or clues which could be made to lead to them.

With this not very cheering assurance, Mr. Kuhn returned to Cheyenne.

Not hearing from the firm for several days, I finally dismissed the matter entirely from mind; but on arriving at the agency one morning, I received instructions from the

Cheyenne firm to proceed in the matter, and with all expedition possible endeavor to cage the flown bird for them.

I at once detailed William A. Pinkerton, my eldest son, and at present assistant superintendent of my Chicago agency, to proceed to Cheyenne, and look over the ground thoroughly there, and also, if necessary, to proceed along the line of the Union Pacific, and, after ascertaining who were Taylor's friends and companions, work up a trail through them, which would eventually bring him down.

The latter course was not necessary to be followed, however, as on arriving at Cheyenne, with some little information gleaned from the firm, he was able to ascertain that a young lawyer there named La Grange, also originally from the South, had been a quite intimate friend of Taylor's—so much so, in fact, that La Grange had for the last six months regularly corresponded with the captain's sister, who had been described to him as not only an exceedingly beautiful woman, but as also a lady possessed of unusual accomplishments and amiability.

My son "cultivated" La Grange largely but could secure but little information through him. He seemed to know nothing further concerning either Taylor or his family, save that he had incidentally met him along the line of the Union Pacific; they had naturally taken a sort of liking to each other, and in that way became friends in much the same manner that most friendships were made in that country. He further recollected that he had always directed his letters to a certain post-office box, instead of to a street number; but seemed perfectly mystfied concerning the action

of the brother.   He had just returned from a three months
absence in Kentucky, and it was the first intimation he
had had of the Captain's crime. La Grange also said that as he
had been very busy, he had not written to Miss Lizzie (evidently referring to the sister), nor had he received any communication from her during that time.   He had had a photograph of Harry, taken in full dress uniform while stationed
at Atlanta, which had been copied in Philadelphia, but a
thorough search among his papers failed to reveal it.

This was all that 'my son could secure, as La Grange,
evidently suspecting that, in his surprise at Taylor's crime,
he might say something to compromise himself and endan-
ger Taylor or wound his beautiful sister, to whom he seemed
greatly attached, positively refused to have anything further
to say concerning the matter ; and with what information he
had, William returned to the hotel in a brown study, determined to take time to exhaust the material at Cheyenne
before proceeding on the proposed trip along the Union
Pacific.

After summing up and arranging the points he had got
hold of, he telegraphed me fully, adding his own impression that Taylor was in Texas, but expressing a doubt as to
whether he had better proceed along the Union Pacific for
more information, or go on to Philadelphia at once and in
some way secure information of the family as to their son's
whereabouts.

On the receipt of this telegram, which arrived in Chicago
about noon, I at once resolved upon a little strategy, being
myself satisfied that Taylor had proceeded *via* St. Louis

and New Orleans into either Texas or Mexico, and was then engaged under his own or an assumed name, in some business agreeable to his taste, as formerly explained to Mr. Kuhn, and immediately telegraphed to my son :

" Keep La Grange busied all day so he cannot write, or mail letters. Study La Grange's language and modes of expression. Get LaGrange's and Taylor's handwriting, signatures, and Miss Taylor's address, and come next train."

Agreeable to these instructions, he secured several letters from Taylor to Kuhn & brothers, concerning business matters, with the last one, containing the announcement that he would be in Cheyenne on the tenth of October with collections ; and immediately sent by a messenger a courteous note to La Grange, desiring an outline of Taylor's life so far as he might feel justified in giving it, and requesting an answer which was politely but firmly given in the negative over Adolph La Grange's own signature, which completed a portion of his work neatly.

The balance was more difficult. He ordered a sleigh, and after settling his hotel bill, but reserving his room for the night, at once drove to La Grange's office, where he in person thanked him for his courteous letter, even if he did not feel justified in giving him the information desired. A little complimentary conversation ensued during which time my son's quick eyes noticed in the lawyer's waste-basket an envelope evidently discarded on account of its soiled appearance, addressed to " Miss Lizzie Taylor, Post-office Box——, Philadelphia " which on the first opportunity he appropriated. The next move was to *prevent* La Grange's mailing any letter, as it was evident he had written several, including one to Taylor's sister, which were only waiting to be mailed.

Seeing that he had made a pleasant impression upon La Grange, who appreciated the courtesy of the call under the circumstances, and informing him that he had decided to make no further inquiries there, but was to proceed west on the following morning, he prevailed upon him to take a ride in his company about the city and its environs. In leaving his office, La Grange hesitated a moment as if deciding the propriety of taking the letters with him, or returning for them after the sleigh-ride; but evidently decided to do the latter, as he left them, much to my son's relief.

The drive was prolonged as much as possible, and the outlying forts visited, where, having letters of introduction from myself to several army-officers stationed there, both he and his companion were so hospitably treated that the afternoon slipped away quickly, and the two returned to town evidently in high spirits. La Grange felt compelled to reciprocate as far as in his power, and billiards with frequent drinks for the lawyer and a liberal supply of water for the detective, were in order until within a half hour of the eastern bound train time, when La Grange succumbed to an accumulation of good-fellowship, and on his own suggestion, as he "wash rising y'n'g 'torny y'know!" accepted the hospitalities of my son's room, at the Rawlins House, where he left him sweetly sleeping at a rate which would prevent the mailing of the letters he had left locked in his office for at least two days to come; as "rising young attorneys," as a rule sober off in a carefully graduated diminishing scale of excesses of quite similar construction to the original.

On the arrival of my son in Chicago, I immediately caused to be written a letter addressed to Miss Lizzie Taylor at her post-office box in Philadelphia, of which the following is a copy:

"Sherman House Chicago, Jan. 1868.

"Miss. Taylor,

"My Dear Friend:—You know of my intended absence from Cheyenne in the South. During that trip, I really never had the time when I could write you so fully as I desired and even now I am only able to send you a few words. I am *en route* to Washington on business, and have now to ask you to send the street and number of your father's house, even if it is not a magnificent one, as you have told me, to my address, at the Girard House, in your city, on receipt of this; as I shall be in Washington but one day, and would wish to see both you and your people without delay. I not only greatly wish to see you for *selfish reasons*, which our long and pleasant correspondence will suggest to you as both reasonable and natural, but there are other good, reasons, which you all will readily understand when I tell you that I met *him* accidentally just before my return to Cheyenne, and that I have a communication of a personal nature to deliver. While not upholding him in the step he has taken, I cannot forget that I am his friend, and he, your brother.

> "In great haste
>> "Your true friend
>>> "ADOLPH LA G——"

P. S.—I leave here for the East this morning. Please answer on immediate receipt.

>>>> A. L.

This was posted on the eastern-bound train not an hour after my son's arrival from the West; and another note was written upon the back of an envelope which had passed through the mail, and had got a very much used appearance, and ran thus:

"FATHER OF LIZZIE:

"Treat Adolph well, you can trust him. Give him one of the 'photos' taken at Atlanta in my full-dress uniform; keep one other of the same for yourselves; but destroy all the rest. Have been so hurried and worried that I don't remember whether I have said anything about photographs before. But this is a matter of *imperative necessity*. Adolph will explain how he met me.

> "Good bye,
>> "H——."

It was impossible to detect any difference between this handwriting and that of Captain Taylor's in his business correspondence to Kuhn Brothers; and, armed with this document, with the assistance of the epistolary self-introduction which had preceded it, I directed my son to leave for Philadelphia that evening, secure admission to Taylor's residence, and the family's confidence, agreeable to the appointment made by mail, and thus not only secure the man's photograph, but other information that would be definite.

On arrival at Philadelphia, he secured the services of an operative, from my agency in that city, to follow any member of the Taylor family who might call for the letter, to their residence, in the event of an answer not being received at his hotel in due time from the one assumed to have been sent from the hotel in Chicago from La Grange, who found Taylor's home, an unpretentious house on Locust Street, while my son remained at the hotel, fully expecting the coveted invitation to visit the Captain's beautiful sister, which arrived at his hotel only a half day after he did, and strongly urged him to call at his convenience.

He was satisfied from this that our theory regarding his being in Texas, or Mexico, was correct, that the family had not the slightest suspicion of his identity, and that, wherever Captain Taylor might be, communication with his people had been very infrequent, and that, with what he would be able to invent after being received at Taylor's house, he could secure at least sufficient information to put him upon his son's trail. Not desiring to play upon their feelings and friendship as another person any longer than necessary, however; and he sent word by a messenger, not daring to trust his own handwriting, that he would call that evening, though necessarily at a late hour ; and, accordingly, that evening, about nine o'clock, found him at the door of a pleasant Locust street cottage, ringing for admission.

A tall, handsome young woman greeted him at the door, and accordingly bade him enter, saying pleasantly, as she ushered him into the cozy little parlor, that she was Miss Lizzie Taylor, and presumed he was Mr. La Grange, with whom she had had so long and so pleasant a correspondence; and of whom "poor Harry," as she said with a shade of sadness and tenderness in her voice, had so often written, before he had made his terrible mistake, and become a wanderer.

After hastily satisfying her that he was the genuine La Grange, and profusely apologizing for his not having written for so long a time previous to his arrival at Chicago, from Cheyenne, he took up the thread she had dropped, as quickly as possible, and said that he felt sure that Harry would retrieve himself soon, and return the money, as he had no bad habits, and everything would be all right again.

"But, yet, Mr. La Grange," she continued, " it makes me shudder whenever I think of all my brothers being away off there on the Rio Grande, among those terrible people !"

" But, you must remember," he replied, encouragingly, " they are strong men, and can well defend themselves under any circumstances."

"Harry is strong and brave, I know," answered Miss Taylor, rather admiringly ; " but brother Robert is not fit for such a life. Why, he is but a boy yet."

"Ah, a younger brother?" he thought, making a mental

note of it, in order to assist in shaping his conversation, after which he said aloud : " I almost forgot to give you this note ; " and he took the piece of envelope out of his note book, as if it had been sacredly guarded, and handed it to her.

Miss Taylor read the hastily written lines with evident emotion ; and after studying a moment, as if endeavoring to reconcile matters, while her face was being searchingly read by an experienced detective, she rose, and, apologizing to him for the absence of her father, who was in New York, on business, and of her mother, who was confined to her apartment a confirmed invalid, she asked to be excused so as to show the note to her mother.

The instant the door closed, my son had seized the album which he had located during the preceding conversation, and rapidly turned its leaves to assure himself that he was not treading on dangerous ground. He found a half-a-dozen different styles of pictures of the captain, including three of the copies taken in Philadelphia of the original Atlanta picture, and felt reassured beyond measure at the lucky turn things had taken. He would have abstracted one of these, but it was impossible, and had barely time to return the album to the table, and himself to his seat, when he heard the woman's step along the hall, and in a moment more, she entered the room.

CHAPTER III.

GIVING the door a little impulsive slam, as she closed it, Miss Taylor at once came to where my son was sitting upon the sofa, and seated herself beside him. She said that her mother was anxious beyond measure to learn how and where he had met Harry, how he was looking, and what he had said.

The imagination and resources of the able detective are fully equal to those of the most brilliant newspaper reporters, and a pleasant and plausible fiction was invented, how he (as La Grange, of course,) having taken a run from Louisville down to New Orleans, by boat, was just landing at the levee when he suddenly came across Harry, who had hastily told him all; how great had been his transgression, how deeply he had regretted it; but that now he was situated in his business matters, so that if let alone, he would be able to return to Kuhn & Brothers every dollar which he had taken, and have a fine business left; how it had been necessary for him to come to New Orleans on imperative business, and that he should not come east of the Mississippi again under any circumstances. He further said, that Harry seemed hopeful; that he had stated that his younger brother, Robert was well and enjoying the frontier life; and that, further than that, he had no time or disposition to talk, as he was on the very eve of departure for Texas, only having time to write the little note concerning the photographs.

Miss Taylor excused herself for a moment to convey the truthful intelligence to her anxious mother; and on her return suggested that they go through the album together at once and attend to the photographs, an invitation which was accepted with unusual readiness.

Every gentleman who has had the experience, and there are few who have not, know that looking over an album with a beautiful woman who has some interest in her companion, is a wonderfully pleasant diversion. In this instance it was doubly pleasant, for it meant success to my son, whose zeal is as untiring as my own when once on the trail of a criminal.

"I wonder why," asked Miss Taylor, as if wondering as much about Mr. La Grange as about any other subject; "I wonder why Harry desires those photographs destroyed?"

He was turning the leaves for her and, as La Grange, of course, had a perfect right to take plenty of time to explain the matter soothingly and sympathetically.

"But do those horrid detectives track a man out and run him down, when, if he were let alone, he might recover from his misfortune and right the wrong he has done?"

Mr. LaGrange remarked that he had heard that some of them were very much lacking in sentiment and sensibility, and would go right forward through the very fire itself to trace the whereabouts of a criminal; and all those little things helped, he could assure her.

She began to see how it was, she said, but suddenly firing

11

up, she shook her pretty fist at some imaginary person, ex, claiming :

" Oh, I could kill the man who would thus dog my brothe Harry."   And then, after a little April shower of tears, quite like any other woman's way of showing how very desperate they can be under certain circumstances, began slowly taking the Captain's pictures from the album, commenting upon them, and then handing them to the bogus La Grange to burn, who would occasionally step to the fire-place for that purpose, where he would quickly substitute miscellaneous business cards which answered the purpose excellently.

An hour or two was passed with Miss Taylor in conversation upon various topics which might lead the really estimable young lady to divulge all she knew about the Captain, or concerning his whereabouts and business, which was certainly not much.

It appeared that, immediately after the embezzlement, and while at St. Louis, Taylor had telegraphed to his brother Robert to meet him at New Orleans at a certain time, as he was going into business in that section, and should need his services for which he would be able to pay him handsomely ; the brothers had met there and had proceeded to some other point ; the captain claiming that it would be injudicious to make that fact known, as he had also sent a full and complete confession to his parents regarding his embezzlement from Kuhn Bros., which he had directed them to burn, and which he finished by requesting his family not write to either himself or his brother for some time to come ; or at least until he should indicate to them that it would be safe to do so ; and under no circumstances to give any person an iota of information concerning himself or his brother.

My son left Miss Taylor's hospitable home with a pang of regret for the deception which had seemed necessary in this case ; for whatever may be the opinion of the public regarding the matter, a detective has often quite as large and compassionate a soul as men of other and apparently more high toned professions.

So long as intelligent crime is the result of a high standard of mental culture and a low standard of moral conscience—conditions which now exist and have for some years existed—intelligent minds must be trained to battle criminals with their own weapons ; and these two questions of speedy detection of crime and swift punishment of criminals will be found quite as essential to a preservation of law and society as lofty arguments or high moral dissertations on the right or wrong of the expediencies necessary to bring wrong-doers to immediate and certain justice.

As soon as 1 had received a full telegraphic report of the success of the Philadelphia experiment, I directed him to proceed to Louisville, where he would be met by Operative Keating, from Chicago, who would bring him letters of introduction from myself to Col. Wood, commanding the first Infantry at New Orleans; Captain White, chief of the Detective force of that city ; General Canby, commanding the Department of Texas, at Austin ; Col. Hunt, Chief Quartermaster of the Department of Texas, and other army officers, requesting them to render my son and his assistant any aid in their power, should the necessity for such assistance arise, the requisition from Governor Foulke, of Dakotah Territory, for Henry G. Taylor, upon Governor Pease, of Texas, and general instructions concerning his conduct of the search for the handsome captain after he had got beyond mail and telegraphic communication.

I was sending him into a country which was at that time in many portions utterly unsafe for the securing of a criminal should the pursuer's mission become known so as to allow the person desired time to apprise his friends of his danger, or give him even an opportunity to rally any number of acquaintances for defence; for the reason that, as Texas had become a sort of refuge for ruffians, they became clannish through the general peril of being pursued each experienced; and would, as a rule, on the slightest provocation, assist in the rescue of any person under arrest, not knowing how soon it might be their turn to cry for help; but I have invariably sent my sons into danger with the same expectation that they would do their duty regardless of consequences, as I have had when sending other men's sons into danger. Happily I have never mistaken their metal; and, in this instance, felt sure that I could rely upon him to exercise both discretion and intrepidity in exigencies to which his long experience and careful training have at all times made him equal.

The two detectives met in Louisville, and at once proceeded to New Orleans, where they arrived early in the morning of the 7th of January, 1868, and were driven to the St. Charles Hotel. No time was lost, and while my son presented his letters to different parties, and made cautious inquiries regarding the recent appearance in New Orleans of Taylor, Keating, in the character of a provincial merchant, investigated as far as possible the business houses dealing in stock, leather, or wool, as to whether any such person had made arrangements for consignments from the interior or seaport Texan cities. No trace of their man was found, however, until my son was able to get at the register of the St. Charles Hotel for the preceding three months, which was attended with some difficulty, on account of the crowded condition of things at that house ; and any detective, or other expert, will understand how much time and patience are required to discover one signature from among ten thousand, when that one may be an assumed name, and perhaps five hundred of the ten thousand be so similar to the one sought, that a disinterested person could scarcely be convinced it was really not the person's handwriting desired ; but after a good deal of trouble and searching, the names of " H. G. Taylor & clerk," were discovered on the last half line at the bottom of a page under date of November 30th, 1867, which, by constant wear and thumbing in turning pages, had been nearly defaced, but which in his handwriting beyond a doubt told the story of their presence.

Further inquiry of the clerk on duty at that time, and with his memory refreshed by a glance at Taylor's photographs, developed the facts that he had certainly been at the St Charles on the date shown by the register, and that he was accompanied by a young man about nineteen years of age who was recognized as Taylor's clerk.

The peculiar register then kept at the St. Charles Hotel in New Orleans was also instrumental in assisting the detectives. It gave the guest's name, residence, hour of arrival, and hour of departure, with name of convayance at arrival and departure in the following manner :

H. G. Taylor and Clerk, | *Mobile,* | 12 *m.* | *Ped.* | 2 *Dec.* | 7 *a.m.* | *'Bus.*

This told anybody curious about the matter that H. G. Taylor and clerk, assuming to reside in Mobile, arrived at the St. Charles Hotel, New Orleans, at noon on Saturday, the thirtirth day November, 1867, either afoot or by some mode of conveyance unknown to theclerk of the house and that they left the house in an omnibus at seven 'clock on the morning of the third day following.

Naturally the next inquiries were directed to ascertaining to what boat or railroad lines omnibuses could be ordered at that hour of the morning ; if to different ones, then to discover who had driven the particular omnibus which conveyed Taylor and his brother from the hotel ; and then make an effort to learn to what point they had been conveyed. This, however, proved less difficult than had been feared ; for it was found that on the morning in question the omnibus had gone from the hotel to but one point, and that was to the ferry connecting with Berwick Bay route, by the New Orleans and Opelousas Railroad and the Gulf, to Galveston, although a large number of passengers had been booked, and it was impossible to ascertain whether Taylor and his brother had actually gone that route or not, though everything was in favor of that presumption.

The death of General Rosseau had caused quite a commotion in New Orleans, and it seemed a pretty hard matter to get anything further of a definite character in that place; and I therefore instructed my son and Detective Keating to proceed slowly to Galveston, stopping at Brashear City, where Taylor might have diverged,—suyposing he had taken that route with the other passengers from New Orleans,—and to particularly search passenger-lists aboard any lines of boats, and all hotel registers, before arriving at Galveston, so as to have the work done thoroughly nearest the base of operation ; as I knew that for any party to get on the wrong scent in that vast State, thinly settled as it was, with no means of quickly conveying needful intelligence, was to enter upon both a needless waste of money for my patrons, and an objectless and wearying struggle against insurmountable obstacles for my detectives, whom, whatever may be said to the contrary, I have never in a single instance needlessly or injudiciously exposed to privation or danger.

In Brashear the conductors of trains were applied to ; the hotel and omnibus men were questioned, the postmaster was appealed to, and even the passenger-lists of the boats which had been in port, and to which they were able to gain access for a period of three months, had been searched in vain. Every trace of the man seemed lost ; and I was appealed to for a decision as to whether they should proceed to Galveston by boat with the presumption that Taylor had taken passage under an assumed name, or take a few days' trip up along the line of the New Orleans and Opelousas Railroad and seek for information of their man at different points through Central Louisiana.

J decided on the former course, and they accordingly embarked from Brashear immediately after the receipt of my telegram of instructions, on the handsome steamer Josephine, the only boat whose books they had had no opportunity of examining ; and, having received my telegram but a few minutes before the steamer left, were obliged to do some lively running to reach it ; for, in anticipation of a message from me to take that route, my son had directed Keating to settle the hotel bill, and with both valises in hand wait at a convenient corner, where, should Willliam receive a dispatch from me of the character expected, within a certain time, they might yet make the boat. Everything transpiring as my son had hoped, they were just in time, after a lively run, to be hauled up the gang plank by two stalwart negroes, and were soon steaming down the bay and thence out to sea.

CHAPTER IV.

A S the two ascended to the cabin they were congratulated by the officers of the boat and many of the passengers on their graceful and expeditious boarding of the
steamer ; and being something of objects of interest on account of the little incident, they concluded not to lose the
opportunity to blend the good feeling evoked into a thoroughly pleasant impression, and consequently took the
shortest way to accomplish that desired end by at once walking up to the bar where the assembled gentlemen, to a man,
apparently in compliance to general custom, seemed to understand that they had been invited before a word had been
uttered by either of the detectives, so that when my son
asked, " Gentlemen, won't you join us ? " it was an entirely
superfluous request ; for on either side behind, and extending
a solid phalanx beyond, the " gentlemen " had already joined
and were describing the particular liquor that in their minds
would do honor to the occasion in the most lively and familiar manner possible, and interspersing their demands upon
the leisurely bar-keeper with such remarks as " Gen'lemen
had narrow 'scape : " " Gen'lemen made a right smart run of
it ; " "Gen'lemen not down from Norlens (New Orleans),
reckon come down Opelousas route," and other similar com-
ments ; but invariably prefacing each and every remark with
11*

the stereotyped word "Gen'lemen," which men were, with-out exception, assumed to be in that country at that time, at least in conversation ; as any neglect to preface a remark with the word laid one liable to become immediately engaged in a discussion regarding the propriety of the use of the term, behind navy revolvers, rifles, double-barrelled shot-guns, or any other available pointed or forcible means of argument.

After the thirst of the crowd, which upon a Gulf-coasting steamer is something terrible to contemplate, had been in a measure assuaged, my son excused himself, and with Keating repaired to the office, remarking to the clerk :

" I presume you would like to transact a little business with us now ?"

"Any time to suit your convenience," returned the clerk, but getting at his books with an alacrity which showed that he would be a little more willing to attend to the matter of fares then than at any other time.

William handed him an amount of money large enough to pay for both the fares of himself and Keating from Brashear to Galveston ; and, while the clerk was making change, said by way of getting into conversation with him, " I'm afraid we're on a fool's errand out here."

The clerk counted out the change, inked his pen to take the names, and then elevating his eyebrows, although not speaking a word, plainly asked, " Ah, how's that ?"

" "Well, you see," replied the detective, "we're hunting a man that's had right good luck."

" He can't be in these parts," replied the clerk with a slightly satirical smile. "Names?" he then asked.

"James A. Hicks and Patrick Mallory."

"Where from?"

"Pittsburg."

"Which is which?" asked the clerk in a business tone of voice.

"I am Hicks, and that pretty smart-looking Irishman by the baggage-room is Mallory," was the reply.

"Your age and weight?" asked the clerk mechanically, at the same time looking at my son keenly and getting the rest of his description at a glance.

These questions were properly answered and as the clerk was noting them he asked, "Might I ask what was the gentleman's good luck?"

"Certainly; he has fallen heir to a coal mine in Pennsylvania, and we are endeavoring to hunt him up for the executors of the estate."

"Ah?" said the clerk, driving away with his pen, "will you be so good as to ask Mr. Mallory to step this way?"

My son stepped up to Keating and remarked aloud, "Mr. Mallory, Mr. Mallory, the clerk would like to see you;" and then as Keating stepped to his side, remarked as if for his better information, "He knows your name is Patrick Mallory and that we are from Pittsburg, hunting Taylor, so he can come home and enjoy the property the old man left him; but he wants your entire description."

"Quite so;" said the quick-witted Irishman dryly.

"You've got me now," said Keating, winking familiarly at the clerk, "when we came over we went under; and so many of us was lost that those saved wasn't worth mindin' as to age, ye see; but concerning heft why, I'd not fear to say I'd turn an honest scale at a hundred an' sixty."

The clerk smiled but concluded not to ask Mr. Mallory from Pittsburg any more questions.

As soon as he had made his notes, however, William told him that he had examined the lists of all other boats plying between Brashear and Galveston, save those of the Josephine, and requested him to look through them, concluding by describing Taylor and stating that he might register either as H. G. Taylor and clerk, or under an assumed name, as he was somewhat erratic, and through family troubles not necessary to explain, he had got into a habit of occasionally travelling *incognito.*

The clerk readily complied with his request, scanning the pages closely and repeating the name musingly as if endeavoring to recall where he had heard it. By the time he had got on with the examination of a few pages, William had selected a photograph of Taylor, and on showing it to the clerk the latter seemed to have a certain recollection of having seen him, but a very uncertain recollection as to where, or under what circumstances. He went on repeating the name, however, turning back the pages with his right hand and tracing the names back and forth with the index finger of his left hand, occasionally looking at the photograph as if to assist in forcing a definite recollection, but without any result for so long a time that Messrs. Hill and Mallory of Pittsburg became satisfied that their last hope before arriving at Galveston was gone, when suddenly the clerk carelessly placed the picture beside a certain name and in a manner very similar to a dry-goods clerk on securing a successful "match," in two pieces of cloth, quietly remarked :

"Yes, can't be mistaken.   There you are ; I've got him."

"Then *we've* got him !" exclaimed my son, in the excess of his gratification shaking the hand of Mr. Mallory from Pittsburg.

"It's a joy," said the latter beaming.

"Think of the immense property !" continued my son.

"And the surprise to his friends !" murmured Keating.

"The surprise to himself, I should say," interrupted the clerk.

"Quite so," said Mr. Keating.

It appeared that Taylor and his brother had missed one or two boats at Brashear from some cause, but had finally taken passage on the Josephine, November seventh ; and as the detectives had not been able to ascertain whether the Josephine had carried the fugitives or not, on account of her being belated by adverse weather, and was now returning to Galveston after having had barely time to touch at Brashear, they had felt that perhaps they might be upon the wrong trail, which, with unknown adventures before them, had been peculiarly discouraging ; so that now, when they ascertained that his apprehension was only a question of time and careful work, they could not repress their gratification.

Nothing further worthy of note transpired on the voyage from Brashear to Galveston, save that the trip was a pretty rough one, and they finally arrived in the latter city hopeful and encouraged, notwithstanding the unusually dismal weather, which seemed to consist of one disconnected but never-ending storm, the "oldest inhabitants" of the place contending with great earnestness that "it 'peared likes they'd never had nothin' like it befoah!"

Arriving in Galveston early Sunday morning, they went to the Exchange Hotel, and after breakfast set about examining the hotel registers of the place, ascertaining that Taylor and brother had been in the city, stopped a day or two, and then, so far as could be learned, had gone on to Houston. They were satisfied he had made no special efforts to cover his tracks, although he had not made himself at all conspicuous, as the difficulty encountered in getting those who would be most likely to recollect him, to recollect him at all, clearly showed; and it was quite evident that he had not anticipated pursuit, at least of any nature which he could not easily compromise, and intended going into some legitimate business under his own name and with his brother's assistance.

Before he could be arrested in Texas, however, it would be necessary to secure Governor Pease's warrant, which obliged a long, tedious trip to Austin, the capital of the State; nearly the whole distance having to be done by stage, which at that time seemed a forbidding piece of work, as it had rained every day of the year, so far; and it might be a question of helping the stage through rather than being helped through by it. Besides this, according to my son's reports, which gave a true description of things in Texas at that time, everything beyond Houston had to be paid for in gold, as sectional sentiment and counterfeiting had pronounced a ban upon greenbacks, and not only in gold, but at exorbitant prices; hotel rates being five dollars per day; single meals from one to two dollars; railroad fares eight cents per mile, and stage rates nearly double that amount; with no assurance that you would ever reach a destination you had paid to be conveyed to; all attended by various kinds of danger, among which was the pleasant reflection that you might be called upon at any time to contribute to the benefit of that noble relic of chivalry, the Ku Klux Klan, who at that day were particularly busy in Texas.

All of these pleasant considerations made the departure from Galveston for Austin, in a Pickwickian sense, unusually agreeable.

At Houston they discovered from different persons, including the postmaster, that Taylor had been there, but had made inquiries about points further up country; and the general impression was that he had gone on, though at Brenham, the terminus of the railroad, where they arrived Monday evening, they could find no trace of him.

The next morning, when my son arose and looked on the vast sea of mud,—a filthy, black earth below; a dirty, black sky above; with nothing but driving rain and wintry gusts between; while the lackadaisical Texans slouched about with their hands in their pockets, with only energy enough to procure tobacco or " licker; " their sallow faces, down-at-the-heels, snuff-dipping wives desolately appearing at the doors and windows, only to retire again with a woe-begone expression of suspended animation in their leathery faces,—he fully realized the force of the remark attributed to General

Sheridan, and more expressive than polite : "If I owned Texas and hell, I would live in hell and sell Texas!"

The stage was crowded, however, and the dreary convey-ance splashed and crunched on until noon, when dinner was taken at Wilson's Ranche, a long, low, rambling, tumble-down structure, which, like its owner, who had at one time been a "General" of something, and now retained the thriving title out of compliment to his departed glory, had gone to a genteel decay with a lazy ease worthy of its master's copy. The dinner was one long to be remembered by the detectives, as it was their first genuine Texan dinner, and consisted merely of fat boiled pork.and hot bread of the con sistence of putty cakes of the same dimensions, which, when broken open after a mighty effort, disclosed various articles of household furniture, such as clay pipes, old knife handles, and various other invoices, probably playfully dumped into the flour barrel by some one of the half-score of tow-headed, half-clad children which the "General" and his buxom helpmeet had seen fit to provide for torturing another generation with rare Texan dinners at a dollar a plate.

It was an all-day's labor getting to La Grange, but thirty five miles from Brenham, where they arrived at ten o'clock, tired and exhausted from the day's banging about in the stage and out of it, for they were obliged to walk many times in order to rest the jaded horses so that they could get through to La Grange at all ; but before retiring made all the inquires necessary to develop the fact that their man had not been at that point.

The next day, Wednesday, was rather more trying than

the previous one. Two miles out of town the stage got "bogged," and the entire load of passengers were obliged to get out and walk through three miles of swamps, the stage finally sticking fast, necessitating prying it out with rails. After this Slough of Despond was passed, the Colorado river had to be forded three times, and then came a "dry run," which now, with every other ravine or depression, had became a "wet run," and was "a booming" as the drunken driver termed it between oaths. There was at least four feet of water in the dry run, and the horses balking, the buckskin argument was applied to them so forcibly that they gave a sudden start and broke the pole off short, which further complicated matters. My son, being on the box, sprang to the assistance of the driver, and stepping down upon the stub of the pole, quickly unhitched the wheel horses, so that the stage could not be overturned, and then disengaged the head team, finally appropriating a heavy wheel horse, with which he rode back to Keating, who was perched upon a rear wheel to keep out of the water, which was rushing and seething below, sweeping through the bottom of the stage and at every moment seeming to have lifted the vehicle preparatory to sweeping it away like feathers, and also holding on to the baggage which he had got safely upon the roof of the stage; and, taking him aboard his improvised ferry, after securing the valises, rode to the muddy shore, forming with his companions about as fine a picture of despairing "carpet baggers" as the South has ever on any occasion been able to produce. The bedraggled passengers ascertained that the next town, Webberville, was several miles distant, and that there was no house nearer, save on the other side of the rapidly rising stream ; and as night had come on, the best thing that could be done was to penetrate the woods, build a rousing fire, and shiver and shiver through as long, wet, and weary a night as was ever experienced.

There was never a more longed-for morning than the next one, and the moment that the sickly light came feebly through the mist and rain, and straggled into the dense cotton-wood trees, where the discouraged passengers had a sort of fervent out-doors prayer-meeting, they started forward for Webberville, hungry, drenched, and so benumbed as to be scarcely able to walk. It was five miles into town, but one mile of that distance stretched over a quagmire known and described in that section as " Hell's half acre ; " and the truthful inhabitants of Webberville related of this delectable ground that during the rainy season its powers of absorption were so great that it would even retain the gigantic Texan mosquito, should it happen to take a seat there.

This bog was impassable to the travellers, who finally bartered with the owner of a hog wagon to be carried over the marsh for a silver half dollar each. This was far better than remaining on the other side, and they finally trudged into the town more dead than alive.

Fortunately for the detectives, the brother of ex-Governor Lubbock, of Texas, was one of the party, and as they had all become so thoroughly acquainted, as common misery will quickly make travellers, he took my son and Keating to the residence of Colonel Banks, a merchant of Webberville, whose good wife never rested until she had provided the party with a splendid meal, something with which to wash it down, and beds which seemed to them all to have been composed of down.

After they had a good rest, the passengers for Austin were got together, and explained the situation of things. The creek the other side of Webberville was a mighty river. The driver thought he could possibly get the stage across, but was certain he could not do so with any passengers or baggage to make it drag more heavily; but he thought that if once on the other side, they might get to Austin the same day. William was anxious to push ahead, and looking about town discovered a rather venturesome negro who owned a monstrous mule, and at once entered into negotiations with him for the transfer of the party and baggage, sink or swim. So when the stage arrived at the creek, the baggage was unloaded, and the stage successfully forded the stream. But as the water covered so broad an expanse, was so deep and rapid, and altogether presented such a forbidding appearance, the passengers refused to try the mule experiment unless William, who had proposed the mode of transfer, and had secured the novel ferry, which stood with the grinning negro upon its back ready for passengers, would first cross the Rubicon to demonstrate the convenience and safety of the passage. So handing the captain one of the valises, he mounted the mule, which, after a few whirls, a little "bucking," several suspicious sidewise movements, and a shouted "Ya-a-oop, da, Dani-el!—done quit dis heyah foolishness!" plunged into the current without further ceremony.

The passengers saw that Dani-el and his master were up to a thing or two in that section of the country ; and after seeing Keating cross the stream in safety also, they one by one ventured upon the transfer, which was finished without accident, but with a good deal of merriment; and the colored clown paid even beyond his contract price, the stage was enabled to go lumbering on to Austin, where it arrived at a late hour of the same day.

CHAPTER V.

RAIN, drizzle, and mist ; mist, drizzle, and rain. It seemed all that the country was capable of producing ; and the same preface to the befogged condition of the English chancery courts used by Dickens, in his introduction to "Bleak House," with a few of the localisms expunged, would have fitly applied to the condition of things in Texas, which afterward culminated in a flood which swept everything before it.

In Austin—though the seat of the State government and the head-quarters of the military department of Texas, full of legislators, lobbyists, officers, and soldiers, everything had the appearance of having been through a washing that had lasted an age, and had been prematurely wrung out to dry, but had been caught on the lines by an eternal rainy day. Involuntarily, with the spatters and dashes of rain and the morning wind, Longfellow's "Rainy Day" came drifting into the mind, and the lines :

> "The day is cold and dark and dreary ;
> It rains, and the wind is never weary ;
> The vine still clings to the mouldering wall,
> While at every gust the dead leaves fall.
> And the day is dark and dreary !"

were never more appropriate than when applied to any

portion of Texas during the months of January and February, 1868.

The very first man my son met in the office of the hotel, the next morning, was a member of the Legislature from Besar County, who, hearing his inquiries of the clerk concerning Taylor, informed him that he had been introduced to him in San Antonio a few weeks previous; that he was in company with a much younger man whom he represented as his brother, and that he had ostensibly come to San Antonio to make some inquiries concerning the hide and wool trade; but whether with an idea of settling at that point, or whether he could yet be found in San Antonio, he was unable to state.

In any event this was cheering news; for it assured my detectives that their long and weary search would not prove unavailing; and William directed Keating to make himself useful about the different hotels and hide and stock dealers,—as it is a detective's business to work all the time, and the slightest cessation of vigilance after the beginning of an operation might at the most unexpected moment cause the beginning of a series of circumstances eventually permitting a criminal's escape—while he himself sought out General Potter who escorted him to General Canby's head-quarters where he was most cordially received, and not only given an order for military aid, should it be required, but General Canby himself went with him to the Capitol and introduced him to Governor Pease, vouching for the reliability of any statement made in connection with the business which had brought him so far from home; as, while I had charge of the secret service of the Government, during the war, with myself and sons had had an intimate acquaintance with, and personal friendship for him.

Governor Pease frankly stated to William that the affidavits were rather weak, and that should some of the "shysters" of that State who did a thriving business in *habeas corpus* releases, get an inkling of his business and the nature of the papers, they might give him a deal of trouble, even if they did not get his man away from him eventually. He said he would make the requisition as strong as possible, however, and expressed his hope that the reputation for ingenuity in devising and executing expedients possessed by Pinkerton's men would be more than sustained in this instance; and General Canby terminated the interview by giving the document approval over his own signature.

My son thanked them both for their kindness, and withdrew, only too anxious to get to where his man was before any information that he was being sought for should reach him, and either scare him beyond the Rio Grande, or enable him to act on the defensive, as only a man can act who has plenty of money, plenty of friends, and, as we already knew, a great plenty of bravery on his own account.

Soon after he had returned to the hotel, Keating came in with undoubted information that Taylor had a permanent residence at or near Corpus Christi; that either he or his brother owned a sheep ranche near the coast, not far from that city; while the other dealt in hides and wool there;

and that one or the other penetrated into the interior as far as San Antonio, soliciting consignments.

My son at once concluded that it was the Captain who had done the dealing, as well as stealing, and whose money and business ability had been brought to bear upon the trading at Corpus Christi, and upon the ranche in the country near it; the brother, though probably entirely innocent of complicity in the robbery, or even a knowledge of the source from whence the money had come, only being used for a convenient repository for his ill-gotten funds in case of Kuhn Bros. following him before he was ready to meet them.

He therefore decided to get through to Corpus Christi in the very shortest time in which the trip could be made *via* New Braunfels, San Antonio, Victoria, and Port Lavaca, hoping that he might be able to pick him up along some portion of that route, as it was quite evident he made frequent trips in that direction; and, at whatever point he might be started, should he seem to be going much farther into the interior,—which would be improbable, as San Antonio at that time was quite a frontier city,—arrest him at once, and hurry him back to Galveston along the route he was already familiar with; but, should he be going toward the coast, to let him take his own course, keeping him well in hand until he had reached Corpus Christi or some other seaport city, and, waiting a favorable opportunity, arrest him and get him aboard a boat before he could recover from the surprise.

Not a half hour before they left Austin, he fortunately

met Judge Davis of Corpus Christi, who was there attend-ing some political convention, and who gave him a letter to his law partner at home, should his services in any way be needed, as I had been of some service to him on a previous occasion; so that when my two detectives left Austin on the seventeenth of January, they felt perfectly satisfied of ultimate success, though the same terrible experiences as to staging were again encountered.

It required the entire day to traverse the few miles be-tween Austin and Blanco Creek, where they secured a sort of a supper; the Onion Creek and its branches having been waded and forded numberless times. At Manchell Springs, the stage pole being again broken, they were only able to proceed after improvising a tongue out of a sapling, chopped from the roadside with a very dull hatchet. At Blanco Springs a good rest was taken, and the driver, having the day's experience in his mind, objected to going further that night; but the detectives insisted that they had paid their money to be taken to a certain destination, and, as they had shown a disposition to more than earn their passage besides, no excuse for their detention should be offered.

After a good deal of grumbling, fresh horses were got out, a new pole put in the stage, and the procession again took up its weary march over the then most horrible of roads, crossing the innumerable brooks and runs which now pushed torrents into York's Creek. All night long they slushed and splashed, and tramped and cursed; though the the rain had ceased for a time, there was but little light from the sky, which seemed full of black heavy clouds ready

12

to burst asunder, to again drench them and swell the torrents afresh. My son, Keating, and a man sent along from Blanco Creek, "took turns," trudging along ahead of the lead-team, and, with lanterns, picked out the way. Often they would be misled where the ground was so bad as to almost defy a passage over it, when the patient animals behind them, steaming from the toil of straining along with nothing but an empty coach, would stop, as if guided by a keener instinct, where they would quietly remain -until the united search of the three men had discovered the road, when the intelligent creatures docilely plodded along again.

And so, through seemingly bottomless quagmires; over corduroys, where the shaky ends of timbers, struck by a horse's hoof, would mercilessly splash those walking beside the useless vehicle, or, suddenly relieved from the weight of the ponderous wheel, would fly upwards to heave gallons of slime upon the coach; laboring around the bases of far-extending mounds of sandy loam; descending into unexpected and sometimes dangerous depressions, along coolies, and plunging into streams, where drift, and changing, sandy bottoms always made it a question whether the coach could ever be got across; they marched only as Sherman taught soldiers to march; or as honest detectives will crowd all obstacles between themselves and their duty, and came with the gray of the morning to the beautiful, forest-shaded Guadelupe.

Fording this river without nearly the trouble represented at some of the petty runs and coolies which had been passed, they came to New Braunfels with the sun, which had shown itself for the first time since their arrival in Texas, and which also shone upon the first city which had shown any of that wide-awake "go-aheaditiveness" and thrift so common to nearly all northern cities.

The reason that New Braunfels differed so materially from the ordinary Texan towns lay in the fact that it was almost exclusively settled by Germans; and it was a welcome sight to the detectives to be able to enter a place where, from suberb to centre, up and down long, finely-shaded avenues, it was plain to be seen that the most had been made of everything.

From the pleasantest cottage of the extreme suburb, and past the more pretentious residences,—every home being provided with an exterior bake-oven, the same as in Germany, Pennsylvania, or portions of Wisconsin and Minnesota, to the shops, stores, hotels, and public buildings, every yard, in many instances fenced with stone gleaned and cleaned from the soil, and for that matter, every spot upon which the eye rested, showed that thrift and not whiskey-drinking ruled that place; and that fact alone entitles the little German city to respectable elevation from the obscurity which has heretofore surrounded it.

As nothing at this point could be learned regarding Taylor, though leaving the town and its extraordinary attractions with some reluctance, they immediately proceeded to San Antonio, the roads to which place were quite passable, and arrived at that city Friday afternoon. I had telegraphed to Colonel Lee, of San Antonio, to hold himself in readiness to assist my son and Keating, on the score of personal friendship, whenever they might arrive there, not knowing, from the terrible condition of the roads, at what time it would be possible for them to reach that point, and he, being ignorant from what direction they might come, where they might stay, or under what name they might register, had caused an advertisement to be inserted in the San Antonio *Herald*, of which the following is a copy :

PERSONAL.—WHENEVER THE SON OF A. P., of Chicago, may arrive in San Antonio, he will learn of something to his advantage by calling upon Lieut.-Col. Lee, at the Mengler House.

Keating's sharp eyes first saw the item at the supper table of the Mengler House, where they were stopping, and they both learned by listening to the conversation about them that the Colonel was sitting at the same table.

After supper William made himself known to Colonel Lee without attracting attention, the latter kindly offering him any help needed, after which inquiries of a guarded character were instituted for the object of their search. The landlord of the Mengler House stated that Taylor had called upon him about three weeks before to inquire for letters, but as he was stopping elsewhere but little attention had been paid to him or his questions ; all of which William had reason to believe absolutely true on account of the strong corroborative testimony which would lie in the statement of any landlord that no civility was shown to a man who quarters at any hostelry save his own.

The next morning he called upon Chief of Police, H. D. Bonnet, who extended every imaginable courtesy, went with him to the offices of the different stage-lines, and assisted in examining their lists for some time previous with a view to ascertaining what direction Taylor had taken when he left San Antonio ; introduced him to the Mayor and Chief Marshal, and even went with him on an extended tour through the old Mexican quarter of the town ; but no other information was secured save through the German landlady of a hotel, who was as positive as her limited knowledge of the English language would allow her to be, that Taylor had stopped at her house without registering at all, and had gone directly from San Antonio to Port Lavaca or Corpus Christi on horseback, which, after all, in the exceptional condition of the weather that year in Texas, seemed quite probable.

It was evident nothing was to be gained by remaining any longer at San Antonio, and was quite as plain that all possible expedition should be used in getting on to the coast.

As if the fates were ordained perverse, the moment the two left San Antonio a steady drenching rain again began to fall, and as the stage was crowded, the discomfort of those within could not very well be increased. About twelve miles from San Antonio the driver succeeded in tipping over the stage and giving the occupants "an elegant mud varnish all over," as operative Keating aptly expressed it. The driver remarked that he was "going up the new road," but some of the more profane passengers swore that, if so, he was hunting it three feet under the old one. On arriving at Lavernia station the dismal announcement was made by the lean, long stage agent, who seemed to have never done anything from time immemorial save sit in the door of his tumble-down hovel to make dismal announcement that "the Cibolo (pronounced there 'C'uil-lou') is just a scootin' and a rippin' up its banks like a mad buffler bull ! ye'll all be back to stay at my taven all night."

It was the contemplation of this man's pure cussedness, as he sat there doting on the big bills he would charge when the Cibolo should drive back a stage load of hungry travellers, that nerved them to push on and at all hazards attempt a crossing at some point where the Cibolo "scooted and ripped up its banks" with less ardor than across the regular route to Victoria ; but on reaching Southerland Springs, seven miles distant, it was found that it would be necessary to wait until Thursday morning, when they might possibly make a passage, as the stream was running down to within something like ordinary bounds very fast.

Thursday afternoon came before an attempt to ford the stream was made, when the driver agreed to land the pas_sengers in the middle of the stream on an immense fallen tree, from which point they could reach the other side, when they might be able to get the empty stage across also.

The trial was made, and was successful so far as landing the passengers was concerned, but while this was being done the wheels of the coach sank deeper and deeper into the mucky bed of the stream, and though but a few minutes had elapsed, the strange action of the water had caused deposits to form about the coach so rapidly that it became firmly imbedded and could not be moved by the four horses attached.   At this juncture an old farmer came along, who carried the evidences of some of his propensities strongly marked in his face, which was a thin one, like his conscience, but with bright tips on his cheek-bones and as red a nose as ever the devil-artist in alchohol tipped with crimson.   No importunities, or amount of money could prevail on him to assist the discouraged travellers with his fine mule train ; but a pint of good whiskey, to be delivered the moment the stage had been drawn from its peril, with a small drink by way of retainer, accomplished what would not have been done in any other manner and set the travellers joyfully on their way again.   They journeyed on at a snail's pace until one o'clock Friday morning, when they arrived at Kelly's Ranche, kept by Bill Kelly, uncle of the " Taylor boys," notorious for their connection with the Ku Klux and various other gangs of villainous desperadoes.

The family were unceremoniously awakened, and at once good humoredly proceeded to provide the ravenous passengers with something to eat ; after which they made a " shake-down " on the floor, into which substitute for a bed everybody turned and slept late into the morning, awakening stiff in every joint and scarcely able for that day's journey, which, with its complement of accidents and delays took them safely over Esteto Creek and into Yorktown early in the evening, where the detectives secured certain information that Taylor had been in Corpus Christi the week previous, and was un-doubtedly there at that time, as Texas by this time had become a net-work of resistless streams, almost impassable quagmires and far-reaching lagoons.

L ATE the next morning they left Yorktown, having taken on a passenger of no less importance than ex-Confederate Governor Owens, of Arizona. He was a pleasant, voluble old fellow, and my son at once fell in with his ways, and treated him so courteously that it perhaps averted a greater disaster than had at any previous time occurred.

Gov. Owens was largely engaged in the Rio Grande trade of supplying frontier points with provisions and merchandise, and was just on his way to Indianola, on the coast, where he was to meet his Mexican freighters, comprising thirty wagons and carts, of all characters and descriptions, driven by the inevitable lazy greaser. Even as late as the same period, 1867-8, a vast amount of freighting was done between St. Paul, Minnesota, and Fort Garry Manitoba, in the famed Red River carts, driven by the inevitable, lazy half-breed.

William, knowing the position held by Gov. Owens during a portion of the war, and realizing that an ex-office-holder will never lose his tenderness for the political régime which made him titled, assumed to be a Mississippian, from Vicksburg, with an Irish acquaintance, on a trip of inspection through Texas, and, so far, terribly disappointed with the State.

During those periods when, owing to the depth of the

mud, the passengers were oblidged to walk, they would fall behind or walk ahead of the stage, when they would chat pleasantly upon general subjects. On one of these occasions Gov. Owens eyed his companion sharply a moment, and then asked :

" Can I trust you, sir ? "

" Certainly."

" On the word and honor of a gentleman ? "

" Yes, and an honest man, too," William answered.

" I believe you ; thank you. You know stages are robbed out this way ? "

" I do."

" Did you ever see it done ? "

" No ; nor have I any desire to be around on such an occasion," he replied, laughing.

" I reckoned you hadn't better, either," said the Governor earnestly. " It wouldn't make so much difference if they would do the work a trifle genteelly, in a gentlemanly way , but the fact is, we have low fellows along our Texas stage lines. They have no regard for a man's family. Why, he continued, warmly, " they'll just pop out from behind the trees, or up through some clumps of bushes, ram a double barreled shot gun, loaded to the muzzel with slugs and things, into the coach from both sides at once, and just blaze away—all that are not killed outright are scared to death. There's nothing fair about it ! "

William expressed his curiosity to know if the drivers were ever killed.

" Drivers ? Never, sir, never. Why, those ruffians are too

smart for that.   Let it be known that they have begun kill·
ing drivers, and there isn't a stage company in Texas that
could send a coach past the first timber.   They couldn't
afford to kill stage-drivers, for the moment they began it, that
would be the end of staging."

My son expressed his thanks at learning so much of the
business principles of these land pirates, and the old gentleman continued :

" You see, it takes a peculiar kind of a driver for a Texas
coach.   You want one, first, that can drink right smart
of whiskey, for the water isn't good along some of these
branches.   You want one that can swear a hoss's head
square off, too.   He's got to be a coward, or he would
help put this robbing down ; and yet, he has got to be
rather brave to drive right along up to a spot where he
knows he is to see his passengers butchered ! and that,"
continued the Govenor, earnestly, " is just what I want to
talk to you about, as I feel sure that I can trust you."

The Governor then explained to him that a certain member of the Ku-Klux, whom he was sorry to say was too intimate with those roadside plunderers, had informed him
that morning, just as he was leaving Yorktown, that preparations had been made to rob their stage at a point
between Clinton and Mission Valley; and that he very
much desired some organization among the passengers
for defence, as he himself had upwards of thirty thousand
dollars, to be paid out at Indianola, for goods, and to his
freighters for wages.

On the receipt of this alarming intelligence, my son took

the responsibility of informing the rest of the passengers what might possibly be expected; and, as Gov. Owens had six fine carbines, which he was also taking down to Indianola for the protection of his freighters on the Rio Grande, preparatory to any attack that might be made.

About six miles from Mission Valley the stage route traversed a low piece of bottom-lands covered with timber, and a considerable growth of underbrush. A corduroy road had been built through the place, and as the coach was obliged to be driven slowly across it, the locality offered particularly fine inducements for a robbery of the character described by the Governor, so that the precaution was taken of walking along with the coach, three on either side, with carbines ready for instant use.

Just before entering the timber, two men were seen prowling about, and, evidently fearing their actions might cause suspicion and frustrate the plan they had in view, made a great effort to appear to be two respectable hunters in search of only wild game; and, before leaving the timber at the other side, two more persons were seen, who, evidently, not having been given any signal, had come as near to the stage as they dared, to ascertain for themselves why their comrades had failed in their calculations; but skulked away after seeing the force which grimly trudged along, guarding the empty vehicle, into which the passengers were glad enough to climb when the danger was gone by, and be carried with sound bodies and whole pockets to the supper which had been some time in waiting when they reached Mission Valley.

Dinner the next day was taken at Victoria, from which city William and Keating expected to be able to go by railroad to Port Lavaca, only twenty-eight miles distant. They were doomed to disappointment in this, as the railroad had been abandoned since the war, either the Union or Confederate soldiers having taken it up bodily and turned it upside down, like a gigantic furrow, from Victoria to the sea.

After many years somebody had come along and turned it back ; but to this day the steam-engine has never thundered over it again, the most that has ever been done having been to drag an occasional freight car over the road by the not peculiarly thrilling application of mule power ; and so it was said a hand-car, worked by a gang of negroes, was used for transporting passengers, the trips being made back and forth whenever a load could be got, and not before.

As they were obliged to remain for this new mode of conveyance, their time was entirely unoccupied, and they could not but have leisure to make something of a study of Texan life, as it then existed ; and on Sunday afternoon were witnesses to one of those little episodes which sometimes make extremely lively certain periods that would otherwise remain hum-drum and ordinary.

The bar-room of the hotel had been crowded all day, and a good deal of liquor had been drunk, while there had also been a large amount of money lost and won over cards, so that there was that feverish, explosive condition of things which always follows large winnings or losses at games of chance, although there had as yet been no disturbance of a serious character.

At one of the little gaming tables, John Foster, County Clerk of Victoria County, and another person, named Lew Phillips, who had been one of the Andersonville Prison-keepers during the war, but had drifted out to Victoria and had secured charge of a large livery-stable there, were engaged at a game of poker, when Foster was heard to quietly say:

"See here, Lew Phillips, you stole that card!"

"You're a liar!" was retorted with an oath.

The two men were up over the card-table in a twinkling, looking at each other, and both very white.

"Apologize!" demanded Foster, still quiet, but with a terrible earnestness in his voice.

"I don't do that sort of business, you white-livered coward!" shouted Phillips.

Without another look or word, the two parted, one passing out one door and the other out of another, while the crowd in the hotel canvassed the matter as coolly as though there had been no difficulty worth mentioning, while a few quietly laid wagers on who would get the first shot.

In about fifteen minutes more, Foster was seen returning with a double barrelled shot-gun, and Phillips, who had a wooden leg, came stumping up another street with an immense navy revolver in his hand. It was noticeable that the space between the advancing men was made very clear, so that nothing should interfere with their sociability. In a moment more, Phillips had fired at Foster, and evidently hit him; for, as he was bringing his gun to his shoulder, his aim had been badly disturbed, and before he had time to fire, Phillips had fired again and wounded his man the second time. Foster now leaned against a porch column, desperately resolved to get a good aim;—his antagonist, all the while advancing, attempted to fire again, but missed this time, the cap refusing to communicate the deadly flash to the chamber of the revolver;—then there was a blinding flash from Foster's gun, accompanied by a thunderous report, and the two men fell almost instantaneously.

Foster had discharged both barrels of his weapon, heavily loaded with buck-shot, at Phillips, the entire charge having entered his wooden leg, and sent him spinning to the ground, like the sudden jerk and whirl of a nearly spent top, the recoil of the gun also "kicking" Foster flat as a Tennessee "poor whites" corn pone.

The "gentlemen" who had been looking on and quietly criticising the little by-play, now rushed forward and surrounded the combatants, the anxiety of each of whom was to be assured of the other's death; or, in case of his being alive, to have some one be the immediate bearer of tender regards and profuse expressions of friendship; thus terminating satisfactorily to all parties what the chivalrous inhabitants of Victoria informed my detectives was called a "stag duel," the most common and effective method known for settling the little difficulties liable at any time to occur among gentlemen, the only conditions imposed by custom being that neither party shall offer to shoot in a crowded room, or be allowed to fire at his opponent unless he is also prepared, when other citizens who may be using the streets, at those times withdraw from them as rapidly as consistent with the proprieties, when the occasion is immediately made interesting to the participants, who advance and fire upon each other as rapidly as a liberal practice in this and other "codes" of taking human life, will permit.

As the next sensation to a "stag duel" in Victoria was the arrival of the "train" from Lavaca, in the shape of the hand-car manned by four burly negroes, who with the original superintendent of the road had formed a soulless corporation with which nothing could compete, it was not long before the detectives had secured seats with four other passengers, making ten persons in all, to be conveyed twenty-eight miles on a broken-down hand-car over probably the most villainous excuse for a railroad ever known.

The fare was six dollars in gold for each passenger, which might seem to have a shade of exorbitance about it when it was considered that the accommodations consisted of two very insecure seats, constructed over the wheels, upon each of which three persons might cling with a constant expectation of being jolted off by the unevenness of the road, or of falling off from sheer fatigue in endeavor to cling to the ramshackle boards beneath them.

"All abo'd!" shouted the negro conductor, with all the style and unction of the diamond-pinned aristocrat of a New York Central Train; and then, as the "train" started out of Victoria the passengers and the admiring lookers-on were greeted with the following song, turned to the "Ra-ta-tat" of the wheels upon the rails, and sturdily sung, or chanted rather, by the jolly but powerful crew:

> " Heave ho !
>> Away we go——
>>> Winds may wait or de winds may blow !
>> Heave ho !
>> Away we go——
>>> For to cotch de gals at Lavac—o ! "

In the sense that this mode of travelling had the charm of novelty, and the thrilling attraction of danger combined, it was a success. There was freshness and variety about it too ; for, whenever one of the negroes had "done gin out," the conductor would call for volunteers from among the passengers and give the demand a peculiar emphasis by the remark, "Takes brawn 'n sinyew to pump dis hy'r train into 'vacca ; 'n de' Lo'd never did make no men out o' cl'ar iron'n steel ! "

The argument was so forcible that some one would work wirh the negroes while the " clean done gone " man and brother rested and meditated upon "catchin' the gals of 'vacca ! " which the song brought out so feelingly.

Besides this, new interest would be added to the excursion whenever the wind was favorable ; for, stopping the car, a mast, to which a sort of " mutton-lig sail," as they termed it, would be attached ; the conductor would brace himself and would lengthen or shorten the sail as was most judicious, and then the hand-car ship would speed along the billowy track like a majestic thing of life for a mile or two, when the party were again forced into a realizing sense of the plodding nature of the means of transit, which, after all, at times became monotonous.

On one of these occasions of momentary fair sailing and enthusiasm, they were also favored with a down grade of quite a stretch ; and, as everybody was happy at the wonderful rate of speed acquired, while the negroes were sing ing snatches of songs in the gayest manner possible, a " spread" of the track let the car upon the ties from which it leaped at one bound into the swamp, completely immersing several of its occupants in the muddy slime.

No damage was done, however, as the spot where everything and everybody alighted was too soft to cause anything to be broken ; and after righting the car, and repairing the disaster as much as possible, William and Keating safely arrived in Lavaca early in the afternoon, were at once driven to Indianola where they cleaned up, including a most welcome bathing and shaving, at the Magnolia House, embarked on a little schooner carrying the government mail down the coast; were becalmed in Aranzas Bay, and late during the night of the twenty-seventh of January, the light from a quaint seaport city danced along the waves of its beautiful harbor, and welcomed the worn-out but indefatigable detectives to Corpus Christi.

OING ashore, the two proceeded to a sort of hotel or boarding-house on the beach, where they found Judge Carpenter, formerly of Chicago, who had become District Judge there, and who, on learning my son's name, inquired if he were not a relative of Allan Pinkerton the detective.

He replied that he was very *distantly* related, which was a literal truth at that time, when the Judge claiming any acquaintance, proffered any assistance which might be desired, whatever his business. The courtesy was courteously accepted, but no questions were asked concerning Taylor.

After breakfast the next morning, they strolled up-town with Judge Carpenter, when passing a Mr. Buckley's store, Keating, while catching step, took occasion to nudge my son, who carelessly looked into the place, as any stranger might, and there saw the object of his long search pleasantly chatting with one of the clerks; but they walked on quietly with the Judge as far as the post-office, when he kindly introduced them to another Mr. Taylor, the postmaster.

After a few moments' pleasant conversation, William asked the postmaster if he could direct him to ex-Sheriff John McLane's residence. It proved to be but a block distant, but on inquiring there, it was ascertained that he was absent at his store farther down-town.   He was the only person in that city, besides Keating, whom my son felt that he could trust, as I had not only previously rendered him service, but also held him in the light of a friend ; and he had already been requested by me to render him any service in his power, should William pass that way, so that he knew the first thing he should do was to go to him, explain his business fully and secure his immediate advice and assistance.

Finding him, he told him that he did not feel justified in arrèsting Taylor unless the mail boat in which he had arrived was, in some way, detained for an hour.   McLane said he would attend to that, and brought Captain Reinhart to the store, but not telling him why the delay was desired, arranged or the same, and at once hunted up Sheriff Benson, to whom my son delivered the warrant and demanded the prisoner.

Benson at first hesitated, expressing the utmost surprise, as Taylor was a fellow-boarder, and he could not realize, so he said, that he was other than a brave and chilvárous gentleman, and began to question the validity of the requisition, but William told him that there was the order of Governor Pease approved by General Canby, and that he did not propose to be dallied with or imposed upon in any manner.

Seeing that my son had come too far and undergone too many hardships to be trifled with, he went with him to Buckley's store, where they found Taylor, who was given into the detectives' hands, though utterly astounded and completely unnerved at the idea that the strong hand of the law was upon him.

In this condition, and before he could collect his scattered senses and decide to make a legal resistance, which would have caused my son a vast amount of trouble, if indeed it had not resulted in the liberation of the elegant swindler, he was placed on board the schooner.

After they had left Corpus Christi behind, William began a system of soothing argument, with the end in view of convincing Taylor, who was now becoming nervous and restless, and evidently ashamed of being carried away so ingloriously, that it would be the best thing for himself, his brother, and even his people in Philadelphia, to go along quietly, without creating any disturbance, as, should he do so, he would treat him like a gentleman in every instance; but should he give him any trouble whatever he would be obliged to put him in irons, and not only treat him like a criminal, but would serve him roughly in every particular.

Taylor saw that he was in my power, and that I had put two men after him who would have gone to Cape Horn for him, and that his only chance of escape lay in strategy.

He had the perfect freedom of the boat, and, when he desired, chatted with the captain and the crew, who were not apprised by my son of the character of his new companion, and everything was done to make him comfortable.

At first he kept entirely to himself, but of a sudden his manner changed entirely, and he became particularly pleasant, especially to the captain of the boat; and as they were nearing the little barren Saluria Island at the entrance to Matagorda Bay, William accidentally overheard the captain say to Taylor, "The tide is high enough, and I will be able to run close to the island." This caused him to have nc particular suspicion of Taylor, as the remark might equally apply to a hundred other subjects besides the one to which it did; but in a few moments after, he noticed the schooner, which had hugged the island pretty closely, now suddenly take a still closer tack and rapidly neared the barren coast. Feeling alarmed lest the helmsman was not attending to his duty my son yelled:

"Captain, what under heaven do you mean? Don't you see that in another moment you'll have us beached?"

He had scarcely uttered the words when Taylor was seen to spring into the waves, and then disappear, and the boat at the same moment stood off from the island, as if in obedience to the warning my son had given.

The truth flashed into his mind in an instant: Here, after this hard unremitting toil, the discomforts, the annoyances, the dangers, everything through which they had been obliged to pass, after their hopes for success, and after they had earned it,—if two men ever had earned success, just when they were beginning to feel the pleasure of work well done, and be able to experience the genuine satisfaction it is to any man who is honest enough to acknowledge it, in securing the regard of the public for assisting in its protection, the commendation of one's employer for good sturdy care for his interests, and the self-respect one gains in doing one's duty, even if it has led him a hard life of it,—they were to be cheated and outwitted. Half crazed, my son, with anger and indignation, and a perfect flood of humiliating thoughts filled his brain in the first great question, "What was to be done?"

His first impulse was to plunge in after him, and in pur-
suance of that impulse he had freed himself of his boots
and coat, when, seeing Taylor rise to the surface and
make but little headway against the tide, which was ebbing
strongly, he called to the captain to round to, and began
firing with considerable rapidity, so as to strike the water
within a few feet of the man who was so unsuccessfully
struggling against the tide, but whom he could not blame for
making so brave and desperate an effort to free himself.

He was provided with two magnificent English Trenter
revolvers, which will carry a half-ounce ball a fourth of a mile
with absolute accuracy ; and as he could use it with great
precision he could easily have killed the man in the water.
Both the captain and Taylor were terribly scared, and as
Taylor held up his hand and yelled, " I surrender ! " the balls
were cutting into the water all about him savagely, and
the captain shouted, " For God's sake, don't kill the man !
Don't you see I'm rounding to ? "

Keating, who had been almost worn out from the Texas
trip, had been sleeping in a bunk below, and who had been
roused by William's firing and the strange motion of the
schooner, now came on deck rather thinly clad, and the two
detectives covered Taylor with their revolvers ; while the
captain, himself at the wheel, handled the schooner so that
it was only necessary for him to keep himself above water
in order to float with the tide against the side of the boat,
when my son, rather too indignant to be particularly tender,
grabbed him by the hair and his luxuriant whiskers, drew
him aboard, and soundly kicked him into the cabin, where

he began crying from excitement and fright, even going to such depths of discouragement that he begged for a revolver with which to kill himself, which being handed him by my son for that purpose, he very properly refused, and was put to bed for the purpose of drying his clothes, like a truant school-boy.

It was my son's intention to take the steamer at Indianola for Galveston immediately upon arriving at the former place; but on account of a heavy "Norther," which had blown all day Friday, the steamer had been obliged to put out to sea, and the party were consequently compelled to put up at the Magnolia House and wait there until the following Monday; and it required all the detective's shrewdness to keep Taylor quiet, as he had learned from some source that the creation of Wyoming Territory, which occurred a short time before his capture, had caused Cheyenne to be a city of quite a different territory than when the requisition was issued, which would have amounted to so grave a technical flaw that the requisition would not have held against a *habeas corpus*.

Court had just set at the place, and Indianola was full of lawyers, hungry as vultures for just such a rich case; but by constant persuasions, partial promises leading to a hope, at least, that a compromise might be effected at New Orleans, and dark hints of irons, and that, should his brother come on there and create any disturbance, he would be immediately arrested as accessory both before and after the crime; with constant drives out into the country, rambles down the seashore, and every pretext known to the mind of the ingenious detective, everything was managed successfully , a receipt for nearly two thousand dollars in specie secured ; the turning over of the money to Taylor's brother stopped ; and Taylor himself taken to New Orleans without an attempt at rescue ; and receiving a dispatch there from me to the effect that a compromise could not be for a moment considered, the party left that city Thursday, February 4th, arriving in Cheyenne six days later, my son accounting for his prisoner to the authorities into whose hands the case then passed, the last being seen of " Harry G. Taylor, the Man from Somewhere," being behind the bars of the guardhouse at Fort Russell, where he had been placed for safekeeping previous to his trial ;—and I have related these facts, not so much to show any startling phase of crime, as to give the public a single illustration, out of thousands upon my records, of how men must overcome every known obstacle while leading the hard life of the detective.

THE END.

www.ingramcontent.com/pod-product-compliance
Lightning Source LLC
Chambersburg PA
CBHW020928120726
47905CB00008B/2424